# PARADIGM

## John Chapman

# PARADIGM


John Chapman

**Your Books Press**
121 Holly Trail, NW
Cleveland, TN 37311

This book was printed in the United States of America.

To order additional copies of this book, contact:

Your Books Press
1-423-475-7308
www.parsonsporch.com

# LUCK

It was luck that I saw a redbird outside my
window this morning
But not luck that the same bird found
a most proficient mate this afternoon
It was luck that it rained yesterday
But it was not luck that it did not rain today
It was luck that I was born with three brothers
But it was not luck that my father was a preacher
It was luck that I crashed my car
But it was not luck that someone was there to pull me
out.
It was luck that it snowed and luck that in came
in time to ruin my game
But it was not luck that the sun came out
and melted it all away.
It was luck that I was born
But not luck that I know so much.... about luck

Anonymous Poet

The year is 2044. A twelve year old boy was standing in the garden. His mother called to him. "Neyhume, come into the house, your father wants to speak with you."

He went into his house and into his father's bed room where Gilbert lay sick and dying. "You wanted to see me Father?"

His father, named Gilbert Waddles, had named his son Neyhume after dreaming about the soon to be born child. In the dream an angel descended from heaven and spoke to Gilbert. "*Your child shall be called Neyhume,*" the angel said. "*For Neyhume is a great prophet, and your son to be born is he.*"

"Your mother has told me something about you that disturbs me greatly," Gilbert said to his son. "She told me that she had seen on some of your school papers that you were spelling your name N-a-y-h-o-o-m. Is that so?"

"Yes," his son answered.

"It is spelled N-e-y-h-u-m-e. That was my dream. You should respect that."

"I do," his son said. "But it is my name, and I choose to spell it my way. Did the angel also spell the name for you?"

His father did not respond to the question. Instead he coughed and cleared his throat. "You are Neyhume, spelled N-e-y-h-u-m-e. Do you understand?"

"In your world, your universe, it is, I am certain. But in mine, it is spelled my way, my universe, my life. Do you understand that?"

His father coughed and waved his son away from the bed and out of the room. In two days time he would die. A month later the boy's mother would also die. As he was the only child, he was collected by the authorities and sent to an orphanage. There, he signed his name Nayhoom Wadell, until the name was finally accepted. From that time on he would be Nayhoom Wadell.

## TWENTY THOUSAND,
## OR MORE, YEARS AGO
## A COMMENCEMENT

The youngest one a male, and the pretty one a female, the small one's sister two years older than he, were gathering nuts from beneath a very large scaly bark hickory nut tree. She was a young person who did what she was told to do, and this was always expected of her. The boy was less dependable, and not old enough to hunt, though his father and brother had argued with his mother about it. They needed him to carry supplies, extra spears and arrows, flints and water. But she put up such a commotion and defense against it that the older man and his eldest son always abandoned the notion and went off without him. But it was only a matter of time, and the boy would absolutely side with the men, and the mother's defenses would be over ruled. The boy and his sister bent heartily to their task and gathered many nuts that September day.

His first hunt would occur the following summer. He would be twelve years old then, nearly thirteen, and even more interested in the tales his father and brother would tell about locating and killing game. The boy had fashioned a good bow by himself with the sapling wood and sinew traditionally used, and had even killed a few birds with the sharp, stick arrows he had also made using cane that grew along a nearby creek. He was not proficient yet at napping flint, but he had tried, and being proficient at it would happen soon enough. Until then he shot cane arrows, the added hardwood points he sharpened and then fire hardened. And with bloody sinew he bound a few of his crudely fashioned points, his first attempts at napping flint the way his father and brother had taught him, to some of his arrows, and other more sharp scraps of flint to the ends of other arrows.

These flint pointed arrows were meant as special and would not be used unless absolutely necessary. When his father and brother were alone together they sometimes laughed about his toys. But they knew he was coming along, and could soon be as adept as they at making weapons, and maybe even better.

Cold days and nights were in the near offing. The leaves were turning colorful, and often the nights were so cool that it was necessary to build a fire under the stone overhang. The father and older son had been busy propping long limbs against the protruding rock ledge, and covering them with cured animal skins in anticipation of the coming cold weather. It had been only two years since they were expelled from their tribe, when they had a much more stable and warmer structure to live in, and the convenience of friendly neighbors.

But those good times were over. An elder's granddaughter had accused the oldest son of raping her. And though he had not, it was assumed that he had, and to avoid the son's death, the family of five left amid the jeers and stone throwing of the people of the tribe. They were warned that they could never return.

They had been banished from their people because of a lie believed. There was no way of proving the eldest son's innocence so they resigned themselves to making it alone, at least until they might meet up with people who would accept them.

The youngest one continued to complain during the summer, fall and winter, of his eleventh year, about not being allowed to go on hunts with his father and brother. But reneging he considered that the older ones knew best, and imagined it was his job to stay behind and protect his mother and sister. Fall turned to winter and he grew taller, and so did his desire to hunt with the grown men. When the deep cold of winter came they struggled but without tragedy or sickness.

His father knew his youngest son wanted to go hunting, and near the end of the following summer he decide to defend the idea against his mother if she protested. She did, but the boy was growing fast and was becoming a man. After a lengthy argument with him and his father, she realized that his childhood days were over and he must go.

With great enthusiasm, his bark quiver full of cane arrows, flint tipped with crude points he had napped himself, he waved goodbye to his mother and sister as he left the rock overhang with the two older men on their way deep into the mountainous forest in search of big game.

The day before they left, the mother and her pretty young daughter had together picked a large, bark basket full of late summer berries, and they had plans to mash most of them and make berry slush. The grown men loved to come home from hunting to berry slush. The slush would be waiting for them in a large clay bowl. While the women watched, the men would sit together before the bowl and dip the slush out with mussel shell spoons. The remaining berries would be eaten later with meat.

In the afternoon, after the men had left, going to their favorite hunting places in the forest, and with most of their daily chores done, the two women sat inside the shade of the rock ledge and worked at softening skins for making clothes. The chatted constantly, the older woman offering instruction, and the younger one debating the finer points of what her mother was saying. They heard footfalls in the dry leaves not far from the ledge. They assumed it was the men returning. But it was not them. It was four men from the tribe who had previously expelled them.

The men approached the shelter and entered. The women screamed and began protesting the intrusion. But the men had been watching and knew the man and his two sons were away. The young, pretty, girl was grabbed quickly and carried out of the shelter, and after the animal skin clothes were stripped from her mother, three of the men raped her violently, and then one of them strangled her with his bare hands. They then left, taking the young girl with them through the woods, and back to the village from where they came.

It had been a successful hunt. They had caught a deer, a large doe that struggled in the snare. At the very close range of one foot, the young boy shot the trapped deer in the eye with one of his flint tipped arrows. The arrow penetrated the thin, bone eye socket and pierced the deer's brain and it died immediately. His father and brother laughed, and they knew they would laugh more telling the story that night while eating with the others, and lounging around the open fire pit.

When the father and two sons returned from hunting, it was late in the day, about three hours before dark. They discovered the woman's naked, lifeless body, and the father fell to his knees beside her and wept. The sons stood by horrified and shocked. And then the father became extremely angry, saying he knew who had done it. He grabbed a spear and walked out of the shelter, and found signs in the leaves the marauding men had left when leaving. He took off at a trot, through the woods, following the signs. His sons followed him.

In the waning hours before sunset they came to the village. The man and his sons slowed to a quiet walk and approached the perimeters. A fire was being built in the center of the gathering area, and a few people were starting to gather around it. The man motioned for his youngest son to stay put and out of sight. The boy ducked down behind a large boulder, and watched his father and brother sneak closer to the village.

When they were nearly at the clearing, six men jumped out from behind cover and thrust heavy spears into the man and his son. They died there and then, while the young boy watched from behind the big rock. The man and his sons had been expected and the six men had been waiting. They knew the young boy was somewhere out there, but they chose to look for him at a later time. They dragged the bodies of the dead man and his oldest son toward the fire, and the young boy ran deep into the woods away from the scene of the murder of his father and brother.

\*\*\*

He went straight up the mountain, away from the village, until it was so dark he couldn't keep from stumbling and falling. He stopped from time to time to look down in the direction he had come to see if he was being followed. He was not, and he heard nothing but the sounds of a darkening forest.

On a steep slope he climbed a tree in the dark, and nestled his body in among the tight growth of branches and rested, and listened for footfalls in the dry leaves on the ground down the mountain. Continuing to hear nothing he dosed until dawn.

Visions of his mother's naked, dead body, and his father and brother being slaughtered with spears, were interwoven in his fretful dreams that night. He almost fell out of the tree twice. But he was very tired and also traumatized by their deaths, and his body and mind needed rest. He struggled to stay awake but nervous sleep ruled.

When birds began to chirp just before daylight, he awoke for a last time and climbed out of the tree, and resumed his climb up the mountain side.

By noon he had gained the top, and from up in a tall tree he observed the village below, and smoke rising in the sky from fires there. He climbed down from the tree and looked around, making mental notes about the location. He found five stones, and imagining they represented the five members of his family he placed them at the foot of a very large oak tree. And then he went north along the rugged spine of the mountain.

He walked for ten days along the mountain spine, his bow always loaded with an arrow and gripped ever ready to shoot if necessary. To keep count of the days, he put a small, round, stone for each in the raccoon skin satchel that he carried slung over his neck to hang within the reach of his left hand. He carried points and flints, and a flint knife in the bag, and anything else he might use such as a mussel shell spoon, a heavy piece of leather for napping flint, and pieces of deer antler for shaping the flint material against the leather.

He killed a large rattle snake and dried the meat over a small fire during the day. The snake kept him alive, along with certain berries and plants he found in the mountain forest. He knew that soon he would drop down to the lowlands where the game would be more plentiful.

After ten days he did start down the eastern slope of the mountain, though he had no idea where he was going, he was just going, and heading east down the mountain. At the bottom of the mountain he noted the surroundings, and again gathered five large stones and placed them at the foot of the largest tree in the vicinity. He had seen his father gather stones this way to mark where they were in the forest.

He elected to go always in the direction of the rising sun, realizing that as the season changed so did the position of the sun's rising. The alignment of night stars told him when in the late summer it was. He intended to return one day soon and seek revenge for the deaths of his mother, father and brother, and possibly rescue his kidnaped sister who he assumed was being raped repeatedly. But he did not know this for certain.

\*\*\*

He traveled down the mountain on the east side, going toward the rising sun. He had never been in this part of the country, and found the trees and shrubbery much different from those he was accustomed to. But he noticed immediately upon reaching the foot of the mountain that the game there was abundant. A young pig crossed his path and he shot it with an arrow, and then chased it down and beat it to death with a rock. Fresh, warm blooded, meat would be very welcome after his diet of rattle snake. The area was prolific with small game, as he knew it would be. But the insects were prolific also. He was bitten hundreds of times by mosquitoes and other small insects while he traveled eastward quickly but miserably.

The boy was very tall for his age of twelve, very

soon to be thirteen, and strong, and could run very fast and far. But he was alone, and he knew that being alone was a dangerous position to be in. Other than keeping alive, his objective was to find other people he could join with. He traveled toward the place in the sky where the sun rose, and hoped that soon he would come across friendly people.

He turned from time to time and looked back toward the mountain he had walked the ridge of, thinking ahead to when he would return to walk it again, and carry out his revenge against the killers of his father, mother and brother, and hopefully rescue his sister, if she would still be alive.

During the second day in the lowland, while waiting in hiding at a place along a creek where he had seen deer tracks, he heard voices. It was three people, and they were walking through the woods toward him. He crouched lower in his spot.

Soon, two old men and a middle aged woman appeared along the creek bank. They stopped and chatted to one another, but he could not understand what they were saying. Their language was different from his. But they seemed friendly and not aggressive in any way. He drew his courage up and stepped out of hiding. "Hello," he said, in his language. The three people turned quickly, pointing their spears menacingly toward him. He smiled, dropping his bow, and held his arms high in the air. "I only want to be friendly," he said.

He saw that the three people were relaxing. He continued to smile. Slowly he reached in his pouch and brought out a hand full of berries and offered them to the three. They smiled and laughed and motioned for the boy to come closer.

*** 

The woman was thirty years old, but more than half as old as she would become. She was strong and not very feminine, but she was friendly, and her word superseded anything the old men might say. The boy realized this immediately. And he also noticed that the woman liked him. He decided he could use this to his advantage. The old men saw that too, but had nothing to say about it.

The boy and the three older people labored to understand one another. But the rift in language was not great and they managed very well. He would soon learn the meanings of their words and they would come to understand his. And from that, things would get better.

They took the boy back to their village with them, and for the first time in over three years, he met people his own age and many other older people too. As best he could, he told his story, and the people were amazed. They knew of the boy's village on the far side of the mountain, and they regarded the people there as being savages, and ruthless killers. He agreed with their assessments.

The woman took care of him, insisting that he stay in her wickiup style dwelling. She was once a mother to a boy who would be about his age, but the boy and his father were killed by bears. He complied, and soon essentially became like a son to her. Her husband had been a chief in their tribe, and she had taken his place in the tribal council and was much respected by the other members of the village. It appeared to them that it only made sense that she adopted him.

At the beginning of fall he continued to think about his sister and the deaths of his other family members. He told his new mother about his feelings and she seemed to understand. When he told her he had planned to return to the village and attempt a rescue of his sister, the woman protested. But she knew he was determined and would go no matter what she said or did to stop him. That is when she decided that she, and a grown man friend of hers, would go along with him. She was very brave, and felt it was her duty to help and protect him if she could. He agreed to let them go, but insisted that he would be the one to take the risks. He was thirteen by then, but he was tall and strong, and all of the tribe was very impressed with his skills as a hunter, and lately as a young man. He had earned their respect.

At the very end of September, the three packed provisions in skin carrying bags, filled their bark quivers with arrows, took up their spears and headed for the mountain and the marked places there he remembered.

He found the first pile of five rocks right away. And after they climbed the mountain and walked the ridge for ten days, he had a harder time finding the pile he had made above the village, but smoke from below told him more specifically where it was. From there it was simply a matter of hiking straight down the mountain.

He wanted his companions to stay on top, but the woman protested until he gave in and said they could go at least halfway down. But they would not stay where he wanted them to, and would follow him all the way. He reminded them of their agreement, that he would take the risks. That is when they said they would stay hidden in the forest while he surveyed the village and its surroundings.

He assured them that he would attempt nothing until the following day. They had reached an agreement and would let him go by himself to inspect the possibilities of gaining access to his sister. He said he would return to the spot where they were sometime soon after sundown.

*\*\**

He crept ever closer to the village until he stood beneath a tree he could climb that would give him a good view. He climbed slowly, careful to not shake limbs which might alert the sentry standing guard in the watch tower in the center of the gathering area.

Near the top of the tree, and well hidden by limbs and leaves, he could see the roofs of all the dwellings. And he had a decent view of the central clearing amidst the circular grouping of houses. He watched and waited and thought, and made plans, which involved making a torch. And then he saw his sister.

She was walking with a man across the center clearing. He would recognize her anywhere. She went with the man into a house and did not come back out. But the man emerged and went into another house. The boy continued to watch.

When he was again with his companions he told them about seeing her, and told them his plan of rescue. It was a risky one and his new mother complained about it. But he told her that he was determined to try, and that he could never abandon his sister. The woman relented and nodded her head in agreement.

He found a large, dry, pine knot to make a torch with. And using many small, straight tree branches he bound them around the knotted limb in such a way as to create a circular wind screen around the potential torch flame, which would also hide the flame from view. Next he wrapped small, dry vines around the knot, and with a stick worked the bear grease he had brought, down in, and around the vine wrapping.

Early the following morning his mother's friend built a small fire. The boy was charged and ready with the torch and several arrow tips wrapped with fur and dry grass, and soaked with bear grease. He lit the torch and put the newly built fire out, and told them to wait where they were until he returned, and to be ready to run back up the mountain with his sister. He would then go in another direction, creating a false trail. He told them to not stop until that night when they would be far away, and he would eventually join with them back at their village. Very reluctantly they agreed to do as he wished. The time for action had come.

The sun was rising, and the shadow of the mountain darkened his surroundings as he silently approached the back of the wickiup up house he had seen his sister enter. The flame of his torch burned steady and low. He heard voices inside the house. He recognized his sister's voice and also heard a man's voice. He stepped back and to the side of the house and lit one of his arrows. And then, when the watchman in the tower was looking away, he shot it across the open area, hitting the thatched roof of a house on the far side. Within seconds the roof was ablaze and he heard women screaming. He also heard the man's voice inside the house his sister was in. The man ran out of the house and across the open area, and the boy tore a hole in the backside of the stick dwelling and spoke to his sister. She screamed, and then realized the voice was that of her brother who held out his hand for her to come to him. She did, and crawled through the hole and they ran from the house. They heard a man's voice and turned. It was her captor. Her brother, with an arrow already loaded in his bow, turned and shot the man in the chest. He fell back into the house and died. The boy ran with his sister to where his companions were waiting.

As the trio were leaving him standing there, his fingers slowly loosed from those of his sister's hand, and they took one last look at each other before she was pulled away by the woman.

He ran first to the south, but then he stopped and ran west through the woods back to the far side of the village. His torch was still burning. He lit another prepared arrow and shot it into the roof of another house, and then another. He shot four flaming arrows, igniting four other houses, and then he fled toward the north, breaking branches and purposely scaring the ground with his feet as he ran.

On a small rise two hundred yards from the village, he hid behind a rock and waited. Soon six men with spears came into the small clearing a hundred feet away. He shot one in the shoulder and another in his right eye, and then he ran. The four men not wounded followed.

He stood behind a large tree and waited. When he heard them arrive near enough, he stepped out and shot one of the men in the chest, who then fell hollering like a child before dying. His comrade threw his spear at the boy. But it missed him. He had stepped back behind the tree just in time. And then he stepped back out and put an arrow in the same man's groin. The other two men ran. They were very young, barely men, and extremely afraid.

He too ran, this time in a long arch, around the north end of the village, and then up the mountain side. He considered his mission accomplished and would head back to his new home and mother, and his sister.

*** 

On his way along the spine of the mountain, he discovered signs where he and his companions had trekked to his old village, and signs of them with his sister traveling back to the new home. It was a comforting find, even though he knew exactly where he and they were going.

After nine days of traveling quickly, he found the place where he should turn down the eastern slope, and where the others had also turned down it. After two more days he would again be home, and this time with flesh and blood kin, his sister. Anticipating this he was very excited and anxious to be with her.

When he entered the village, he was greeted first by three men guarding the entrance, and then came his sister and new mother. Following that, about fifty of the people who lived there came forward to meet him. Stories had already been told by his companions, about how he had rescued his sister and killed her captor. He would then tell the rest of his story to the people. They listened raptly to his description of how he had burned other houses and killed other men and wounded others. He was only thirteen, but already he was considered to be a grown man. Young girls giggled and swooned when he passed by them, or they him. Young boys and men, and even some of the older men, respected him highly, and talked about him often.

His sister was pregnant, made so by force, by the first man her young brother had killed. But she was very pretty and had no trouble in her new village finding a man, among the many who sought her for marriage, to be the father of her child. And then she had five more children by that same man.

And, two years after the rescue, his new mother, aggressive by nature, one day touched his crotch, and then she gripped his penis. There was no struggle. In all she bore him five children, before dying at the age of fifty-five, when he was thirty-seven years old.

Unable to continue raising to maturity the younger children alone, he took another woman, a young woman, as his bride. She was only fifteen at the time but was a good mother to his growing children. She bore him three more, two boys and a girl. His children numbered four boys and four girls in all. He would enjoy a relatively good life.

When he was much older, after proving himself many times during the hunt, and in battle, and after all his children were grown, he would sit at night around a communal fire with young people, the children of the village, and expound with his sagely words of wisdom. He said men belonged to one of three types. Either they were conquerors or defenders, or, like he had been in his early days, a man who sought revenge. He also said that human life was a constant struggle between man and the elements of nature.

The hero's words were believed, and remembered, and passed along. Though in time, his wisdom about the three categories of men were mostly forgotten. He was considered by most to be a hero. His daring deeds would long be remembered. Other men would emulate his bravery and remember his words about the inevitable, constant struggle between man and the elements of nature. Men ruled, and their eventual visions of God and His purposes became the standard philosophical understandings by which most men, and in general, most people would eventually adopt as their own. A multi faceted, social paradigm was emerging around the world, and the world was man's world: Man, the good, the bad, and the indifferent, battled against nature, and was considered the supreme ruler over nature, if he (man) kept on his toes. Man was considered by most to be at the top of the food chain, and the sole barer of intelligence, cast in God's image! Destination: in the vein of God's will, forever!! But beware of "the evil" side!

# CHAPTER TWO

## FRED HILLIARD'S PLACE

Nayhoom left the orphanage in the summer of his eighteenth year, 2050, and moved in with his aunt Reba, his mother's sister. There were three strange acting men living in the house with her, and he found each one to be intolerable in some way. She had prepared him a room like one might for a young child. He felt out of place immediately, and did not like her, or her friends, and left after only three days. He left at five AM, and it was late morning that day when it was discovered that he was gone. By that time he was miles away, riding in a stranger's electric car never to return.

He had walked several miles in the hot morning sun, and there was almost no traffic, and there had been very little traffic for several years. Gasoline was extremely scarce. Only people with fortune or power could obtain any of it. The man who gave him a ride was such a person, a local government official, though he drove an electric car as did many people. He told Nayhoom he stopped for him because he looked like his deceased son Mitchell.

Nayhoom was five feet and eleven inches tall and medium built. His hair was brown and straight and he was not outstanding in any way, except that he was exceptionally handsome, at least many people thought he was. He was strong and strong looking, but without the obvious, big veined, muscularity of many young men his age. He had been told by several people he had a face that could be trusted. But before that he knew he was trustworthy, and he was.

He got a ride out of town that morning, which was all he really cared about. The sun was climbing in the sky, and at ten AM it was one hundred and ten degrees Fahrenheit, and would get hotter as the day progressed. The air conditioner in the man's car did not work, and though the windows were all down, it was still stiflingly hot in the car as it hummed down the highway along with a few other electric cars, and an occasional hybrid.

"Where are you going?" the man named Roy asked.

"I don't know, and I don't care," Nayhoom said. "I can stop riding with you any time you say."

"I'm going to Hillbrook. Will you ride that far? It is only thirty miles from here."

"I know where it is. Yes, I'll be going that far."

"Are you alright?" the man asked.

"I don't know if I am or not. I hope I am, but I reckon it's debatable."

"Where are you going?"

"You've asked me that already. I'm just going. Do you mind taking me as far as you are going this morning?"

"I don't mind. I'm going to Hillbrook. You look like my son Mitchell. He died last year."

"How?"

"He just died in his sleep, and there was no autopsy. We chose not to have one."

"He just died in his sleep, and there was no autopsy. We chose not to have one."

"Why?"

"We think he killed himself. Well, I'm sure of it. And we didn't want anybody to know."

"Why not?"

"I don't know for sure, my wife and I did not discuss it much. Maybe the reason was our own vanity. It might hurt my reputation. I've never told anyone that."

"I remind you of your son. You felt compelled to tell me."

"I guess that could be. As a young person, are you bothered by that?"

"If I know what you are asking...I'll say no. But I wouldn't have killed myself. What could be the point? I am going to die anyway, at some point down the line in time. But time is something that exists only the way it does in the material world with people. I think in cosmic reality, in the overall reality of existence, twenty, thirty or a hundred years is so minuscule that offing myself now, at any moment in time, in this material world, seems pointless. But, I think I believe that you will deal with whatever you are compelled to deal with, and there can be no escaping it. Even death cannot separate you from whatever it is that you are going to do."

"How do you know that?"

"I think I can't know anything. But I imagine, therefore I am."

"So you don't even know that?"

"Maybe not, but I don't know that either."

"My son was thoughtful like that."

"It might make better sense if you thought is, instead of was."

"What?"

"Your son is thoughtful."

"My son is dead."

"And so you know what that is do you?"

"He's not alive."

"Is that so? What do you know?"

"I know he is not with me or this life anymore."

"Well, in as far as you know, right?"

"He is with me in spirit, I guess."

"You guess?"

"No, I believe that."

"Whose spirit, his or yours?"

"That's a strange question."

"But a good one, right?"

"I'd have to say...mostly in mine."

"More guessing, right?"

"I guess so. What do you think?"

"I imagine that he could be right here with us, in his own spirit, and in yours, mine too. Imagining is something everyone does, like breathing. Some people think imagining answers to difficult questions is like stabbing at a few, very swift fish in a very large pond. But that is just dead end thinking, a place their imagination hits a wall. And I believe they build that wall as an attempt at controlling reality. But the larger reality is that imagination thrives independent of any human control. It exist, possibly allwhere, and may be the very essence of existence."

"That is fancy thinking. But of what practical use is it?"

"What practical use is there in crying, or singing, or say... dreaming? Those functions are complete of themselves in conjunction with everything else, as I imagine imagining is.

"That is deep thinking for a lad your age. How old

are you?"

"Eighteen."

"What do you think about this global warming that is now, apparently the norm?"

"You reap what you sow, and people have sown the seeds that grew these horrible weather conditions. It was their, our, selfish considerations that caused us to do it. It was all a mistake, coal fires, gasoline, kerosene. Live and learn, and also die and learn. That is life."

"Why have people been so foolish?"

"It happened gradually I suppose. Early on, the psychic connection, a natural kinship between animals and other elements of nature, including certain human elements, were slowly lost. And those connections, that understanding, had it survived and thrived, may have provided mental, emotional, even far reaching psychic capabilities, far beyond any thus far experienced or imagined. This global catastrophe might have been avoided. But man assumed he was above all that, even created in God's image.

"If man is only a part of nature, as is every animal, insect, bird, fish or other water creatures, and plants, both of the water and of the land, if man is only part of it all, then that loss of connection, which has been lost with man's insistence that he is above these other lowly elements of nature, is paramount to providing his extinction, and the extinction of many other life forms along with his, and maybe life entire. 'If an eye offends thee, then pluck it out.' Global warming is the natural plucking out of the eye that offends nature, I think. If all else, all other than man, is to be considered nature, and out there, what is he....how can he be different? The answer to that exists in his imagination, his selfish imagination, his pious imagination, his arrogant imagination. He is only a part of the larger whole, and no more important than any other part. It is true that you can lose a finger, an arm or leg and still live, but the total organism suffers with any loss. Man has become like a head without a body. Like the song: "I ain't got no body!"

Roy chuckled. "I am amazed with your insight," he said.

"Is it insight, or just my imagining?"

"I can see the point you make."

"Now that it is hot as hell?"

"Better late than never."

"Yes, never. A strange word invented by man to cover many of his infamous tracks. But psyche!!! Tracks are tracks. If any part of nature is aware of them, they are totally seen. And as we know, or we should know, nature is allwhere."

"I have to turn for Hillbrook just up the way here. I am very glad I met you. What is your name?"

"Nayhoom."

"Excuse me, what did you say?"

"My name is Nayhoom, Nayhoom Wadell."

"It was nice meeting you."

"Nice meeting you too Mitchell's father. What is in Hillbrook? I've been there but I know very little about it."

"Not much really. It is, and has been for many years, a farming town. They have a new internet program that I'm going over to see about. The town is a one red light town, but the red light doesn't work anymore. It just hangs there and blows in the wind. Canfield is only a few more miles on down the road ahead. You might want to go there. I have to turn right up here.

"I'd like to go over to Hillbrook too, if you don't mind. Do you think I could pick up some work there?"

"You might, if you'll work for food and a place to sleep only."

"Eating and sleeping, what else is there?"

"You can ride with me, I certainly don't mind."

"Fine by me," Nayhoom said.

\*\*\*

Hillbrook is a small town in east Tennessee. It is largely locally substantiated, and governed by local, elected people who, anymore, never depend on national aid or government subsidies.

National elections are still held, there is a president of the United States, and a congress, but the function of a national government is concerned anymore, largely with climate catastrophes and national defense, and there is actually little need for national defense. They are also accountable for maintaining communication and weather satellites, governmental number one priorities worldwide. The internet is the world's chief source of communication, news and entertainment, though there is much dubious usage of it and a person needs to be aware of the realities of cyber corruption.

Problems associated with global warming have reduced threats of invasion, and attacks on Americans, including the once popular suicide bombings, to a scant minimum. It is hot everywhere, and economic growth all over the world has slowed dramatically, or has stopped altogether.

The oceans worldwide are inundated with a multitude of acids and other pollutants, including oil pollution, as many of the oceans oil wells have been sabotaged by pirates and other outlaw types. Most river fish and seafood is inedible, and only the foolish partake of it. Terrorists and would-be terrorists, would-be attackers of innocent people, are busy trying to stay alive in their own locales throughout the world.

But there is much thievery, especially in second and third world countries. And there is much thievery elsewhere, including the constant threat of looting any unguarded place holding valuably goods all across America and elsewhere abroad. Most people in America own guns, and many carry them holstered on their belts like in movies about the old west. It is now considered legal to carry concealed or unconcealed weapons.

People in the US who work for money still pay a portion of their earnings through taxes, withholding taxes, to the national treasury, the government. They also pay sales tax on purchased items, but there is no social security, no Medicare, and no governmental aid of any kind.

Because of the bizarre weather conditions on earth, economic growth in the United States and elsewhere around the world has found walls too high to surmount, and the halt of it has become indefinite. Almost all world trade has been reduced to a stark minimum. Oceanic and transportation by air is near nil for the lack of fuel. Sailing ships are again, around the world, being built and used.

The police force in Hillbrook is a volunteer one, and there is no shortage of men and women who apply for law enforcement jobs. They are compensated mostly with food and clean drinking water, and other things useful though hard to obtain, but are hardly ever paid with money. Minute men organizations are becoming common all across

America. Bartering, worldwide, is fast become a normal mode of exchange: goods and services for goods and services.

Being a cop, or as it is commonly called *peace officer*, is a much sought after position in Hillbrook and other small towns in the US. After a year on the job, each officer is evaluated by local citizens through an election process, overseen by an elected city council, after which they are released, fired actually, or re-upped.

Personality problems are not tolerated. Egotistical, loose cannon, police officers are chiefly concerns of the past. A public police officer has become one of the most respected positions a qualified person can secure, but it is dangerous. Three qualities, or personality attributes, specifically required are: compassion and bravery, and the willingness to help others. And you need to be strong.

Nayhoom had a positive feeling about going to Hillbrook, and he really couldn't say why. But as Roy had thought he would be, he was questioned by men guarding the main entrance to the small town.

"We know you Mr. Steel, but who is your passenger?" the guard holding an automatic rifle asked.

"My name is Nayhoom Wadell and I'm visiting your town for basically the first time. I think I was here once before when I was a child. I think I may stay, if I can find work."

"You'll need to find work if you stay. And the population in Hillbrook is nearly maxed out. I'll need to inject a tracking pill into your arm, if you don't mind."

"I don't mind. Will it dissolve soon?"

"After about a month, OK?"

"Sure."

The man put the pill gun to Nayhoom's bare shoulder and pulled the trigger. There was no pain. A man in the nearby guard shack looking at a computer monitor, waved at him. "Thank you," the guard said to Nayhoom. "There is nowhere in Hillbrook that you cannot be detected, even far out in the country. There are monitors everywhere." "Fine," Nayhoom said, and Roy pulled away.

A Big Brother fear was not an issue in Hillbrook. Only the city council could together authorize an electronic search, and the activation of search equipment, and codes, which was sometimes necessary. Many small towns used the new tracking devices. Only small towns could manage them well. But larger towns were starting to divide themselves into individually governed warrens, or burrows so they could. Tracking was beneficial for many reasons. The use of such tracking equipment with children was much in demand and never contested.

Populations in towns across America had died down to less than a third of what they had been just ten years prior in 2040, when Nayhoom was eight years old and living at his parent's home. There were now many nomadic groups of people living primitively in the country sides, and in abandoned buildings throughout America. They were generally referred to as hooligans.

Kidnappings by hooligans happen regularly and the kidnapped held for ransom. To be tracked means that you are being looked after. The children of Hillbrook are tracked from the early ages of five and six, and some earlier, with a longer lasting tracking pill. Kidnappings rarely occur in close-nit communities.

A few public schools exist in America, largely without air conditioning, but home schooling is safer and becoming more the norm almost everywhere. Illiteracy is growing, but there seems little hope for any immediate, positive change to that.

Nayhoom was fortunate to be allowed to survey the town of Hillbrook and possibly live there. He knew that and intended to make his stay there a clean one. He told Mitchell's father goodbye and watched him drive away from where he stood beneath the now defunct traffic light, swinging back and forth and creaking loudly in the hot and humid breeze that was blowing up from the south.

\*\*\*

A girl with her boyfriend walking beside her

stopped and asked Nayhoom if he was lost.

"I might be," he said, "but I know about where I am, and I'm going to start looking for work. Y'all got any idea where I might look first?"

"Try Fred Hilliard's farm. A friend told me he needed help out there," the girl said.

"Out where?" Nayhoom asked.

"Out on the Golly Gee Creek. Anybody out there can direct you to his place."

"Where is the Golly Gee Creek?"

"That'a way," she said, pointing down the road to the north, "about four miles."

"Thanks," he said, and started walking in that direction. The sun was already blisteringly hot. Sweat trickled down the back of his neck and his arm pits were slick with it.

"When he finally got to a sign that read: Golly Gee, he looked for a creek, or anything that would give him a hint where he should go next. He saw nothing, so he walked on. Shortly he saw ahead on his right, three very long greenhouses, and on the other side of the road on a small hill, a house with a barn behind it. When he reached the dirt road that went to the house he saw a large, white mailbox at the beginning of the long driveway. The name Fred Hilliard was hand written in bold black letters on its side.

Fred Hilliard was a divorced man, stout, vigorous and fifty years old, who was a devout Christian, and committed to what he considered to be his life's calling: providing freely as much food as he possibly could for the people of Hillbrook. He answered the door shortly after Nayhoom knocked.

"Yes sir, can I help you?" Fred said.

"Someone told me you might be hiring. I'm looking for work."

"What is your name and where do you come from?"

"My name is Nayhoom Wadell, and I have lived for the past six years at The Aubrey House Orphanage over in Canton. I just got out, and I need to be somewhere, work somewhere. I have nothing, and want nothing except a place to sleep and call home, and food and water, and to get out of this heat. I understand that might be all you have to pay help with. It is all I require."

"That is all I have, and I'll try you out for a day or two. If all goes well, we'll think about more days. Talk to the woman in charge of the green houses. Her name is Patty Sorenson. She will show you where you can stay. I'll call down there and tell her you are coming. What was your name again?"

"Nayhoom Wadell. I didn't make that up, my father did."

"OK Nayhoom, I'll see you tomorrow."

It was getting extremely hot that morning as Nayhoom walked to the green houses. He could take the hot weather pretty well, but lately it had started getting even hotter each day, and he wasn't used to staying out in the heat quite so much. He needed shade and water fast.

The woman in charge of the greenhouses, Patty Sorenson, was forty years old, attractive and strong looking. She greeted him at the entrance to one of the greenhouses. "Fred said you were coming down. Your name is Nayhoom?"

"That's right. I need a drink of water and some shade bad. Do you mind?"

"Not at all, come on in and sit in front of the big fan there and I'll get you some water."

The big fan was six feet in diameter and situated at the west end of the greenhouse. Water, pumped up from a deep well, ran down many pieces of chain wrapped with strands of burlap. The chains hung down from the wooden frame incasing the very big fan with four blades reaching out from the center arbor three feet on all sides. The fanned air blew through the cool, dripping water. It was a homemade cooling system that Fred Hilliard had devised. It worked very well cooling the west end of each greenhouse.

At the middle of each were two smaller fans rigged the same way with cool water from the same deep well, pumped up to trickle down burlap wrapped pieces of chain that dangled before the spinning blades. They pushed cool air on toward the back ends of the greenhouses. All three of Fred's greenhouses had cooling systems like this, that worked wonderfully well, and each greenhouse was covered with white nylon shade cloth. The thermometer outside had twice registered one hundred and thirty degrees, but inside the greenhouses the temperatures had stayed below one hundred degrees Fahrenheit.

He had solar arrays, solar panels, nearby that generated the electric power that fed the batteries, which sent direct current to current inverters, before traveling on as alternating current energizing the water pumps and fan motors.

Both Patty and her husband Steve, had worked for Fred Hilliard, and had lived on his farm, for five years. They were highly respected by the other employees. Patty returned with a tall glass of cool water and handed it to Nayhoom. She asked him where he came from and he told her about the orphanage.

"I have a niece named Vickie Blount who lives at that Orphanage. Did you know her?"

"Yes," Nayhoom said. "We called her Tiny."

"That's her," Patty said. "She weighed two hundred pounds when her parents died seven years ago."

"She's gained another hundred," he said.

"That poor girl. How can anyone, a kid especially, let themselves get that huge?"

"No one ever put a stop to it with reasoning that made any real sense to her. She was left to her own thoughts about it and her thoughts were childish."

"No guidance. My Sister Gail, her mother, was a very miss guided person. Heroin took her life and her husband's too. Would you like to see where you will be staying?"

"Certainly," he said, and followed her to the east end of the greenhouse and out the back door into a huge soybean field. The beans had been grown and harvested early to beat the extreme heat. Only the dry, dead, stalks remained.

She lead him to a narrow, low, hillock, that went lengthwise from north to south and ended abruptly at the edge of the bean field. He saw the façades of two small buildings, about twenty feet apart, along the sides of, and near the end of the hill. A window, and a door with a window, was in the middle of each façade. She took him to the one nearest the end of the hillock and opened the door. A cool rush of air met them as they entered, and he closed the door behind.

When she flipped on the florescent light, he saw they were in a ten by thirty feet wide foyer, and he could see that the building they had entered was a long and somewhat narrow one. He saw down a long hallway, a door at the far end whose small glass window revealed light from outside. It opened out to the other side of the hill. The concrete building they were in went underground through the hillock. Another big fan beside the door leading out, at the far end, was the source of cool air.

"This is where you will stay while you are here. After a year you might be eligible for a place of your own. Fred envisions eventually having individual living quarters. But for now, and still awhile yet, this will be your home along with three other guy workers. Your place is on down this way. I'll show you."

He followed her to a small portioned off cubical, just beyond a communal kitchen at the midway point in the tunnel-like, underground building. His enclosed section, enclosed with plywood walls painted white inside and out, was like the others, all with doorways opening out into a passing hallway that went from the front door to the back door of the building. This would be his new home for awhile. The walls of each cubical did not reach the ceiling or the floor to allow for the flow of air from the big fan. But the one foot openings at the ceiling and the floor had half inch hardware cloth, otherwise called mesh wire, nailed over them. The place was clean and cozy, and Patty explained that he, along with the others living there, would always be held responsible for keeping the premises tidy.

"I am a neat person.  They insisted on that at the orphanage," he told her.

There were light switches just inside each door, one for the compact fluorescent lights in the hallway and one for the LED ceiling light in his room.  She said the hall lights were used only when needed, and were otherwise kept off to conserve energy.  She explained that electricity was necessarily in short supply and provided solely by solar panels.  So he would be expected to use electric lights sparingly. "I certainly will," he told her.

"When the other guys come back about one o'clock, which is in about thirty minutes, they will fill you in about other matters."

"This is great Patty. I appreciate it.  What time do we start work?"

"You work from four AM until twelve noon. We have to beat the heat around here. Lunch is at eight AM for thirty minutes.  We provide the meal, and the guys will show you where we eat."

"I understand. I'll be ready. Thank you."

Nayhoom had many more questions, but Patty needed to go back to work, so he intended to learn more from his coworkers, about Hillbrook, Fred Hilliard and his farm, and the people who worked there.

\*\*\*

He sat on his bed and looked around the room. An additional, small, Light-Emitting Diode, (LED), light bulb screwed into a socket on the wall, helped the overhead bulb cast sufficient light on the furnishing of his cubical. He had the small bed he sat on, a soft lounging chair, and a table with straight-back chairs beneath the light bulb on the wall. A three cubic foot refrigerator hummed softly on a table in a corner. A small sink with cold water only was attached to the eastern wall. A communal bathroom with a cold water shower was down the hall. An old flower-patterned rug covered most of the concrete floor. And he could feel the cool air moving over his feet as the walls of his new space, not reaching the floor, stopped about a foot above it, being supported by heavy, corner post. The walls did not go all the way to the ceiling for the same reason: allowing for the circulation of air from the big fan. There was an old chest of drawers beside a small door to a small closet. "Home sweet home," he said.

He lay quietly on his bed and listened to the motor and the sound of the big, spinning fan blade at the east end of the partially underground, worker's dorm. "You can do this," he told himself.

A little after twelve o'clock he heard a door open and the voices of men as they entered the building. He listened as they walked down the dark hallway, and then parting each other they went into their private spaces. Nayhoom walked into the hall and called out? "Hello, I'm the new guy. Somebody come out and let me meet you."

Three young men stepped out into the hallway. They each wore white cloth head wraps that looked to Nayhoom like turbines. "Hello," one said while walking toward him and unwrapping his head. "My name is Jason Winters."

"I'm Nayhoom Wadell, call me Nayhoom."

"Hello Nayhoom," Jason said, "this is Carl Porter, and that one coming is Boris Storm, we call him Bore, like a wild hog." A big and strong, handsome looking young man, twenty one years old, with very broad shoulders, waved to Nayhoom. "Guys, this is Nayhoom Wadell. You are not from Hillbrook, are you?"

"No, I'm from the Aubrey House Orphanage over in Canton. I was just released from there."

"Released?" Carl said. "It sounds like a prison."

"It sort of was, but not really. They are all OK over there, but I was glad to be leaving. And I'm glad I found this job. Lots'a folks don't have jobs or places to live. I'm very fortunate."

"You will like it here," Jason said. "Fred is easy to work for, and Patty is very nice too. I guess you've met them both."

"Yeah, Fred, Mr. Hilliard, said he would try me out

for a couple of days, and Patty was really nice. Is the work hard?"

"Not really, Carl said. "It's just hot and dry. You can't drink enough water."

"He might not get as addicted to it as you have," Bore said.

"I'm not addicted, just dry."

"If the three of you would tell me what goes on here, I'd appreciate it. Patty said you would. I know very little."

"Let us get showers and change clothes, and we'll meet up at the lounge at supper time and we'll tell you what we Know."

"Great. Where is the lounge and when is supper time?"

"Back up front, you'll see, and supper is usually around 2 PM." Jason said.

Nayhoom found the lounge area where he had first entered the building, but had not paid much attention to it before. It was the foyer space you enter when coming in the front door. It was at least twice as large as his room, with a window beside the entrance door, that along with the door window allowed enough light in that an interior light during the day, and early evening, was unnecessary, unless you needed or wanted extra light. The visible concrete walls and plywood partition walls were painted white.

There were lounge chairs, a book shelf, old magazines on end tables, a center round table and chairs, and a desk close to the window supporting a computer and a microwave oven. Two writing tablets and a can of pens and pencils were also on the desk. He moved the mouse, but the computer was not turned on.

He sat at the round table and waited for his new friends, who came shortly and sat with him.

"So do y'all hang up here often?" he asked.

"Most every evening I guess," Jason said. "We watch videos and live feed on the computer there, news and weather too. What was the orphanage like? Were you abandoned? Is that why you were there?"

"My parents died when I was twelve and I was taken there. I got out a short time ago. I'm eighteen now."

"So how did you land this job?" Carl asked.

"I hitched a ride almost to downtown Hillbrook, a boy and a girl walking by said I should try for a job out here. So I walked out and got it."

"That is phenomenal," Bore said. "I tried for three months before I was hired. Jobs are very scarce, especially one that takes on borders. You might be the luckiest person alive."

"I don't think luck is a reality," Nayhoom said. "I am very fortunate, that's for sure."

"I'll say," Jason said. "There are people in Hillbrook who would do about anything to get on out here."

"What goes on out here," Nayhoom asked.

The three young men laughed. "Lots a hanky-panky," Bore said.

"He wishes," Carl said. "This is a vegetable farm. There are three greenhouses, but Fred wants many more. And other than growing regular vegetables in the greenhouses we are now growing soy and mung beans in the fields. Fred works hard with his bean laboratory plants, trying to engineer hardier and hardier, heat resistant beans. But the increase in temperature, and heavy rains, seems to always stay just ahead of his efforts. Still we produce a lot of food for the people of Hillbrook."

"And he makes a living doing that?"

"He gives the food away free to the farmers market in town. Fred is a devoted Christian who believes it is his calling to grow food for the people of Hillbrook. And he is doing just that. This was his father's vegetable farm before he died, and it is paid for, and Fred has money, and no desire for more. So he grows food and gives it away. We all work here for food and a place to live. Fred is a great person, and wonderful to work for. You fell into a bed of roses Mr. Nayhoom."

"I guess I did."

"We will eat supper soon. You don't have anything

to eat do you?" Jason asked.

"No."

"Then you are invited to eat with us. We are going to have Bore's famous soup. Well, it's famous in his mind, and Carl and I don't want to mess with putting together something ourselves."

"He's not telling the whole truth," Bore said. "Him and Carl love my soup."

"Is love the right word Bore?" Carl said.

"Adore may be more accurate," Bore said.

Carl and Jason sniggered. We'll be back in a few," Jason said. "Water is all we have right now to drink. Is that OK?"

"Sure. Thanks guys," Nayhoom said.

***

"Where did y'all get those turbines you came in wearing?" Nayhoom asked after the three men had rejoined him.

"briansconnections.hbrook," Carl said. "He can get about anything with his connections."

"Did you buy them?"

"What with? Bore does pencil sketches. He's great at it. He traded with Bryan, a pencil sketch of Bryan's wife for four turbine wraps. Roscoe left his when he left. You can have it, you'll need it, believe me."

"Yes, I'll need to look as staggeringly dapper as you three."

"Good man," Carl said. "The world is our oyster."

"So it's just us and Patty and Fred?"

"Oh you haven't met the girls, and the two other married couples?"

"Girls?"

"Right through the wall there about twenty feet, there lives four of the most beautiful women on this farm, in the world even," Jason said. "And they are all available."

"Accept one," Bore said.

"Ah yes," Carl said, "the one who'll have nothing to do with any of us. Naomi, she stays off limits and Bore is crushed."

"She is the prettiest girl I have ever known," Bore said, "and she looks right through me."

"So there is a softer side to the employed. That is good to know. What are the other girls like?"

"You will meet them all tomorrow and see for yourself, but they are all good girls, hard workers and very friendly. But not friendly enough though, if you know what I mean," Carl said.

"Bummer!" Nayhoom said. "And the married couples, where do they live?"

"Over in the woods on the far side of one of the

bean fields.  Patty and her husband Steve, the Sorensons, live there.  You'll meet them all tomorrow."

"I'd get the chill off this soup in the microwave, but it'll be OK at room temperature, don't y'all think?" Bore said.

"You're the chef," Jason said.  "As long as it will eat!!"

"It will," Bore said.  "Y'all proved that last evening."

Nayhoom was a little surprised when Carl said a short prayer before they ate.

"I hope you are not a staunch carnivore," Bore said before they started eating, "because there is no meat in this soup, or anywhere on this farm."

"I guess I'm a carnivore, but maybe not a staunch one.  I've never thought about it."

"When is the last time you ate meat?" Carl asked.

"A week ago, I guess.  Everybody out here is a vegetarian?"

"Vegans," Bore said, and ladled out four bowls of soup. "Where and when did you last have meat?"

"One of my last meals at the orphanage, it was meatloaf."

"Animal flesh!" Carl said.

"That would be meat," Nayhoom said.

"We vegans think of life as an absolute phenomenon to be highly respected, even treasured.  A true vegan does not see animals as the enemy to be conquered, or as food, or as being created in any way for humans to use. Vegans see themselves as a part of the natural world and not its owners or masters."

"I see," Nayhoom said. "So there ain't no pork meat in this soup?"

"Nodda," Bore said. Carl nodded at Nayhoom and appeared to be waiting for an answer.

"I wouldn't shoot Bambi," he said. His three new friends laughed at him. And then they started eating Bore's soup.

***

Bore told Nayhoom, when he handed the white head wrap to him, that he had washed it twice with bleach, so it would be as clean as possible. "You want me to show you how to wrap your head with it?" Bore asked.

"Nah, I can do it," he said, and took the wrap back to his room and stood before a small mirror and proceeded to wrap his head. When he was finished wrapping, he stepped out into the hallway, and waved to Bore standing beside his door, and walked to the east end of the building, and stepped outside to wait for the others. It was three thirty AM, and a very pretty girl wearing white, baggy, khaki pants, a white sweatshirt, and holding a white turbine head wrap like his, was standing in the darker reaches of the outside light just outside the backdoor.

He could not see her face very well by the light of the one outside light bulb, but he was certain that she was very pretty. He thought he could tell that by the way she spoke to him. As the day became brighter he would see just how pretty she was. She had short blond hair, gray eyes, and needed no makeup. And she moved with an air of elegance, naturally displaying a beautiful womanly shape, though she was only seventeen.

"Hi," she said. "I'm Naomi. Who are you?"

"My name is Nayhoom Wadell. I came here just last evening." He could now see her pretty face better in the light of the outdoor light as she moved closer to it.

"Your head wrap is all wrong. You'll burn up with it like that. Let me fix it."

"Sure, I thought it would be simple. I guess not."

"It is simple, but you just don't know how it works best. You want most of the cloth on top of your head to protect you from the hot sun. I'll show you, come here."

She removed the turbine and rewrapped it, folding and layering the majority of its length on top of his head, and then wrapping the final three feet of it around, and tucking in the last bit of it. "There, now maybe you won't have heat-stroke."

"Thanks Naomi. When you don't know, you don't

know, and I didn't. I'll have to find some white sweatshirts and pants too."

"briansconnections.hbrook," she said. He operates a kind of swap and shop web-site. If he can't get something right away, he will eventually. Bore can show you."

"I'll check that out. The guys said there were four girls, where are the other three?"

"They'll be along. Girls run late. I'm just out here early for some reason."

"You came out to meet me."

"Did I?"

"We met didn't we?"

"Yes but..."

"It's a done deal, and a pleasant one too. How many people work on this farm?"

"Hmmm, fourteen, I think. I've never really counted or heard the number mentioned. You'll meet everyone today though. We are planting mung beans in the south field. And it's going to be another early scorcher. The days seem to all be scorchers lately. It hasn't rained on the farm in two months. Maybe it will rain soon."

"How can the beans grow without rain?"

"Well, part of what we do is pump water up from the creek to water the plants. It is a hand operated pump, so the process is slow. It has to first be primed and then most of what we pump has to be carried to the plants in buckets. It's not easy, but it is also not very hard, just hot. Are you healthy?"

"I think so. I'm not the sickly type, and I can stand a lot of heat, even without white clothes and a turbine."

"Good, you'll need to be tough to keep this job."

"My head is already sweating. Will you help me tie this thing up again later? I've got to take it off now."

"Sure, take it off," she said.

Suddenly the three other young girls, and the other men, all carrying candle light, joined them. The girls were Betty Payne, Shirley Glass and Harriett Deville. They were young and very attractive, and after meeting Nayhoom, all the young field workers walked together toward the south field where they would join with the three married couples, which included Patty and Steve Sorenson.

Carl, Jason and Bore were very talkative that morning as they walked. Nayhoom sensed they were trying to impress the girls, and they were. Bore was the most obvious. He took every opportunity to appear amusing and funny. He commented that Nayhoom had earlier looked silly wearing the white turbine, like "a confused A-rab." But when Nayhoom told him that Naomi had rewrapped it correctly afterward, Bore said that he was sure she had done a great job. Naomi glanced at Nayhoom and he smiled.

"Naomi is out of your league entirely Bore," Jason

said. "She knows you too well."

"I give credit where credit is due," he said.

"Then you won't be giving any to yourself," the girl named Betty said.

That statement caused the others, other than Nayhoom and Naomi, to laugh. They glanced at each other with hints of a smile.

The married couples, minus one husband, had gathered under the big, dying, oak that was the usual gathering place when they worked the south field. They were Stanley and Ruth Crammer, George and Beth Williamson and Steve and Patty Sorenson. They too, except Patty, all wore white cloths, sweat shirts with long sleeves, and had with them white turbine head wraps like everyone else to put on after the sun was up. And the women carried lit candles in candle holders with glass globes. Patty waved, and each in the arriving group waved back.

"Good morning," Patty said. "For those of you who haven't met him, this is Nayhoom." And then she introduced Nayhoom to each of them. "Steve has gone to prime the pump and fill the water barrel. Are y'all ready to hit it?" she said. "How about you Nayhoom, are you ready to work?"

"I'm ready," he said. "You say jump, and I'll say how high."

Patty laughed. We are planting Fred's new strain of mung bean today. The soil is loose enough that we can turn it with hoes if need-be, so if y'all will follow me I'll get you going."

She led them to the edge of a field that needed no plowing because the soil was loose and deeply infused with compost provided freely by many of the residents of Hillbrook. Mostly the compost consisted of leaves and some grass clippings, and much of it was composted vegetable matter from kitchens.

"Y'all will remember we planted the bean for seed last year. Well there is what we gathered," she said, pointing to several, full, fifty pound-sized, burlap bags, "and we can only hope they'll do better this year. Fred thinks they will. We are planting the seed in each row about six plants per foot. Use the one inch depth gauges when putting the seeds down, and George and Steve will follow with water.

"As usual Steve will keep an eye on the progress. You can direct any questions to him.... Nayhoom. He has most of the answers...unless the question is about religion." A few laughed.

"Oh I have all those answers," Nayhoom said. There was more laughter.

"Drink plenty of water and rest when you think you should... Nayhoom. I'll be at the greenhouses if any of you need me. Any questions I can answer?" she said with a smile. "OK, I'll see y'all later," she said, and walked back toward the greenhouses.

Her husband Steve was the foreman, but it was well known that Patty's word trumped anything Steve might suggest doing, but he was respected and there were never any disputes that the husband and wife team could not handle privately.

It got hot early. By ten AM it would be one hundred and ten degrees in the shade. A large thermometer hung on the dying oak displaying a small number of leaves withering under the relentless heat of the everyday sun. Every worker wore a turbine. Nayhoom wore his after Naomi had rewrapped it for him. Bore watched with a look of jealousy and made no attempt to hide his angst.

Carl began drinking water and drank more as the morning wore on. Bore cautioned him against it, but no one else was paying much attention to his guzzling until he starting vomiting. Steve realized suddenly what was happening and walked back to the dormitory with Carl and made him promise to stay there for the rest of the day, and to not drink so much in the future.

Not being used to the kind of work he was doing, stooping and walking bent over that way, poking one inch holes in the loose soil with the one inch depth gauge every six inches, while someone else behind him dropped in the seed, and doing it hour after hour in the oppressive heat, Nayhoom, suddenly had an aching back. He began standing up straight often and arching his back backwards, and then he would rub the small of his back. Naomi saw him doing this and came from where she had been working and swapped places with the person planting the seed behind him. She handed him a stick about thirty inches long.

"Rest your upper body on this stick while you are bent over. That will take the strain off the small of your back. When you get used to bending over a lot it will get easier."

"Thanks Naomi. This works pretty well. I'm awkward at it but it does relieve the tension."

Bore saw this too and sighed. Soon Nayhoom and Naomi were talking to one another and laughing, and Bore tried to ignore it, to ignore them, and stop thinking about Nayhoom doing with Naomi what he would like to be doing. He was jealous.

Nayhoom suddenly realized that there seemed to be something taking place between him and Naomi that was more than the development of a casual friendship. He began casting glances toward her and noticed that she was sneaking peeks at him also. Once their eyes met and neither seemed interested in looking away. Finally he smiled, and she smiled back.

He felt something about her that he did not know existed until that moment he felt it. His back ached, and he was sweating more than he ever had. He was extremely tired and thought he was probably becoming dehydrated. But at one point when they were looking at one another, he forgot completely about his discomforts and wished he could go into her mind and experience what it was about her that was causing him to feel the way he felt. But he realized his thinking was foolish. He even considered that he was having some sort of heat related, mental episode.

She smiled again at him, and he was jolted emotionally. He stopped working and went over to her.

"I'm glad you are here," he said.

"I'm glad I am too. How is your back?"

"I think I'm going to live."

"I hope so," she said, and smiled again, and again he was emotionally shocked at what he perceived as the essence of human beauty. Her eyes shone brightly and were seemingly filled with mirth and the joy of living, and it bore deeply into his heart.

The other girls, Betty, Shirley and Harriett, were busy several feet away planting seed and talking to one another. They were paying no attention to anyone else. Steve operated the hand pump while Stanley, George and their wives carried water in watering cans, to sprinkle over the freshly planted seed.

Everyone took an extra break at nine AM and stood under a shed built to provide shade for the workers. Nayhoom's back still bothered him, and the girls took turns rubbing it while Bore and Jason watched with envy, especially Bore.

When Steve came over and started talking to Nayhoom, the girls, Jason, Carl and Bore, walked off to another spot under the shed and left them alone. "Hi, I'm Steve, and you are Nayhoom, right?"

"Yes, that is right. And you are Steve, Patty's husband?"

"Yeah, we been married for ten years now. There's no finer a'woman alive. I'm a lucky man."

"I like Patty. She seems to have a very level head,"

Nayhoom said.

"Yes, level headed, she is that. How are you and this heat getting along?"

"One hour at a time, I guess. I won't have any trouble sleeping tonight. How big is this farm?"

"About seven hundred acres, but we only work about sixty acres of it. Fred's father farmed a lot more than that, but that was back when you could get gasoline for the farm equipment. Fred would plant other fields if he could get them plowed, but the weeds and saplings have taken over most of it and no one has yet decided to try re-clearing it by hand and with the mules. But we might eventually have to try. There are other people in Hillbrook who would gladly come out and work, but Fred hasn't taken that responsibility on yet. People can be hard to manage."

"I would think so." Nayhoom said. "Has it rained much around here?"

"No, not really. And when it does it sometimes rains too much. About three months ago it poured for days and the creek flooded up two hundred feet into this field. We were lucky it wasn't planted. That's why the rows out there don't go all the way the way to the creek. Fred don't want to risk losing any seed."

"So the ditches between the rows carry rain water back to the creek."

"Yeah that's right. We worked very hard making those ditches down to the creek. We'll need to redo them in the fall, but it won't be as hard as it was to make them last winter."

"The winters around here are getting almost warm

enough to grow something," Nayhoom said.

"Yeah, Fred is working on that. He said that when he was a child it snowed a foot deep one winter right here on the farm. Boy, those times are gone for good."

"Or bad," Nayhoom said.

"Yeah, bad."

When the day's work was finished at twelve noon, Nayhoom walked with Naomi and the girls back to the living quarters. Bore with Jason walked behind them. Occasionally he cast a sorrowful glance at the new arrival walking ahead and bumping elbows with Naomi. But Bore was not a vindictive person, just a disappointed one, and thought Nayhoom to be likeable. But his good looks and big muscles seemed to be doing him no good at all.

That evening Nayhoom visited the girls next door. Betty, Shirley, and Harriett told him they disliked Bore. They thought he was boorish. He went to Bore's defense. "He is a good person I think. He may be suffering from a measure of low self esteem. You would think that a person with his handsome face and great body would have a better opinion of himself. He might never have gotten started with establishing healthy self esteem. He said he has been called Bore ever since he was a child. That might have contributed in some way to the low opinion of himself he seems to have. I struggled with Nayhoom for years. What if your name was Percy Gasfoot, or Cindy Swallows, Dick or Harry Head, Consuela Phoebe, Charlie Magagas, Dick Trickle, or Hans Asperger, which sounds like Assburger? My last name was Waddles. When I was a kid I felt that I just couldn't live with that name, so at the orphanage I changed it to Wadell. I kept the name Nayhoom but I spelled it differently than my parents spelled it. Somehow those changes gave me ownership of the name instead of feeling that I was tagged with it. Bore's name is actually Boris, but people insist on calling him Bore and he may feel tagged with the name, and trying to live with the possibility of being boring, and even boorish, or like a tusk hog."

"That may all be true about him. But still he hits on us girls constantly. We are almost afraid of him," Betty said.

"I'm just saying be willing to show understanding when you can. But of course you have to keep your guard up."

Naomi glanced at him from her seat at their lounge table and smiled. Nayhoom smiled back. "I'd better get back over, supper will be ready soon. What are y'all having?"

"We haven't decided yet. A big salad with tofu, and pintos and turnips on the side probably, right girls?" Shirley said.

"Probably," Harriett said. "I'd like to think of something better, but that will be OK."

"I'll see y'all later," Nayhoom said, and headed back to his dorm.

*\*\**

Chad Pendergrass, Naomi's father, had been a welder. But when jobs of that nature began to disappear he fell to drinking and eventually went insane, and then he died. Her mother Cynthia remarried and moved to Utah.

But Naomi wouldn't leave the south and stayed behind to fend for herself.

She had been working on Fred Hilliard's farm for three years when Nayhoom arrived. She had been there longer than any of the others except for Patty and Steve, who had worked for Fred Hilliard for the past five years, starting long after it became almost impossible to purchase gasoline. Now only people of money and privilege, or people with questionable means, could buy it, and only a few wanted it. Carbon monoxide was seen as one of the biggest contributors to the global warming problem. Around the country there had been many assassinations of people who drove gasoline operated vehicles, many of those assassinations taking place while the victims were driving.

Fred and Patty thought of Naomi as being reliable and steadfast. She always performed her duties as they expected her to. And she respected Fred's commitment to provide as much free food for the Hillbrook residents as he could.

Naomi was not snobbish, but she appeared that way to many who did not know her very well. She was simply distrustful and leery of people. She had always been extremely attractive, and had been taken advantage of before. When she was fifteen, a family member, her father's brother Tim, had tried to rape her. She objected vehemently and yelled for help. A neighbor came and chased him away. Tim was arrested later and put in jail. This incident put her father over the edge mentally, and he was soon afterward institutionalized. And then he died for unknown reasons. That is when her mother remarried, and moved to Utah. Naomi was tempted to go with her and her new husband, but she decided to stay in Tennessee and confront her fears alone. The job at the Hilliard farm gave her the opportunity to do that. But she was shy, and as Patty had put it: "Standoffish."

No one but her really knew how she had been affected by the attempted rape. Tim had managed to remove most of her clothing, and was about to drop his pants when a kid named Wally looked in the window after hearing Naomi scream. He saw Tim unfastening his belt, and Naomi laying on the bed half naked and crying. Wally broke the window with his elbow and screamed: "What the hell are you doing?" Tim ran out of the room and into the street, and was arrested an hour later.

Naomi was put into near shock by the violent act of her uncle. She cried while telling her mother about it, and she cried about her father learning that his brother had tried to rape her. And when her father totally lost control and had to be put in a sanatorium, she cried even more. And then he died, and Naomi was suddenly a different person than the one she had been. Life was evidently full of pitfalls and she considered that she too could be consumed by unseen forces. That is when she was first judged by some people as being overly protective of herself while others thought she was acting conceited. She understood the suspicions and insinuations but chose to ignore them. And then her mother left. Naomi was fifteen and would now have to protect herself. She stayed behind to live with her mother's sister Fran. But Fran soon revealed her darker side and Naomi ran away and found the Hilliard farm.

Nayhoom was the only person she had ever met who appeared to be without some sort of hidden pretense. Even Fred and Patty and Steve seemed to approach her with at least a small measure of falsity, they were hiding something, she thought, but still she liked and respected them. But she was always, in some degree, vigilant of their possible, hidden motives. She had found out the hard way that sometimes even the people you should be able to trust can be like poisonous snakes in the grass.

She didn't sleep very well that first night after meeting Nayhoom, and the second night was equally as disturbing as the one before. Both nights she dreamed about him and her making love, in the dark, out in the soybean field. They were on a blanket, on top of the loamy soil, her arms spread out to the sides, her hands busy digging in the soft earth. But what disturbed her most was how she felt upon waking. She wanted him back the way it was in her dream. She had never felt that way about anyone before, and wished to talk about it, but she trusted no one with her inner most thoughts, especially thoughts about love, and about sex.

She had Betty, Shirley and Harriet to talk to, but they were a little older than her and very self assured people. Naomi knew they considered themselves to be more emotionally mature than her. And she thought they might think she was being childish for having dreams and thoughts about a guy she had just met. So she kept her thoughts and dreams about Nayhoom to herself.

But as days turned into weeks it became obvious to everyone that Naomi and Nayhoom were fast becoming an item, and there was much speculation as to whether they had yet made love. They had not.

One Friday evening after work, and long after supper, about three weeks after Nayhoom arrived and started working at the Hilliard place, Betty, Shirley and Harriett confronted Naomi about her relationship with him.

"Have you slept with Nayhoom yet?" Shirley asked.

"No," Naomi said. "We are just friends."

"Mighty good friends," Betty said.

"So, what if we are? He is a nice person. I like him and he likes me. There is no mystery about that."

"Maybe not to you, but there is mystery," Harriett said.

"In what way? Naomi asked.

"You two are going for each other and you will achieve you goals or you won't. The mystery is with whether you will or you won't."

"Will or won't what?" Naomi asked.

"Don't be coy. Sex, I'm talking about sex!" Harriett said.

It was the first time Naomi had gotten mad at any of her dorm mates. "Should we do it right in front of y'all? Is that what you would like to see? Whatever happened to privacy, and minding your own business?" she said and walked outside.

It was eight pm and starting to get dark. She saw Nayhoom sitting in a chair beside the back door to his living quarters.

"Hi, wanna go for a walk?" she said.

"Sure, where to?"

"Anywhere, I just want to walk a little."

"Sure, we'll go down by the creek. If it gets dark on us we can easily find our way back across the bean field.

"There's supposed to be a meteor shower at dark," he said. "Bore told me about it."

"That would be interesting," she said, as they walked to the field. "Is it a major shower or a lesser one?"

"A pretty big one, Bore said. I saw a couple a few years ago, but they were not so spectacular. A few shooting stars is how I'll describe them."

"It's going to be a clear night. Maybe this one will be showy," she said.

It would be a clear night, and very dark, except for starlight, which came thirty minutes after they left. It was extremely warm and humid out in the big field. The temperature would not go below ninety degrees all night. The moon had set so it was dark. Immediately after it became dark, when they were nearing the creek, they saw five brilliantly glowing meteors go across the sky from right to left. "Oh that was brilliant," she said. "Did you see those?"

"I saw them. I've never seen meteors that bright, or that slow. They seemed to float across the sky."

"Oh there are two more," she said, and put her hand on his shoulder.

"Let's sit down so we can look at the sky," he said. "Here on this grassy spot, well, sort of grassy."

"These are weeds, and dirt," she said.

"OK weedy and dirty, but at least we can look up

easier."

They sat on an area of ground supporting a row of dry soybean stalks, a spot of ground sprouting weeds amidst dead stalks and field grass. But it was dry and there were no briars or bull thistles. The creek was only a hundred yards away. They could hear frogs croaking. Nayhoom cleared the bean stalks away and stomped down the weeds as best he could. Meteors buzzed overhead on their way to earth.

Naomi sat down and immediately one went overhead and she fell back on her elbows to watch it. "They are all high up. We need to be lying back," she said.

"But it is so dirty you'll be covered with it."

"I don't care, I want to watch them fall," she said.

They tried to make themselves comfortable lying on the dry stalks among weeds. But it soon became obvious they were suffering and they had to either sit up or get up entirely and move. But it was very dark and there was no other place evident they could go.

"I should have thought to bring a blanket," Nayhoom said.

"Let's just sit between the rows on the soil," she said.

"But that is all dirt. We'll get filthy."

"So?" she said.

"So if you don't mind, neither do I," he said, and they got between the rows of dead and dry, soybean plants and sat. Naomi laid back on the soil to look up. There was just enough room beside her than he could also lie back. Their elbows were pressed together and their bodies were warm.

A brilliant meteorite fell buzzing to earth, just to the

left of overhead. "That was great," he said. Naomi found his hand and squeezed it. He raised himself up on one elbow to look down through the darkness toward her. He put his hand out and touched her face. "I'm going to kiss you," he said.

She said nothing, and he bent his head over to her. Their lips met. The kiss was tender and light. He did not try forcing a more intrusive kiss on her. He pulled back a little and breathed in the sweetness of her breath. She put her hand behind his head and pulled him back to her and kissed him passionately.

He had kissed only one girl before, at a party at the orphanage. But he wasn't thinking about that. And Naomi had never kissed anyone, especially like she was kissing him now. With no idea of where they were going with the kissing, they kissed in the dark, under flashes of light from falling meteors. And then Naomi began pulling at his back, she wanted him on top of her. And then she wanted him to take his shirt off. He did, and she kissed him deeply while feeling the contours of his naked back. "Take your shirt off," he said. She did.

"You are beautiful," he said.

"It is dark. You can't even see me."

"I can see you with my hands."

Neither would be satisfied with partially undressing. All their clothes were soon off and their hands busy exploring each other. The meteors fell profusely, flashing brightly in the overhead sky. At times they could even see each other's faces and naked bodies. Naomi pulled on Nayhoom's erect penis. "We've got to do it," she said.

He needed no additional urging and slowly they achieved the sexual union each, for their own reasons, had feared. Naomi scooped up handfuls of earth and let it sift back through her fingers, just like in her dream. With meteors flashing above them, Nayhoom came quickly, too quickly he realized and apologized to her about it.

"It doesn't matter," she said. "We are just getting started."

That was what he wanted to hear. Shortly thereafter they were at it again. And that time lasted longer. But still he knew he had been going too fast. "I know what you need," he said. "I can do better. I'm just so excited that I can't control myself. You are wonderful."

"I am happy. Don't worry," she said.

When they put their clothes back on an hour later, they were covered with dust and soil. "The girls will figure out what we have been doing," she said.

"So will the guys, but who cares?"

"Not me," she said.

They did have it figured out. "It's pretty obvious what y'all have been doing," Betty said to Naomi when she entered her dorm. "Bore came over here looking for Nayhoom, and you were gone, so you were both gone. Where were y'all?"

"You said it was obvious," Naomi said, and Betty noticed the dirt on her cloths as she walked away toward her room.

***

About a week after their love making in the soybean field, Nayhoom and Naomi were working everyday as closely as they could with each other, and going off by themselves in the evenings, often out into the bean field again with a blanket, and returning late. Once it had rained lightly and they returned covered with mud. Their friends talked about them but the two did not seem to mind. It was obvious they were energized, and they were cheerful nearly all the time.

On a Wednesday morning they, with all the other workers, met in one of the greenhouses to listen to something Fred had to tell them.

"The mayor of Hillbrook contacted me and said how grateful the residents around town were for our efforts out here providing food. I thanked him of course, and then he asked if I had any ideas about how we might help in other areas. I ask him what other areas, and he said that most of the folks around here are really suffering with the heat. The electrical grid that takes in this area is constantly breaking down so air conditioners rarely work, and when they do, well, people just can't afford to keep them running. We talked about more solar panels, but they are hard to come by and it would take many more panels than most folks have, or could ever afford, to keep their air conditioners operating, so the only option is to bare the heat in the best way possibly. But the folks around here aren't doing that very well. I'm asking you guys to make suggestions about what can be done. You may have no suggestions, and I told the mayor that there may be no answers to the problem, not answers that any of us could come up with, but I said we would try."

Nayhoom spoke up. "Why couldn't they rig up something like you have here in the greenhouses and in the dorms, water cooled fans?"

"They might if they could, but that is just it, they can't handle something like that."

It was a short meeting. Fred had said what he came to say. So he left and the workers went into the mung bean field to continue carrying water to the freshly planted rows. Steve and Bore operated the hand pump, pumping water up from the creek into large barrels, while the others carried it in watering cans to the planted bean seed and sprinkled it out. It would take three days to water completely the twenty acre field, and then they would start over again.

It was mindless but necessary work. Without water the beans would not sprout and later would wither and die, so they carried the water and did not complain. Any worker was free to leave but there was nowhere they could go that existence would be easier. Fred Hilliard was a good person and they all knew that, and Patty and Steve were easy to work with. Life was hard everywhere and getting harder each year as the weather continued to be extreme. Not many people were as fortunate as they to have reliable employment, or a cool residence to return to at the end of a hot workday.

Lying in his bed that afternoon after supper, Nayhoom continued to think about what Fred had talked about. The beginnings of an idea began to form in his mind. He got up and walked to Bore's room and knocked on the door.

"Come in," Bore said loudly, and Nayhoom entered.

"I have a few questions Bore. Do you know where I can get 55 gallon, plastic barrels?"

"Brian can get them for you, why?"

"What about small water pumps?"

"How small?"

"I don't know, not big, or heavy duty. Just big enough to circulate water from a 55 gal barrel of water up to a fan, and do it continuously."

"We'll go down and e-mail him, and get him to looking. What have you got in mind?"

"For every house with electricity, or solar panels, with enough electricity to operate a fan, and a small water pump, I think I can design an air conditioner that people could afford to own and operate."

"How, what....? "

"Like the ones here blowing on us right now, Fred's invention scaled down to something much smaller, something we could manufacture and provide to people who needed it. And according to Fred this morning, many would."

"Tell me about it and I'll make sketches."

Nayhoom described the air conditioner which was simple. The 55 gallon, water filled, barrel would need to be buried in the ground where the water in it, pumped in from a well, would stay as cool as possible. A small water pump would pump the water in the barrel up to pipe spanning the ceiling, or top-side, of an insulated shoot or ductwork attached to the outside of a house. The water, after being pumped up, would trickle down from these pipe with drilled holes, down chains interwoven with pieces of burlap hanging before a strong, squirrel cage fan that would blow the water-cooled air through the ductwork along the side of the house and, after making a right turn at a window, into the house. The air shoot, or air passageway, would be on an incline upward from the fan outside, so that the cool water that was being pumped up from the barrel would, after dripping down the chains, course back down to it, and mix with the original water supply to be pumped up again. A float valve would turn on a water faucet above ground, replenishing the evaporated supply water, and there would always be some evaporation. A person using the AC would need to have a well or an otherwise constant supply of water. Some of the units could be linked directly to the well, depending on the existing plumbing.

"Damn Nayhoom, this will work!"

"I think it will. We stay cool don't we?"

"I'd like to go see Fred and show him this. I think he'll like it."

"Fine," Nayhoom said.

They knocked on Fred's door and he answered it. "Bore, Nayhoom, what's up?"

"Nayhoom has an idea about air conditioning I think you will find interesting. I'll let him tell you about it, and here are some sketches."

They sat on the front porch and Fred looked at Bore's drawings. "So what is your Idea Nayhoom?"

Pointing to various features in the sketches Bore had made, he explained how he thought it would work. "It is your design, just scaled down to work on a standard sized house. If we need to install a water barrel, the barrel will need to be buried in the ground to keep the water cool, but other than digging a hole for it, it's just simple stuff."

"Digging a hole is simple too," Fred said. "I think it will work just fine, and I can't believe I haven't already thought of it."

"You've been busy with genetic engineering," Nayhoom said. "Bore thinks Brian can find what we need. Paying him for supplies will be our biggest problem."

"He has a big family and they all need to eat. I'll back as much as he'll let me with food, from the farm here."

"I did a sketch of his wife and he liked it a lot. Maybe he'll want sketches of all those kids, and her sisters and their kids," Bore said, "his mother and Father too, though they are gone."

"Take some time away from the beans and y'all build a prototype. I'll get two new guys from town to take your places for awhile. Let's see how it works. We'll install it in Stanley and Ruth Crammer's house. They are suffering bad down there. The insulation in that little house has always been scant, and the roof needs a fresh coat of silver paint."

When they were walking back Bore made a comment. "Fred was impressed with your idea."

"It was his actually, just modified a little to hopefully work cooling a house."

"Then he was impressed with your modification. It was there all along but only you thought of it. Stanley and Ruth will be surprised. If it works like we think it will, many will be surprised."

"Maybe we can install them in lots of houses," Nayhoom said.

"I am sure Fred will want to."

That evening Bore and Nayhoom e-mailed Brian Samples. He e-mailed back that he knew he could get the squirrel cage fans, water pumps and barrels, but he would have to search for sheet metal and the insulation they would need to make the ductwork. But he thought in time he could find it.

The following morning he e-mailed them again saying that he had found all the supplies they would need. By the end of that day a deal was worked out between Brian and Bore for exactly what he and Nayhoom needed to make one system. It involved Bore doing pencil sketches of his children. Getting the equipment for others would not be a problem either, and Brian was interested in making a food deal with Fred. But he understood that first Bore and Nayhoom had to build a prototype and test it.

Brian procured the supplies and Fred hitched one of his mules to a wagon and took Bore and Nayhoom to Brian's house in Hillbrook to get them. Brian was a heavyset guy in his middle thirties who lived in a large two story house in the downtown area. The family who had previously owned the house, and the one acre of land it was situated on, had suddenly disappeared five years earlier, and Brian was allowed to, essentially, homestead the place. He was told that if he lived in it, and maintained it well for ten years, and the original owners had not returned, it would become his and his families. The Samples family was halfway there. There had not been as much as a word from or about the previous owners who had vanished.

Brian was the official go-between for hard to find things. He had established many contacts throughout the area and by them, through e-mail, and his web site briansconnections.hbrook, he could find most of what anybody needed. He made a living that way. He had an electric car and two battery powered bicycles. His wife and children wore decent clothes and they were never hungry. He and his wife Becky home schooled their children, as did most everyone, the best way they knew how, and the family lived as normally as could be expected. He was much respected in the community and town of Hillbrook, and was thought to be an essential citizen.

He helped them load the supplies and then had a few words with Bore and Fred before they left and returned to the farm.

"We'll build the thing at their house starting tomorrow," Bore told Fred in Fred's barn.

"OK. Let me know if you need anything."

"That good battery powered drill would be nice," Bore said.

"I'll give it and bits to Patty in the morning. If there is anything else, tell her, OK?" Fred said.

"Will do," Bore said.

The unit was not hard to build. And they got help from the other guy workers digging a hole beside Stanley's and Ruth's house. Just after lunch, about 9'30 AM, after filling the barrel with well water, and securing the float valve, they plugged in the fan and pump which started the air conditioner to working. The squirrel cage fan was powerful and the water cooled air soon began maintaining the inside temperature of the house at a reliable eighty degrees. Stanley and Ruth were ecstatic.

"This house has never been this cool," Ruth said. "Who do we thank, you are Fred?"

"Both," Bore said, speaking for Nayhoom. "It is a simple idea that works."

Patty and Steve were to receive cooling units next, as soon as the equipment could be procured, George and Beth Williamson after that. "This is going to take off like hot cakes," Steve said. "Everybody in Hillbrook will want one."

Naomi was especially nice to Nayhoom that evening. "Fred may have had the original idea, but you made that idea available to anyone with water and a hundred and twenty volts of electricity," she said. "I am as amazed as everyone else. Keeping cool is people's biggest problem, but with your system it is doable. Congratulations Nayhoom, you have saved the day."

"It was Fred's idea," Nayhoom said. "I think it should be called Fred Air.

"Why not?" she said. "Fred Air, I like it, I'll bet other's will too."

As usual lately, they spent the evening together. But this time she visited with him in his room, and they had to be very quiet. "They talk about us enough, we don't need to give them more to talk about," Naomi said.

But being quiet didn't help. The next day their rendezvous was talked about. "Why are we so interesting to everybody?" he ask her.

"Because we are getting it and most of them are not."

"Let's move in together in that old house near Steve and Patties," he said. "We can fix it up really nice. It may take us awhile, but what is time?"

"OK. You think Fred will let us?"

"If you will marry me he will, I know."

"Marry you?"

"Marry me."

"OK."

***

It was a simple wedding. Fred was an ordained minister with an enthusiastic penchant for marrying people. He, with Patty as his helper, conducted the ceremony in front of the little rundown house Nayhoom and Naomi wanted to work on and live in. She had three bride's maids, and Nayhoom had three best men. All the other workers attended the wedding also, and afterward they ate food from the back of a long, flatbed, wagon that Fred pulled down to the house with his mules, and that Patty and others had loaded with prepared food. There was no singing or any kind of music, but it was obvious without music that the two newlyweds were very happy with their union.

Bore insisted on kissing the bride. "No tongue," Nayhoom said.

"I wouldn't do that."

"If you did she might slap you," Nayhoom said.

"Hell-of-a point you make there," his number one

best man said.

The gathering of friends lasted for an hour or more, and then Nayhoom and Naomi were left alone at their new home. At first it would not be exactly comfortable there, but they had decided to start staying in the old house anyway. It would be hot for awhile, until solar panels and Fred Air could be installed. "We will be two happy campers," Nayhoom said. And they were.

\*\*\*

Like most young people they barely knew each other, but they considered their coming together to be a mark of providence. They understood something about it they could not explain, nor did they ever try. There were no questions about their quick marriage that neither he nor she felt necessary to ponder or answer. Nayhoom and Naomi had accepted that their being together was meant to be, and they would not wonder why or how that could be. It just was.

Their compatibility was evident from the start. At first it was something they felt which went with them into wedlock. And then with living together, compatibility became even more evident. Beyond everyday concerns they had deeper discussions, about life and death, and inevitably veganism.

Even though Nayhoom had not yet become totally convinced that being a vegetarian would become his way of living, thinking, and eating, he found Naomi's convictions to be most enthralling and he enjoyed listening to her talk about them.

"I am a vegetarian, a vegan, for deeper reasons than being squeamish about eating animal flesh," she said. "Animals are not enemies, and I don't believe they exist for human pleasure, to subdue them, ride them, make clothes from their bodies, their skins, or to eat them. And though at one time long ago, thousands, millions of years ago maybe, there may have been reason to eat them. I don't know, I don't remember. But in these times it is not necessary. It may be a common acceptance to do it, but I now beg to differ."

"How do you see it?" he asked.

"I'm just part of it all, not special, or heavenly blessed to be lord and master over the fish of the sea, or birds of the air, or the animals of the land. I'm just one among many in this material world. And I think this world and its many diverse inhabitants is together life as we know it. I don't want to take the life of any animal for reasons that are similar to my not wanting to lose a finger, or any other body limb. With the extinction of the dodo bird, the passenger pigeon, and others, I believe a part of life, of me, has also become extinct. Life is precious to all species, be it butterflies, crayfish, white tailed deer or a person. It is life as much as I am life. No life is expendable."

"But it takes life for other life to live," he said. "Animals eat animals."

"Yes and when people were not much more than animals, they too had to kill for a living. But I think that with effort people can realize they have evolved beyond killing for a living, for game, food, and pleasure."

"It is not an easy thing for most people."

"But I believe it is essential," she said.

"Because no one out here eats meat I haven't either. But sometimes I remember, and think about a hamburger."

"I used to eat meat too," she said. "And for a long time I enjoyed the smell of fried chicken. But now I smell it for what it is, and not food."

"I've always liked fried chicken. But I see your point. It is a habit."

"Eating meat is a habit, but it is much more than that for most people who eat it. It is a way of life, of living, and that bothers me."

"Why?"

"It is mindless, blind, and is like a snake swallowing its tail. I believe you are what you eat, and I wish to go beyond animal cravings, but most do not. I think people are eating themselves up and don't know it."

"That is a macabre thought."

"It might be, but I mean eating in that people have centered much of what they do with food, and animal products are at the base of most foods, that and salt. It worries me."

"Why salt?"

"Another bad habit. How did it get started that a vegetable needed salt? I think it started with eating meat, to mask the bloody, flesh taste. And then the habit gravitated to vegetables. But that is just a guess, but it is an unnecessary and harmful condiment. Salt and blood, grease, lard, all are enemies of the human heart! It makes me sick to think about it."

"You are what you eat huh?"

"Don't you think so?"

"One would have to be," he said.

"Yes, and the death of living, warm blooded creatures is also partly what you eat. You are also eating their death and how they died. Why would anyone want that on their résumé?"

"I don't think they do, I just think no one thinks about it."

"Yes," she said, "but people should think about it. At least I think they should."

"That's right, I believe. You think they should, but whether they do or not is up to them. A person comes to a conclusion only when and if they do. I don't see it as a matter of right or wrong, but a matter of doing or not doing. And I'm beginning to see what you mean. One way yields one thing, another way yields something else. I want no part of killing animals anymore, killing them for food or pleasure, or clothes, or whatever."

"I'm glad to hear you say that. Now if we only lived forever," she said.

"How can you know that we don't?"

"I suppose I don't," Naomi said. "But when you die, you die."

"Yes, that is true, but what is death?"

"Well, it is the end of life."

"How do you know that?"

"It appears to be the end."

"But looks can be deceiving," he said.

"There is a dead hawk out in the field there. I'm

pretty sure it is dead."

"What about its spirit, its memories, if it had any, its life?"

"Vanished," she said. "It is the end, right?"

"Who knows anything certain about and end? The right hand, call it living, can't know what the left hand, death, is doing. Science tries to have you believe that dying is the end. But that can only be scientific speculation. The living cannot know specifics about any total vanishing of the self, nor can they know about an after death life. There are those who want you to believe they know what lies ahead for a person after death, but their ramblings are no more than imaginative guesses. Anyone can guess, and anyone does. If an answer about that, about what is in store for a person after death is not prevalent, even after years and years of philosophical and religious debate, and deep scientific probing into the matter, one might believe, as I do, that a definitive answer cannot exist for a living person. And by the same token, there is also no definitive answer that tells of there not being an after death life. As I see it, there is the material world, the world of the living, rocks, birds, trees humans, and there is the ethereal world, an unseen world of activity that people can only theorize a little about. I also include in the ethereal world: radar, radio waves, WI-FI, TV transmissions digital and analogue, shortwave transmissions, electricity, and many, many, more such invisible phenomenon that people have learned to detect, harness and use. Scientist call those things part of the physical world, but scientists are scientist.

"If an after death life has not been substantiated by

now, and yet there is no good reason to believe one does not exist, I put forth the notion that an answer will never be substantiated to the living. And that makes me think that an after death life should not be known to the living as a fact, for reasons cosmically designed, and in a functioning order just as the moon orderly orbits the earth. And by the same sort of order, an afterlife will always be imagined by living intelligence. And it may be that the imagination about an after death life is vitally important to the human psyche, to life itself, as part of the driving force. What would people do if they knew for an absolute fact that life did, or did not, continue after death?"

"I see what you mean. They, we, would probably relax and care less about living if we knew it went on, or maybe we would give up hoping if we knew it ended absolutely." she said.

"I feel certain that is how it would be. My imagination about an after death life would wither and eventually disappear. My entire imagination might even shut down. Many religious types that feel they know what is in store after death, have pretty much stopped imagining about an afterlife. They have become people who know. But each year that I live, I seem to augment my imaginings about what may wait for me after I die. The important thing about that is not that I am ever right about what I imagine, but that I continue to imagine. It will be what it will be as it always has been what it will be. And what that is, or might be, belongs to anyone's imagination. It is their life and death. And I say that life and death are together life. I am not afraid to die."

Her eyes brightened. "I have been afraid, but I think I won't be anymore. What you have expressed to me about what you think and believe has affected me deeply," she said.

Their conversations were always relaxed and easy. They found that talking to each other about such things was free from strife or argument. It was not that they always saw eye to eye, but they realized a benevolent and lenient attitude with each other, and that made talking together very enjoyable.

Prevalent in their conversations was a palpable freedom they both understood. Nothing imaginable was off limits for talking about if one or both desired to discuss it. And there were no set times for when a thing might be talked about. Talking was freedom, and they both cherished it.

\*\*\*

Near the end of that hot summer the young workers at Fred Hilliard's farm struggled against rising temperatures to keep the mung bean plants alive and thriving along the Golly Gee Creek. It was a difficult thing to do because no matter how much water was poured on each plant, the sun pulled it out of the ground fast, and the bean leaves tended to quickly wither and curl. Nayhoom suggested that they cut cane shoots that grew along the creek, and make a shade framework over each row. That is what they did and it took many extra hours to do it. They cut the cane, carried it out into the field, and using string, wire and bits of torn cloth, they lashed lengths of cane to upright pieces of cane driven into the ground, and then tied short, leafy, cross lengths over the rows. The plants responded to the shade in a favorable way, so they intended to store the cane they were using, and use it for the next planting of soybeans, which would be the following spring and maybe even sooner if the weather cooperated. And there was a good chance it would remain relatively warm all winter like it had during the two winters before.

"You make hay while the sun is shining," Fred said. And they intended to, at least make beans.

Nayhoom and Bore helped some with the shade project, but most of their time was spent installing Fred Air in homes in and around Hillbrook. The makeshift air conditioning was much desired and Brian Samples stayed busy negotiating bartering deals between families and various hardware suppliers. But the crux of the negations lay with getting the thing installed free by Nayhoom and Bore, via Fred Hilliard generously agreeing to allow them to be involved. But not a day's work went without their bringing back to the farm, food of various sorts, cakes, pies, or clothes for both the guys and girls, blankets, candles, useful things, essentially in trade for the work the two young men did installing the cooling units.

The most difficult part of some of the installations was digging the sometimes necessary, deep holes by hand for water barrels. They always did that the first day, often starting before daylight when it was cooler. The actual installation of the cooling apparatus would then come the second day. And always, when the cool air began to fill the houses, there would be sighs of relief and cheers for Bore and Nayhoom and exited talk about Fred Hilliard and his simple invention.

Naomi and Nayhoom spent all their extra time working on their little house. It was old and dirty, dust had settled into all the cracks and crevasses, so cleaning was at first the main issue. Fred had several buckets of paint saved from more profitable times, and though the colors, light green and light gray, were not what they would have chosen if they had a choice, the paint went on the outside walls and trim, and they were excited about it. Fred also found enough silver paint for the roofs of theirs and Stanley and Ruth Cramer's house, and white latex for the inside. They used the paint he gave them, and soon the old house began to feel somewhat new again.

After solar panels and Fred Air was installed they invited the others for a house warming, though an actual warming was not necessary. It was October and the outside temperature at midday was 110 degrees, and sometimes more, while inside it remained a cool eighty-two. Nayhoom made a small sign and painted it light green and printed on it with gray paint the words Home Sweet Home, and hung it on a wall in the living room. They were young, very much alive, in love, and happy.

***

A man in the town of Hillbrook had secured a deal to obtain twenty thousand minnows, bass, bluegill, catfish, black crappie, and other types of game fish, and he intended to stock the Golly Gee with them. The Golly Gee was a short, fresh water creek that began with three springs near the far outskirts of Hillbrook, and wound its way through the town and then out several miles and along the edge of Fred Hilliard's farm. From there it went all the way to the Hiwassee River only a half a mile beyond the farm. In 1870 a gristmill had been built where the creek emptied into the river, and though the mill burned in 1920, the limestone sluice remained, as did the ten foot high limestone dam and waterfall above the Hiwassee River it emptied into. The dam kept the Golly Gee from actually connecting with the river the way most creeks do. It emptied into the river, but fish from the river could not swim up the waterfall and enter the creek. So the Golly Gee was essentially a dead creek. It was home to a few brim, crayfish, tadpoles, turtles, carp, salamanders and the like, but there were no bass, or catfish or other game fish in it at all, until a man named Wilson Grunt poured twenty thousand minnows in. His plan was simple, to provide food for the residents of Hillbrook. Everyone in and around the town was excited about the project. Men and kids cleaned and oiled their fishing gear, and everyone contributed to feeding the fish. It would be the following summer before they could try catching small-fry. The idea was very exciting though by that time some of the fish would barely be large enough to keep and eat.

But it was not to be. On Halloween night someone poisoned the creek. And the next day the work hands at Fred's watered the bean plants with creek water and in two days time the plants all died. The poison killed the mature mung bean plants and all the newly stocked minnows. It was a tragedy felt by everyone, and there were no clues as to who had done it. Dead minnows floated on the surface of the creek in town and along its banks all the way to the river.

And then, only a few days later, another more terrible thing happened. A family of four who lived in a house at the outer edge of the little town of Hillbrook, just beyond the city limits, was viciously murdered. Their house was ransacked and anything useful was stolen. This included guns and ammunition. The family's name was Geren, and it was well know that Tom Garen owned a large collection of fire arms.

It was presumed the guns were what the murdering thieves were after, and yet the two women, the mother Phyllis and the daughter Lesley were brutally raped before being murdered. The son, a boy of sixteen named Butch, was stabbed to death with something long and sharp. His three wounds were small but had gone completely through his body. Tom was bludgeoned to death with something heavy and probably metal.

The Hillbrook Police Department lost its state funding four years prior. So accept for the few volunteer peace officers and a locally operated organization, whose members were all well armed men, calling themselves the Minute Men, there was no law enforcement in or around Hillbrook.

The Minute Men were fairly well organized and the leader, Jacob Lawyer, was supposedly under the control of the City Council. However there were leniencies prevalent that were ignored and not usually talked about. But they did not know, and did not have any evidence of who had perpetrated the horrendous crime, but hooligans were suspected to have been the violent offenders.

And then, within days, there came a virulent buzz to the local internet sites. Hooligans had been seen and were running rampant in the area.

Hooligans was the term most used when referring to bands of thieving, malicious people who lived nomadically in wayward places in the mountains and around the countryside, and who were often rightfully blamed for many crimes of theft, rape and murder.

The State Militia and even the National Guard had often been involved in direct conflicts with bands of hooligans around the South. But these military type groups of armed men were most often busy with other matters, bad weather incidents, flood and tornado damage. The hooligan population had grown in number and was growing still. But so were the Minute Men and other locally organized militia organizations in the south, and in other places throughout America. Some people were again starting to use the term civil war. This time, if it truly occurred, it would simply be the bad guys, or as the hooligans referred to themselves: the have-nots of America, against the good guys, the haves of America.

It was when tragedy came to the farm, when Stanley Crammer was found shot to death just outside his home, and his wife Ruth had disappeared, that Nayhoom began to think the fish kill was probably an accident. The intended target from the start could have been the farm and the beans, food for Hillbrook.

The following day, against his better judgment, he left Naomi and went with Bore to complete the installation of a cooling system at a house where three people were very sick and desperately needed some relief from the hot temperatures. Just before he left home Naomi told him that she was certain that she was pregnant. She had done a home pregnancy test twice and both times it was positive.

While he and Bore were working later that morning, word came to them that several hooligan men had been seen at the farm. They left immediately for home. When Nayhoom got to his and Naomi's house, she was not there, and all their food and some clothing was also missing. But he paid no notice of missing things. Naomi was gone and he knew what probably had happened. When he hurried to the greenhouses and the dormitories he found all the doors open and no one around.

While chastising himself greatly for leaving Naomi alone, he went to Fred's house and found Bore with Shirley, Betty and Harriett. Fred was gone and so was Patty. The three girls were hysterical. He heard from them that Bore had saved their lives. He wanted to listen to their tales, but he had to find Naomi. "Naomi is not at home," he told them. And then he rushed out the door and ran back to his house.

# CHAPTER THREE

## PURSUIT

He walked through the house realizing things other than his wife were missing. And then he saw the sign he had made that read Home Sweet Home. It lay on the floor in the corner of the living room. It had a human turd curled on top of it.

With no law enforcement to rely on, he felt he had to immediately go alone after her. There was no question about that. The tracking pill in his arm had long since dissolved, and Fred had taken responsibility for their whereabouts, and had tried several times to get Nayhoom and Naomi to get newer, longer lasting pills. But they had ignored his requests. Now he wished they had both gotten new pills.

He wished also that he had a gun, but he did not. All he had was a wrist rocket given to him by Bore as a kind of present for telling Patty that he was sick one day and couldn't work, when he wasn't sick at all, only lazy. He had also given him a small bag of large, lead split-shot, round fishing sinkers that he could shoot in it. The wrist rocket had not been discovered by the hooligans and stolen. He took it and the bag of split-shot from a drawer, and found an old backpack that had been stashed in the back of a closet. He located his small hatchet with scabbard and belted it and a hunting knife to his side. He took a box of matches from a kitchen shelf and pocketed them, and then he left the house in search of Naomi.

Outside he found footprints in the soft dry ground. They lead him to the creek where he saw that several people had crossed. He wadded the creek. After emerging on the other side he continued following broken shrubbery and a few foot prints until the signs vanished about a mile away. But it was obvious to him that she and her captors had gone across a big field eastward toward the mountains. The hooligans had been known to have encampments in the mountains. And there were many mountains to the east. He had no choice but to try and find where they had gone.

Halfway across the field, and under a large maple tree with yellowing leaves, he picked up their trail again. And he found something he knew Naomi had dropped on purpose. It was her stainless steel bracelet with their names embossed on it. Nayhoom had not yet cried. But after picking up the bracelet and realizing what he had found, he broke down and sobbed. It was positive proof for him that she had been kidnapped and was hoping he would rescue her.

At the edge of the big field the signs again disappeared. He was certain they were headed for the mountains. But that was not a comforting thought because in the mountains he could lose them entirely. An hour later he heard gunfire, and went in that direction, and soon came upon a lone house in the woods. It was quiet, too quiet. And then he saw the front door standing open.

He approached carefully and heard nothing. And then, a few feet from the open doorway, he heard moans coming from inside. He climbed the porch stairs and saw a man lying dead inside the house, on the floor. His head was gashed and bloody. And then he heard moaning again. He went on inside the house and found a woman naked on the kitchen floor. Her throat had been slashed badly. She died while he kneeled over her.

The refrigerator door was open, as were all the cabinet doors in the kitchen. It was apparent what had happened. He rushed out and looked for signs the hooligans might have left. He found some and followed them, continuing his search for Naomi.

Just before dark he found something else she had left. It was a small sheaf of her hair left on a white stone. She had pulled it from her head with her fingers. He put it to his nose and could smell the scent of her. Again he cried.

\*\*\*

At dusk he was lost in the woods and wondering aimlessly a few miles from the foothills of the mountains. He was very tired and his arms and legs were scratched and burning painfully from his salty sweat and from insect bites. His clothes were soaked with sweat, and he was thirsty and hungry. But there was no water or food to be had. He did not care. His only thought was for Naomi and what she might be going through. He might have trudged on, but he heard laughter and crouched behind a small tree. Presently two young boys, about twelve years of age, came running toward him in the darkening woods. There was nothing he could do but be discovered by them. They stopped running and laughing when they saw him, and stood motionless looking at the man crouched behind a thin tree. And then Nayhoom spoke to them.

"Hello. My name is Nayhoom, and I am a bit lost. Can you tell me where I am?"

"How come you are lost?" one of the boys asked.

"I'm looking for someone and I got lost."

"Who?"

"My wife, hooligans took her."

"Hooligans?"

"Yeah. Do you know who I mean?"

"Our house is right back there. You wanna tell my Dad?"

"Yes. I'd like to tell him. Will you go get him?"

The two boys ran back the way they came. Five minutes later two men carrying flashlights and rifles appeared on the path and walked up to him. "My boy said you was lookin'fer yer'wife."

"Yes, hooligans took her, and they came this way, but I've lost them, and I'm lost. I was headed to the mountains where I think they are going, but I've lost my way."

"You don't look so good. Come on back to the house with us and we'll see what we can do."

"OK," Nayhoom said.

The man's name was Doyle Simpson, with his brother Claude. They had made the boys stay at the house while they investigated the man they were told about. They saw that he was harmless and looked him over as they lead him through the woods to Doyle's house. Doyle's brother Claude and young son were visiting and about to leave when the two boys found him. "We ain't never had no trouble with them hooligans, but some have. Did'a hurt anybody?" Doyle asked.

Nayhoom told him and his brother the story about Stanley, and the taking of Naomi, and he told them about the man and woman they killed about ten miles back. "My wife is very pretty, and I think they intend to keep her to rape. I know she is still alive."

"You must be frantic," Doyle said. "I know I would be."

"I am. I feel helpless too. All I have is a wrist rocket against their guns and whatever else they have. I don't know what I can do."

"It's about plumb dark. You can't do nothin' before morning, and I'll bet you are hungry and thirsty. We can help with that. But first thing in the morning I'm going to take my wife and kid to her mother's in Hillbrook."

"That makes sense to me," Nayhoom said. "How are you going to take them?"

"I got'a horse'n buggy."

Doyle's wife's name was Lola, and his son's name was Clarke. After Claude and his son Bo left, Lola set the table and loaded it with food.

Nayhoom washed his hands before he sat down at the table. Pinto beans and cornbread, slaw, wild green and venison were in bowls and dishes before them. He dished out for himself some of everything except the meat.

"Don't you like deer meat?" Doyle asked.

"I'm a vegetarian."

Doyle, Lola and Clarke looked at him like he had just told them he had a disease.

"I'm sorry," Lola said.

"You've nothing to be sorry about. I've just stopped eating meat for personal reasons. But I'll certainly stuff myself with the rest of your fine fare."

"What happened to your wife?" Clarke asked. He had overheard some of the conversation between Doyle and Nayhoom.

"She was kidnapped," he told the boy.

"How come? You think they raped her?"

"Clarke!" his mother said. "Eat and quit asking the man questions.

"How am I going to learn if I don't ask questions?"

"There are some things you don't need to learn," she said.

"It's alright," Nayhoom said. "I don't know what has happened to her. I just know that I have to try and find her."

"If it was hooligans I'll bet they raped her," Clarke said.

"Clarke!" Lola said. "I'm going to make him leave the table Doyle."

"Not another word Clarke or you'll have to take

your supper to your room," Doyle said. "They've been known to hold people for ransom too," he told Nayhoom.

"But there is no one who could pay a ransom. I'm really worried about her."

They ate in silence while it was obvious that Clarke wanted to pursue his rape theory. But he also did not want to go to his room and eat alone, so he kept quiet with the others.

After eating Nayhoom and Doyle sat on the porch and talked while Lola stayed with Clarke inside and packed suitcases for the trip to Hillbrook the following morning.

"You can't just go bargin' in on a band of hoodlums and take her away," Doyle said.

"I know. I'll have to figure something out after I've caught up with them."

"You got no gun. That flipstalk ain't gonna help you none."

"You can kill a person with it if you can get close enough to them."

"Hmmm. I have an extra .45 caliber, semi-automatic pistol in the house and I got an extra telescopic sight for my rifle. I'll loan'em both to'ya, and there won't be no time limits to when you can return'em?"

Nayhoom looked at him. "Really, you'll do that?"

"Shor, just come back with'em some time. And if you can't, you can't. I'll not worry about it. I think you would probably do that for me."

"I sure would."

Before Doyle left the next morning with Lola and Clarke, she stuffed a lot of food into his backpack, along with two blankets. Doyle gave him the rifle scope, pistol, and a box of shells, a canteen filled with water, and last of all he put down inside Nayhoom's backpack a pair of heavy duty, wire pliers. You might need'eze, an' I got four pair. "Don't do nothin' stupid. But I know you will do whatever you have to. Good luck Nayhoom."

They all wished him well and Doyle brought his horse and wagon about and off he went with his wife and son to Hillbrook.

It was just becoming daylight. Nayhoom released the clip of the .45, like Doyle had shown him, and checked its load once again. Then he put the gun into his backpack before shouldering and adjusting the pack to his back, and started walking east, toward the mountains, down a path Doyle had pointed out.

He walked quietly and carefully. When it occurred to him that he might walk up on the party of hooligans any moment, he took the .45 from the backpack and put the barrel of it down inside the front of his white khaki pants, and covered the exposed handle with his shirt tail.

\*\*\*

Naomi would not talk to her captors. But she had not been physically harmed and was kept separated from her friend Ruth Crammer and the two other women. The three were frequently raped by four of the eight men who had abducted them. They were the men who had attacked the farm, and had killed Stanley Crammer, and many other people. Naomi wondered why she was excluded from being raped or killed, but she was very glad that neither had happened.

She had a young body guard who walked behind her. He had been given explicit orders, from the head honcho of their party, a man named Inglewood, to keep her from any harm. This included briars and insects, and anything else that might damage her. But instead of walking in front of her to shield her from briers and flipped-back branches, the young man walked behind Naomi, and kept his eyes glued to her behind.

Just before noon time a house could be seen in the distance, through the trees, across a weeded field. The party stopped and four of the eight men went ahead to investigate.

The four women and the men watching them waited at the edge of the woods by the big field, while the others crossed it to approach the farm house. Soon they heard gunfire and shouting, and then a whistle. "Head out across the field tords the house," one of the men instructed the women.

When they arrived some of the hooligan men were standing on the porch. "We got'chee heart's desire back'in at back bedroom Tim. She's a wait'n on'ye."

Tim was one of the men who had stayed with the women. He smiled and went into the house. Two men lay dead in one bedroom, and two of the hooligans were in another bedroom with two women of the house, raping them. Tim heard the women crying and protesting. He went into the bedroom pointed out to him, and saw a twelve year old girl sitting on a bed. She was also crying.

"Don't cry little-bit. You can go along with this or go

again'it. One way or another I'm gonna fuck thuh shit out'a'ya. Ge'tat dress off."

Naomi was locked in a small, mostly barren, storage room on the back porch, and the other women were left outside. The screams of the women who lived there, and the little girl inside, were heard by everyone. Naomi cried and covered her ears. And then, by the light of a small window in the door, she saw a short pencil stub on the floor. A wadded paper sack was in a cardboard box. She tore a piece of paper from the sack and wrote a message to Nayhoom. It was a message she hoped she could leave somewhere he would find. An old plaque was hanging on the wall that read Home Sweet Home. She put the note behind the plaque just before they came for her.

When the attackers left the house, all who had been at the farm house, and surprised by their arrival, were dead. They were either shot like the men had been or, like the child, strangled by hand. The food pantry was raided and four rifles, including the ammunition for them, were also taken.

\*\*\*

Naomi noticed that when she got tired and complained, they stopped and rested. But if any of the other women complained about needing to rest, they were ignored. That is when it occurred to her that she was being kept for someone special. She asked the man responsible for watching her. "Am I being treated differently for a reason?"

"Because you are so purty Inglewood is taking you to

Ramar. He's hopin' to win brownie points."

"Who is Ramar?"

"The main man. You're gonna find out. At's for sure."

She had other questions but thought it best to not ask them. She trusted none of the hooligan men, and was not allowed to talk with Ruth and the other women. Her main worry was that Nayhoom was following and he would be discovered and killed. She could only hope that he would find her note and heed her warning. And she realized that he might not be on their trail at all, and could even be dead. She was tempted to succumb to her despair, but she considered that without hopefulness and an effort of strength she had nothing. And the other women were worse off. They had been raped, and Ruth's husband Stanley was definitely dead. She assumed the other women had lost love ones also.

Naomi knew they were going toward the mountains to the east, but she wasn't sure exactly how close they were until she could see tall ridges rising close above the tree tops, and the trail they were on began to take an upward climb. A man approached her guard and spoke softly to him. He nodded and directed Naomi to continue walking up the trail. They had left the others behind. After five minutes he grabbed her arm to stop. They sat on the ground and waited.

Three gun shots rang out in succession and her guard stood up. Soon the other men, without the women, came by them. Naomi and her guard, called Tombs, fell in behind. She knew her friend Ruth and the other women had been shot. She cried as she walked up the steepening path.

Night came and they camped among a cluster of huge

boulders. One of the men made ham sandwiches and handed them out, but after taking two from him, when no one was watching, she tossed them out in the dark. The sandwiches landed in dry leaves where she knew some animal, or animals, would find and eat them. Refusing a blanket from her guard, she lay on the ground and tried to sleep. She was exhausted.

*** 

Up in the morning of the following day, Nayhoom stepped onto the porch of the farmhouse. He heard the toenail clicks of several animals as they ran through the house and out the open back door. There was already the smell of death in the air, and he knew that other than the two men on the floor in the living room he would find more bodies inside. He did, and did not investigate them closely other than to see that Naomi, or anyone else he knew, was not among them.

On the back porch he saw the door to the storage room and opened it. He saw the home Sweet Home plaque on the wall and stared at it. He remembered the one he had made and the turd left on it. He turned to leave, and then he stopped and looked again at the plaque. He went to it and took it down, and Naomi's note to him fell to the floor. He picked the folded piece of sack paper up and read what she had written:

*Nayhoom,*
*I am guessing that you will find this note. I don't even*

*know that you are following us, or that you are alive, but I think you are both.*

*I love you more than anything or anyone including myself. I am very worried that you will attempt to rescue me and will be caught and killed. These people are completely ruthless and evil. They care only about their own well being and I believe they hate everyone else. They will have no compunction about killing you. Actually they will enjoy it. I think you probably won't stop looking for me, but please know that your life is precious to me. I would die of despair if you were to be killed. Please be more than careful. Be very, very, smart.*

*I love, love, love, you,*
*Naomi*

He put the note in his pocket and started looking for signs of their departure.

At Dusk he found the bodies of Ruth Crammer and the other two women. He was shocked and horrified to find Ruth dead, but that Naomi was not with them he considered being somewhat encouraging. It was more than obvious that what she wrote in her note about the mercilessness of her captors was very accurate. He climbed the mountain side until dark, and then he found a grouping of rocks a few feet off the trail, and sat among them to eat some of what Lola had packed for him. After eating he found a level spot and bedded down for the night on her blankets.

He awoke before daylight. By morning's first light he gathered his things and started walking up the trail that obviously they were walking also. He carried in his hand the telescopic gun sight that Doyle had lent him. It was powerful to be so small. He could make out the details of leaves a hundred yards or more in the distance. He sighted through it often, looking for any movement or change in color among the leaves and trees up ahead. He checked the ammunition clip of the hand gun he carried crammed down in behind the belt of his pants. But he had no idea what he could or would do if or when he came upon them. His thoughts were like prayers, though he was not specifically aware that he was praying.

The trail he followed became more of a path and steeper all along. He was ascending the west side of a mountain and, by certain signs, was convinced the group of hooligans with Naomi had gone that way before him. Carefully he climbed, careful to make no noise other than the dry, crunching sounds of walking as stealthily as he could on the inclining path.

Presently he heard the faint sound of gunfire ahead far in the distance, and over the top of the ridge he was climbing. His heart sank. He could think only the worst. He hastened his pace and soon came to the top of the ridge. Down below through the trees, far down the steep face of the ridge, he saw a flash of reflected sunlight, and could hear the faint sound of voices. He thought that if Naomi had been killed he would attack the men and probably be killed also. But first he had to see if she was dead or alive.

After ten minutes of slipping down that side of the ridge, he saw movement further down below. He squatted behind a large boulder and sighted through the gun scope and saw three men standing over what appeared to be a deer they were butchering. And then he saw Naomi sitting on the ground a few feet away from the men and their kill. He turned and relaxed his back against the boulder. She was still alive.

He turned and scoped her again. She looked tired but otherwise OK. The men looked filthy and desperate. They also looked dangerous. He wondered if he could just sneak up on them and shoot them all with the pistol. And then he considered that it had been several years since he had fired a gun, and then it was the first and only time, and it was a single shot .22 rifle. He had no confidence at all about any success with an aggressive shoot and kill plan. Just as Naomi had suggested, he would have to be very, very, smart.

He followed them at some distance until on that far side of the mountain the terrain changed. He had come into a wooded depression, and realized he was entering into an area where many people were camped. He could hear and smell them and their fires, and see trash they had discarded.

He found a spot high on a bluff, up from the trail he was following, from which he could scope and see a clearing where many people were gathering to welcome the hooligan party with Naomi. He saw her, and decided he should now rest a little and think.

***

The people all gathered around them and held their hands out for whatever was brought. The men put the spoils on a long table for a man named Cobb to go through and hand out. Naomi watched from the log she sat on. It was mostly young women and children, and a few old men and old women, who were waiting. It didn't take long and everything the hooligan men brought was gone, and still there were people waiting and wanting more. "There'll be more later on, probably today. Y'all'll just have'ta wait," Cobb said.

Two strange men held Naomi by her arms, and led her away through the woods. Soon they came to a small shack. It was cobbled together with logs, plywood, rusty wire and rusty, hammer straightened nails. There was a thick tar paper roof covering it that did not leak, and no smoke curled from its old, rusty stove pipe chimney.

One of the men knocked on the plywood door, and then he opened it and shoved Naomi inside. Then he and the other man stood outside by the door as guards.

She immediately looked for another way out but there was not one she could find. Without knowing where she was, she knew she was trapped. It occurred to her that the dwelling she was in probably belonged to the man named Ramar they were holding her for. She could smell sweat and there were other foul smelling odors.

An hour lapsed and intermittently she heard what sounded like the cheers and jeers of many people some distance away. And though she did not understand what the guards were saying she heard their voices just outside the door.

She was extremely fatigued and had not eaten properly since the day of her abduction. Hungry and tired, she sat on the floor, and then laid on it. And then, without realizing what was happening, she fell asleep.

\*\*\*

Ramar's actual name was Horace Brock. He took the name Ramar from tales his grandfather told about an old TV series called Ramar Of The Jungle. Horace was 33 years old, 6'5"tall, 250 lbs. He kept hair shaved from his muscular body, except the blond, curly, hair of his head. He was very strong, and imaginatively envisioned himself as a type of Robin Hood. He was top dog among many of the local hooligan gangs.

Ramar befriended men like himself, men willing to take from the haves and give to the have-nots. The haves were anyone who had something, and the have-nots were mostly people who would think like him and be thieves. He enjoyed being a bully and, as he put it, breaking heads. He was not dim witted, but also he was not very smart, only strong and charismatic in a crude way. Everyone around him feared him because he was also mean and ruthless, and had a history of violence without ever being punished or brought to justice for being so. He had lived a charmed life and was in essence spoiled and arrogant.

He had fought and had killed one man in an earlier bout that night. Upon entering the cage, the man he would kill looked scared, and he looked not at all sure of why he was where he was, in a cage to fight to the death with a very big guy. A crudely painted sign hung over the gate entrance that read as a sign in an old movie once read: Two Enter, One Leaves. He had not understood clearly his choices, and he had no idea how or why he had been chosen from twelve other men, who like him had been captured and hauled far from their homes, to be locked in a cave for three days, and then eventually plucked from it, and forced to fight a man nearly twice their size.

But that was the situation and the man realized fully that it was no dream, as Ramar toyed with him for awhile, priming the crowd, throwing him around the big, rusty wire, cage built by his men. Then he broke the man's arm. A loud roar rose from the shabby crowd perched along the circular bank surrounding the bowl-like depression in the center of the mountain hideaway. The roar obliterated the man's screams of agony. And then Ramar grabbed his head and looked at his audience. They cheered and many, like in movies, gave him the old Roman, thumbs down sign. He then broke the man's neck.

After Ramar opened the cage from the inside, three fight flunkies dragged the man out, deep into the woods, to a previously dug, shallow grave. After burying him they threw a few large stones on top of the grave to discourage animals from digging, and then walked back to the activity.

After his fight, Ramar mounted his ride and roared back to his dwelling, his shack, which had been built by several of his cohorts. He parked the four-wheeler, and dismounted. The all-terrain vehicle, with a gasoline powered engine, was the only one in the camp. Men wishing to win his favor had stolen it for him along with a hundred gallons of gasoline and two cases of motor oil. Giving big gifts to the head honcho was something each man in the band of hooligans aspired to do. It could be their opportunity to step up.

He was still, wearing his makeshift loin cloth, one

that partially exposed his genitals. He wore nothing else, except a pair of slip-on tennis shoes necessary for shifting gears on the four-wheeler. The guards almost bowed as he approached them.

"Inglewood brung you a women," one of the guards told him. "She's inside."

Ramar said nothing to the two men, except: "Stay put," and went inside. Naomi had awakened when she heard him arrive.

"Dammmm," Ramar said after getting a good look at her by candle light. "Inglewood did good. I'm Ramar. I guess you heard about me."

She said nothing.

"You can talk can't you?"

Again she said nothing.

"Take your clothes off," he said.

"Go to hell!"

"So you can talk. I'm gonna fuck you, you know that don't you?"

"I'm pregnant. Doesn't that mean anything to you?"

"Nothing," he said. But he was lying. His father and his mother were both superstitious. Ramar was too, and like his parents he believed that screwing a pregnant woman could make him impotent.

"I'm tired right now. But tomorrow is another day."

He went outside and told the guards to take her to Becky. "An y'all check in over there often and watch that she don't get away, or damaged. She better not! You hear me?"

The men nodded that they understood.

After the two men left with Naomi, Ramar took his loincloth off and stood before a full length mirror, and by candle light he admired his sweaty, muscular body. And then from a drawer in an old chest he pulled out a large, paper wrapped parcel containing the hind leg bone of a pig, and bit into the meat. The hog leg had been cooked along with the rest of the pig over an open flame. It was only two days old and not yet rancid.

After eating his fill he drank from a stolen, Quart bottle of Old Barton. Soon he was buzzing and fell asleep on his feted, sweat soaked bed.

\*\*\*

At first light, Nayhoom made his way down from his perch high on the bluff, and went stealthily closer to the compound. A hundred yards from it he climbed a tall sycamore tree and found a pretty good view of a clearing near the center. From that vantage point he had a fair observation of the entire campsite, though much of it was hidden by the last of fading, fall leaves. No one was yet awake and stirring around, but soon two women appeared with buckets. They were going for water at a spring not far away. He watched through the rifle scope, and eventually saw the spring and the women dipping water from it. He watched them through the matrix of limbs and sparseness of shriveling, and paling, fall foliage, and saw the women fill their buckets and then return.

After they were inside their shabbily fashioned tents again, fearing that he could eventually be seen, he climbed down from the tree, and went through the forest, and climbed a ridge, and then another tree. From high in the red oak he had an even better view of the compound's clearing, though he was at least another hundred yards away. But it seemed to him unlikely that he could be seen, so he relaxed and considered that coming up with a good plan was going to be very difficult.

He ate the last of what Lola had given him, and he drank the last of the water. He thought then he would soon have to go to the spring he had seen and fill his canteen. And it wouldn't be long before he would be hungry. Water was an absolute necessity and so was a bit of food. He climbed down, and when reaching the ground his foot rolled on a hickory nut, He realized then what he must do right away.

He walked further east, away from the encampment, looking for something he could eat. He wasn't hungry yet but he knew that he would soon be.

As he walked through the woods, he stopped from time to time to gather hickory nuts that lay on the ground. He filled his pockets, and then began putting them into his backpack. Being careful to not lose his way, he walked only a few hundred yards from the big, red oak he had climbed. He was in a draw, a small valley between ridges that suddenly started down an steep slope. He saw that the trees were becoming smaller, and possibly were replacing trees recently cut, and then he saw what he knew to be kudzu vines hanging from the branches of small trees a bit further down the draw.

Kudzu is eatable, and when he was fourteen he had once gone to gather it with a kid at the orphanage. The boy, named Grady, had taught him a lot about wild eatable foods, but he had never used any of the knowledge. One day he and Grady found plenty of Kudzu, and had cooked and eaten it, so he knew it was eatable and tasted OK. But it was early summer then, when the vine is tender, and the weather was not yet quite so hot. It was now November and almost five years later. And though the vine he could see was clearly alive he didn't know for sure if he would be able to eat any of it.

With closer inspection he found many purple blossoms peeking out among its leaves, and he knew also the blossoms were eatable. He had eaten them before too. The weather was very hot and detrimental to some plants, but the inclement temperature had not harmed this particular patch of kudzu, up in the shady, cooler mountains. It seemed to be flourishing, and though it was late summer it was still blooming.

✳✳✳

From another tree close to the compound, he found an even better view of the central clearing inside the encampment. While looking through the scope he saw Naomi with a woman. They were sitting under a big, ragged, umbrella covering a table. She looked well. He wondered if their baby was well. His eyes filled with tears and he had to wipe them. When he looked again she was walking away from the table with the woman, and they went inside a tent and did not come back out right away.

The tent was made of a light colored cloth, so he was

certain it would be easy to see from wherever he might choose to observe the encampment. He moved closer still, and climbed another tree, and again saw the same light colored tent. He realized again it was going to be nearly impossible getting her away.

He climbed back up the bluff and found his original view point, and there, using the scope, he saw again through the trees the light colored tent. She emerged from it with the woman and they went to the table with the umbrella and sat. It began to come to him at that point what he must do next.

After spending most of the day cracking and eating hickory nuts, and munching on kudzu blossoms, and then sneaking to the spring to fill his canteen, he decided that at dusk he must try to get close to the light colored tent, and possibly let Naomi know that he was trying to find a way of rescuing her.

Taking ample time, precaution, and a wide berth around the campsite, he worked his way to a place on the side of the ridge he thought was just above the tent where she was kept. Slowly, and as silently as he could descend the wooded ridge, he crept to a spot just above the tent. From there he could hear Naomi and the woman talking. He could not make out what they were saying, but he recognized Naomi's voice. After an hour of watching and waiting for an inspirational idea to occur to him, the woman left the tent and went to another one.

He eased closer still, until he was about ten feet away from the tent and crouched behind a tree. He was certain the tent before him was the one she was in, but there was a possibility that someone else could be in there with her. If so, and he called to her, it could be the end of him and his attempt to rescue her for sure. There was no time to think about it. He had to try.

"Naomi," he whispered loudly.

There was no answer so he tried again.

"Nayhoom, is that you?"

"It's me. I've been following you. I found your note. I'm trying to think of a way to free you."

"I just knew you were behind us," she said softly. "I am handcuffed to the bed and can't leave this tent. You must be careful. They will kill you for sure. A man called Ramar is the big boss man around here. He rides an all terrain four wheeler and he kills men for the fun of it. If he knows you are here he will run you down, and kill you for sure. Please don't let that happen. I love you."

"And I love you. I'm trying like you said, to be very smart. But this place is well guarded and it will not be easy taking you away. But I'll never stop trying until I do. I love you. How is our baby?"

"So far so good."

"Has he or anyone hurt you?"

"No, not yet anyway."

"Shhhh," Nayhoom said.

The woman was returning. She stopped outside the tent door and looked directly toward him. And then she went inside. Nayhoom cautiously sat for nearly another hour, and then slowly he crawled as silently as he could back up and away from the tent, and to where he thought it would be safe to stand up and walk. He climbed the ridge in the dark and found a place, on the mountain slope among some large rocks, to spend the night.

At first light he took the same wide berth around the encampment, back to the ledge where he felt safe. He considered that if and when he could get her away, they would need food to maintain them while they were returning to the lowlands. He decided to go nut gathering, and then gather more Kudzu blossoms.

His orientation with the hooligan camp, its position in the mountains, and the way he had arrived, was now secure in his mind. At the top of the ridge above the bluff, he looked through the trees, back down in the direction of Hillbrook, and thought he saw, far away in the lower foothills, a flash of reflected light. The morning sun was very bright. He thought what he saw might be more hooligans arriving. The only way to know for certain was to be where he could see clearly whoever it was when they came nearer. So he went in that direction, stopping from time to time to gather hickory nuts and store them in his backpack.

From another tree he scoped the most often used way up the mountain and saw several men approaching. He climbed down and took another position in another tree. From there he could see the men clearly coming on, and they did not look like hooligans. And then he saw his friend Bore. Bore and many men were looking for him and Naomi. He would soon learn that the men were a large number of Minute Men from around Hillbrook, and Bore had joined-up with them.

He waited on the trail and just as they were approaching he stepped out with his hands in the air. The men stopped when they saw him and Bore came forward.

"Nayhoom, we are looking for you and Naomi. And it looks like you found us first. Is she alright?"

"She is being held by the hooligans. I know where she is and she knows that I am trying to find a way to rescue her."

\*\*\*

Bore showed him a tracking device and told him that Ruth Crammer had a new tracking pill in her arm so they were able to easily find her body and the bodies of the other women. He said that Brian had learned that there was a large hooligan camp in the mountains to the east which could be reached on foot from the town of Hillbrook. The hooligans had killed ten people on the day Naomi was taken, and Stanley Crammer's wife Ruth and two other women were abducted. Bore made clear the details of how he and the Minute Men had found their bodies, and had also found several people dead at a farm house. Nayhoom told Bore about the first house he came to where the hooligans had attacked and killed people, and that he also had come across the dead people in the farm house Bore and the Minute Men saw. It was where Naomi had left him the note. And he told him about finding Ruth's body and those of the other woman who had been shot.

"Naomi told me that the man in charge of the hooligans was a man they called Ramar. She said he was a murderer and would kill me for certain if I was caught. I don't know how I can ever sneak her out and away."

"Has she been harmed in any way?"

"I asked her and she said no. She is pregnant with our baby and she said that so far she and the baby were OK."

They devised a simple plan. Nayhoom would return and go down close to the white tent. At dark Bore and the Minute Men would attack the encampment. Hopefully the ruckus created would give Nayhoom an opportunity to snatch Naomi away. He drew a generalized map of the compound and showed Bore on it where Naomi was and told him which way he thought he and she would go. Bore offered to give him a pair of wire cutters to cut her handcuffs, but Nayhoom showed him the strong pair Doyle had given him. He brought out the pistol. "I'll get her free. I just hope I won't have to shoot anyone."

"Those people are dogs, pure trash. Don't worry about killing any of them. Just save Naomi."

He knew the plan had to work, there were no other choices. The circumstances were obviously dire. He left Bore and the men. Trotting, and then climbing quickly up the mountain path, he went directly over the ridge to the other side, and straight to a place above the white tent, and Naomi, and waited for darkness to come.

\*\*\*

Ramar had thought often about the woman Inglewood brought him. He thought she was the most beautiful woman he had ever seen. But there was something about her that he was totally unfamiliar with. She seemed to loath him for one thing. But that was not it, and he had no good ideas as to what it was specifically that interested him so. She was a different kind of woman creature altogether, he thought, so seemingly self reliant. Many women appeared that way to him, but he saw that at bottom they were all as needy as the next. But this one gave him a different impression totally, she was different, and she seemed so strong, like him, he mused. He was definitely attracted to her, but she was pregnant. He considered that she might be lying about that to save herself. But he knew she was being truthful. He wanted to see her again. After removing his shirt and donning a skin tight pair of jeans, he rode his four-wheeler over to Becky's tent.

He parked it nearby and walked to it, and went inside without calling out. Becky was naked though he hardly noticed. She did not respond either. Naomi sat on her pallet, but stood with her hands cuffed behind her back when he came in.

"You are one pretty woman," he said to her, and flexed a pectoral muscle. She scowled at him and looked away.

"I'm not such a bad guy. Ask Becky, she'll tell'ya. Ain't you even gonna talk to me?"

"I don't need for anyone to talk to me about anything. I've been kidnapped and I want to be released to go home. I am pregnant and I need to be close to a doctor. If you had any decency about you at all, you would take me back and leave me to the only life that matters to me."

"I just think that before long you will learn to like it around here, and like our way of life."

"Why don't you bet your life on that," she said hatefully.

126

"I'm a good guy when you get to know me."

"Your way of thinking is at its end. You are among the last of men who have thus far believed that life is a contest and only the strong and aggressive survive to be winners...winners of what?

"Winners of whatever is available. Winners of the moment."

The people you kill. They are the losers of the moment. Is that right?"

"That is obvious."

"You are disgusting!"

He looked sternly at her, and then at Becky who was fully clothed now. "Don't let her out of your sight. You hear me?"

"I hear you," Becky said.

"And don't harm a hair on her head, or let anybody else."

"I won't," she said.

\*\*\*

While he waited at the top of the ridge above the tent where Naomi was kept, Nahoom rehearsed in his mind what could happen after Bore and his men commenced the raid. Bad things might happen, and he knew this. There would be one chance to take her away, and that would probably be all. With the scope he sighted down through the woods and picked the best route back up the ridge, as they would be hurrying in the dark, and he did not want to be running into trees. But it was very thick with trees all the way down to the tent, so it would be difficult to negotiate the woods on the way back up in the dark. But that had to be as it would be. He didn't attempt to pray exactly, but he was asking God for help when the time came to flee with her and their unborn baby.

He checked his backpack to make sure of what he had they might need. He checked the automatic pistol to see if it was loaded and ready. Should he need to use it he hoped he could do it without screwing up. He cocked and released the mechanisms several times, and then he put it in the front pocket of his pants. There was nothing now to do except wait for dusk and then darkness.

When the time finally came he slipped as silently as he could down the ridge in the darkening light of day. A hundred feet from the tent he stopped and squatted behind a large tree. He would be able to traverse the last few feet quickly when it was time.

Slowly total darkness came, and he heard gunfire near the beginning of the encampment and wooded gulch. When the gunfire increased, the girl watching Naomi came out of the well lit tent and looked toward the loud sounds. Nayhoom grew tense and troubled by the aggrandizing of gunfire and the screams of women and children. The girl just stood in front of the tent, looking toward the loud sounds like she was waiting for a parade. And then she dashed back inside the tent. He could hear her talking loudly to Naomi.

"There is big trouble up the way there. We got'a get out of here. If you run away you'll get us both killed. Do you understand me?"

Nayhoom knew he had to move quickly, and he

hoped he would not have to shoot the girl. He was poised and ready with his gun, and was going to confront the girl and take Naomi when he heard the four-wheeler and saw its lights headed toward the tent. He could not decide what to do, so he crouched again behind the tree.

Ramar stopped just outside the tent.

"Becky!" he shouted. She emerged with Naomi still handcuffed. "Bring her over here," he said against a backdrop of gunfire and loud voices.

Becky shoved Naomi forward. "You're taking me...too aren't you?" she said.

"I'll have to come back for you," he said while unlocking the handcuffs.

"You ain't commin' back, you're runnin'."

He forced Naomi to get on behind him, and then he fastened her hands around his waist with the handcuffs. "I'll be back," he said.

"You're lying!!" she screamed frantically.

"Get away Becky. I don't want to have to shoot you," he said, and roared off through the woods in the dark with Naomi. Becky picked up a stick and threw it after them.

Nayhoom was shocked. Naomi was gone again. He scrambled back up the ridge hoping to see which way they were going. At the top of the ridge he could intermittently hear the motor vanishing somewhere to the east further into the mountains. And then, briefly, he saw the vehicle's lights. He watched and waited for some time as the lights would appear and then disappear. Eventually he could hear the motor no longer, but occasionally he saw flashes of light until he saw them no more.

The encampment below was falling to the Minute Men. The hooligans were out gunned and out smarted. And then he saw fire, a lot of fire. Bore and his companions were burning the tents with flame throwers and then extinguishing the flames before the woods could flare up. He heard the screams of women and children, and the yells and curses of hooligan men.

There was no choice to be made about waiting for Bore and the Minute Men, or leaving now to continue his quest to rescue Naomi. He considered that every minute he was not in pursuit, was a minute that later might ultimately mean the life or death of his wife and unborn child.

He stumbled through the woods until he found the logging road Ramar had taken. He could still smell the oil that had belched from the vehicle's engine.

A bit of moon had risen in the east which allowed him barely enough light to continue walking in the road without walking off it. He was determined to search for her for as long as it took. He felt that he and Naomi were one, and without her he was only half alive.

# CHAPTER FOUR

## TRACK DOWN

Nayhoom followed the four-wheel tracks through the mountains all the following day, and then they vanished. The road bed was becoming very rocky so he thought that further on he might pick them up again, but he did not. Naomi was gone, and he was essentially lost. There was nothing he could do except continue on until the old logging road led somewhere that hopefully he would find a trace of her again.

Hungry and nearly exhausted he sat by a small, dry, brook and cracked nuts and nibbled at the goodies. He longed for a large bowl of pinto beans, beans cooked by Naomi. And then he cried. A voice spoke to him from behind: "Hey young feller. What's ye problem?"

He turned quickly and saw an old man standing several yards up the road. "Are you lost?" the man said.

"I guess I am," Nayhoom replied. "Where does this road lead?"

"I guess you can go dang near anywheres on it ye'ont to. Where you goin?"

"I'm looking for someone. I think they went this

way."

"On a motor'sickle?"

"Yeah, an all terrain four wheel vehicle."

"I heared it go by early this morning. Friends's a'yorn?"

"My wife."

"She run off with another feller?"

"She was kidnapped."

"Oh. If that was them, they long gone by now. The main highway ain't but about five mile from here. Do you know which a'way they was goin' after that?"

"I don't have a clue. He was a big man with the hooligans."

"They might'uv gone left then. They's lots'a hooligans ou'tat way, further up in'a mountains. You wanna come wi'me back at my place an' get som'm'ta eat? You look like you could use som'm."

"I probably could. I'm pretty whipped."

The old man lived alone in a small, eighteen foot camper trailer situated permanently up on concrete blocks. It had a small, cobbled together porch with a tin roof across the front of it, and old pieces of tin roofing were tacked around the bottom to ward against cold air in the winter. But the winters in East Tennessee were never cold anymore. The rubber tires had long since dry-rotted, and fallen apart. It was perched on the side of a gentle wooded rise near a spring the old man said was almost dry. But it had not yet dried completely, and the water was sweet, but above all it was cool and wet. Nayhoom guzzled it.

"You don't need to drank too much," the old man

said.

"I'm plumb dry," Nayhoom said. "But you are right. I should take it easy."

"What's you had to eat?"

"Hickory nuts and Kudzu blossoms, and some greens I found along the road back there."

"That ain't much. In got meat and samp an tators inside. Ye'ont some'at? I got plenty."

"I'll pass on the meat. What is samp?"

"How come? Hit's just squirrel an' possum."

"I'm a vegetarian. What is samp?"

"How come? Meat's good fer'ye."

"I just am. I reckon I can't explain it. What's samp?"

"Cornmeal mush. Ever had any?"

"Sure, lots'a times. I like it. What is your name? Mine is Nayhoom."

"Nayhoom? I ain't never heard at'n. Mine is Howard, Howard Free."

"Nice to meet you Howard. I'm Nayhoom Waddell."

"Nice to meet you. Veggearian, what's the opposite of a veggearian?"

"A carnivore I guess."

"Yeah, that's me, a carnivore."

The old man farted. "Vegearians fart don't'a?"

"Yeah, but veggearian's farts don't stink," he said with straight face.

The old man looked perplexed until he saw Nayhoom's wry smile, and then he laughed. "Just li'ol popcorn farts, Right? They even smell like popcorn, right?" he said laughing. Nayhoom laughed with him.

*\*\**

He ate loudly, sucking on the squirrel and opossum bones. He had also cooked cornmeal mush, and Irish potatoes that he had grown. Nayhoom ate a big bowl of cornmeal mush the old man called samp. It was sweetened with the goo of a big locust bean, and he ate some of the boiled potatoes. "You're a good cook Howard, and I appreciate you letting me eat with you. I guess I was headed for starvation."

"It takes a long time to starve. But this grub will hold it off a bit longer," he said, and sucked loudly on the thigh bone of a young opossum. "You ought'a dive in on some'iss meat. Hit'll stick to'ye ribs a lot longer'n at samp'n tatots. I couldn't live without meat."

"There's lots'a people in the world older than me or you that don't eat meat."

"Who?" Howard wanted to know.

"I don't have any names. I just...."

"Ah! At's what I thought. Man's an animal. Animals eat meat. It's natural."

"How did you get this? Did you shoot them?"

"I ain't got no gun. I trapped'em. I got lots'a traps. I trapped'em. Squirrels and possums are stupit. Squirrels are the smartest though. But I'm smarter. Tough shit if you ask me!"

"I see."

"See what?"

"I mean I thought you might have shot them. But you trapped'em."

"You damn right I did. You want some comfrey tea?"

"No, I'm full Howard. I really liked that samp with the locust bean. I'll not forget it."

"Well. I wish I had some sugar, and some coffee, but them thangs are hard to come by. Cornmeal is hard too, but I got a bunch last time."

"Where, where did you get them?"

"A little store called Green's over in Brad Town, bout five mile from here. Take a left down on the main road. You'll see it directly, if'n you go lookin' fer'em hooligans. They hang out over at'a way."

"I'm going, but I don't know what I'll do when I find'em."

"Steer clear of'em."

"But they have my wife."

"You shor she didn't take up with'em?"

"I'm sure."

"Well. Just don't do nothin' stupit."

"I'll try to remember that."

"Well. Let's sit on the porch. There might be a breeze ou'tair."

\*\*\*

There was no breeze, it was hot and humid. They sat silently, letting the food digest, and then Howard began telling about the days when he was in the logging business. According to him he was the hardest worker with the company he worked for. All the others were slackers. He talked about his two wives. "Women are evil," he said. "My two daughters were both whores, and my son Jimmy overdosed on pain pills and died."

"I'm sorry about that," Nayhoom said, "Life is hard on everybody."

"You dang right it is. Even rich folks struggles with it," Howard said.

They sat without talking for a long time. Squirrels scampered noisily among the dry leaves. Soon Nayhoom began to nod sleepily. "I go to bed early," Howard said, "cos I get up early, real early. You reckon you can sleep on the floor? I can throw some blankets down, make it a bit softer."

"Sure, I'm tired. I could sleep anywhere."

"Well, I'm goin'ta head at way. You can sit out here long as ye'ont to. I'll put the blankets in a chair in'air, an' you can spread'em out anywheres ye'ont to. I get up early. You get up wi'me?"

"Yeah, I want to get an early start."

"Well, see'ya then," Howard said, and went inside his camper.

Nayhoom sat on the porch until he heard the old man snoring and farting, and then he decided he might sleep better on the porch. He went inside and got the blankets and took them back and made his pallet on the porch floor. It was a hot, sultry night, but while thinking about Naomi and their unborn baby, he went to sleep, sweat trickling down the sides of his head.

\*\*\*

Howard was awake at three AM and boiling water to

make tea. Nayhoom awoke and joined him. "What kind of tea is that you're making?"

"Comfrey. Hit grows in'a woods all around here. You'll like it I bet. Can you eat some more samp?"

"Sure, that yesterday was good."

"I'll fix us some directly. Let's sit out on the porch and drank iss tea, OK?"

"Thanks again for your hospitality Howard."

"Yer welcome."

Again they found little to talk about that morning, so they drank the tea, and then ate, and quietly listened to the awakening sounds of the woods. An hour before daylight a thermometer on the old man's porch read 88 degrees. After breakfast and another cup of comfrey tea they discussed the weather, global warming. Howard told him he thought he wouldn't live much longer. "This heat will get the last laugh. I've dreamed about my death several times lately." Nayhoom said that he could only speculate about when he would die.

"Spec-e-ate?"

"Guess," Nayhoom said. "There is no real way of knowing when you are going to die."

Howard smiled. "Is'a uh real way'a knowin' about anything? You see what you see, thank what ye thank, an' know what ye know, an' do what you do."

"No truer words have ever been spoken," Nayhoom said, shouldering his backpack and stepping off the porch to leave.

The old man smiled again. "You ought'a stay another day. Get's ye a good plan up."

"I'll have to plan while I walk."

"Well, make a hundred. Nice meet'n ye," he said, and waved goodbye.

"Nice neet'n you too Howard. Thank you very much."

He found the old road again easily enough, and set out down it at a quick pace. His stomach was full, but good nutrition had thus far been very thin, and would probably continue being thin. Walking down the logging road just before daylight he considered that he wasn't getting enough protein. And then he decided that his fate depended on more than protein.

Parts of a string of quotations from the Bible popped into his head, quotes he partially remembered from his days at the orphanage. The exact quotes from Matthew are this: *Therefore take no thought, saying, What shall we eat? or, What shall we drink? or, Wherewithal shall we be clothed? (For after all these things do the Gentiles seek:) for your heavenly Father knoweth that ye have need of all these things. But seek ye first the kingdom of God, and his righteousness; and all these things shall be added unto you. Take therefore no thought for the morrow: for the morrow shall take thought for the things of itself. Sufficient unto the day is the evil thereof.* Meaning each day has enough trouble of its own.

He stopped at a small brook, water trickling from beneath a limestone shelf, and took his clothes off to rinse the sweat from his body. "I'll eat what I eat," he said to a squirrel watching him from a nearby oak tree.

\*\*\*

Nayhoom was headed for Brad Town. He thought he might complete the five mile walk by eleven AM or maybe before. He checked the clip in the pistol and put it back in the front pocket of his, now very dirty, white khaki pants.

Eventually, when the logging road became soft again, he saw the wheel tracks left by Ramar's vehicle. That was an encouraging development. But the only thing he had been able to think of for rescuing Naomi was shooting Ramar, and riding away with her on the four wheeler. But he had never shot a pistol, and had never been on a four wheeler, and he had no idea how to operate it. He thought he might see Ramar operate it, and if it was simple, he could then do it. He realized that crippled plan was no plan at all. He was discouraged completely. But he felt he had to follow them and attempt something, but not something that might jeopardize her safety or his own.

When he came to the main road it was ten-thirty in the morning. The old paved highway was essentially abandoned. An occasional delivery truck, going to the grocery store in Brad Town was about all that ever traveled it anymore. But there were numerous droppings of dung from horses, and other domestic farm animals, on the paved surface. Owning a mule, pony or horse, was a sign of prosperity for the local mountain people. If you did not own such an animal, you needed to know someone who did.

After seeing where the wheel tracks crossed a muddy section between the logging road and the highway, and turned left toward Brad Town, he went left also. He remembered Howard saying that he would see the store directly. And he did, around the first curve he came to.

He saw first, tacked to the side of an old, concrete building, a Pepsi Cola sign, and a Snickers Bar sign. And then he saw other signage at the front of the store. The name, Green's Grocery, was hand written with a broad brush and green paint on the side of the building. A cow stood at the rear, looking lonesome and forlorn, chewing its cud. There were no people about. The old store looked deserted.

But it was not deserted. When Nayhoom walked into the weeded parking lot, a man came from the store pointing a shotgun at him. "You can just get on back out on the road there," the man said.

"I don't mean any harm," Nayhoom said. "I'm looking for my wife. She was kidnapped by hooligans."

The man lowered the shotgun. "You look like you might be a hooligan yourself."

"I'm not though. I just spent the night with a man named Howard Free, back up that old logging road back there. Do you know him?"

"Yeah I know'im. What's your name?"

"Nayhoom Waddell."

"Nayhoom? I don't know nothin' bout your wife, but I know a little about them hooligans. Come on in the store here an' we'll talk."

The store appeared bare of many normal things. There were a few canned foods, salt, sugar, flour, cornmeal and some other staple goods, and topical medicines, but the candy, cake, and chip racks were empty. There were no cold drinks, bread, or vegetables. There wasn't much of anything.

Three other people were in the store, two older women and a young boy. One of the women was the man's wife. They owned the store. The other woman and her young son were there to shop. They lived close by.

"We thought you was a hooligan," the man's wife said.

"I'm looking for my wife. Her name is Naomi. She was taken by a guy named Ramar."

"We've heard'a him," the other woman said. "He's a killer."

"That's what I understand, and he is a kidnapper."

"How you gonna get'er back?" the man asked.

"I don't know, but I have to do something."

"You might be killed," the man's wife said.

"Well I might, but I can't worry about that. I love her. I have to do something."

"They's Minute Men in the area around here. I'm one of'm. There ain't no law. Maybe you ought'a try'n get organized with us," the man suggested.

"I'm afraid she will get hurt."

"Well what chance do ya have alone against a bunch'a hooligans?" the man asked.

"I don't know." he said. "Where is their camp?"

"Somewheres back in the mountains yonder. They ain't nobody knows exactly, but they all go in on highway three, just out yon-way, bout ten mile. You go walkin' out it and somebody'll shoot you for sure. They got watch dogs, men, all along the ridges ou'tair. You'll be spotted quick?"

"How have y'all managed to stay clear of them?"

"I shoot to kill and they know it. But it is just a matter of time and they'll get me. I know that. We're leaving early next month. But meantime, we have friends around here that depend on us. The same friends who help watch the store at night. They tried to burn us out oncet. But Wendel Payne shot the guy tryin' to torch the place. Me an' other Minute Men took out a bunch of'em right after that, but it's just a matter of time an' they'll try some'm else. Lee here wants to leave now. But we owe these folks around here. We're stayin' a little bit longer. But the hooligans have won. If they's to commence on us all at oncet, we'd be overrun quick. An' we think that is their plan, eventually. You ain't safe around here even if ye'own ye'own home."

"I've got to try going out that way. Are there any short cuts you can tell me about?"

"They's a creek that crosses the road out yonder bout a mile. You can foller it back up in the mountains. We've seen'em come'a walkin' out'a it. But I wouldn't advised it. Them folks camp out all up an' down that creek, so I've heard."

"Thanks a lot y'all. I'm going after her."

"We'll pray for'ye," the wife said.

The man walked with him across the parking lot. Halfway across they heard the sound of a motor coming down the road from where Nayhoom planned to go. Soon an all terrain vehicle appeared and went by the store going fast. It was Ramar with Naomi sitting behind him, her arms around his waist, her hands handcuffed together. Ramar paid no attention to them, but Naomi saw Nayhoom, and he waved.

"That was my wife and Ramar," he told the man. "Now back I go in that direction."

\*\*\*

When he came to the logging road going toward Howard's where he had spent the night, he saw in the mud that the tracks had not changed. Naomi and Ramar had continued on down the highway. And there was no way he could know where they were going. All he could do was go in that direction and hope he would discover a clue.

He started walking and five minutes later he met a horse drawn wagon with car tires, driven by a man with his son beside him holding a deer rifle. Nayhoom waved to them, but they ignored him and went on their way. He thought they might be going to the same store he had just left.

About an hour later he was a few miles further down the road and they came up behind him, and the son called out.

"Are you Nayhoom?"

Nayhoom turned around. "Yes I am."

"Charlie told us about you, that you was lookin' fer ye wife. We seen her an' that hooligan feller on our way out the highway here. They was bookin' it on that four-wheeled motor sickle. "You wanna ride with us? We're goin' about another five mile."

"Yeah I'd like to ride with you."

The man's name was Clarence Walker, with his son James sitting beside him on an old car seat fastened to the wooden wagon with large nails driven into the bed and bent over the bottom frame of the seat. Clarence was forty and his son James was sixteen. They had been to Charlie Green's grocery store to get items for themselves and their neighbors. The groceries were in cardboard boxes in the wagon.

"I'm Clarence Walker an' this here's my son James. We made a grocery run, if you can call it that. Green's store ain't got many groceries left. We'll have to go all the way to Gambles perty soon. Where you think your wife and that Hooligan feller went?"

"I don't know. They could have gone anywhere. But I've got to try and figure it out. He is a very bad person and I'm really worried about her. All I can do is try to follow them and hope something occurs that will allow me to get her free and away from him."

"They's Minute Men that would be glad to help."

"I may have to do something like that, but I'm afraid that would only get her hurt."

"You gotta a gun," James asked.

"Yeah I got one but I really don't know how to use it."

"I bet I can show ye," James said.

"Here it is," Nayhoom said. "I've never shot it or any pistol. I shot a single shot .22 rifle once a long time ago."

"Shoot, there ain't nothing to this old thang. Look here, you just cock it, take the safety off and pull the trigger, the gun does the rest. Shoot in the bank over there."

"Shoot once and let the horse get used to it," Clarence said.

Nayhoom aimed at the red clay bank and pulled the

trigger. The pistol shot was loud, and the gun bucked, and the horse perked its ears and got tense. Clarence talked to it and then told Nayhoom to shoot again. He did and the horse did not react.

"You keep pulling the trigger an' the gun will shoot every time. You just need a little practice. Go to our house with us an' me an' you'll go out back an' shoot some. I got a pistol too. Dad likes to shoot to, don't'chee Dad?"

"I'll shoot some wi'yins," he said.

"I would but every minute I'm not looking for Naomi is a minute that later on she might need me there to help. I'll have to keep moving."

"I bet you would like my sister. She ain't the smartest rock in the box, but she'll do anything you ask her to...so I'm told. He'd like'er wouldn't'e Dad?"

"Everbody likes Megan. She's real personable."

"I'm in love with my wife. That will never change. But thanks for the thought. Where does this road take you?"

"It goes to the main highway about fifteen mile further on. You can go left to North Carolina there, or right down to Blairsville and Dahlonega Georgia, and then on down south. There is a big store called Gamble's there on the highway that might have some gas. He might have stopped there for some. You can ask," Clarence said.

"I will. So that store is where I'm now going. You say y'all are going about five miles?"

"Yeah. It's less than that now, about four more. Shoot that gun a few more times. Let James help you."

"OK, but I don't want to shoot too many shells. I doubt that I would ever find more."

\*\*\*

Where they turned left to go to their home, they stopped and let him off. He walked on assuming that ten or eleven miles would take a long time to walk. It was very unlikely that anyone else would come along and give him a ride. He was dirty, unshaven, and with the pack on his back he thought he would probably be mistaken for a hooligan and passed up, unless other hooligans came along and offered him a ride. That was a possibility just occurring to him. He bristled and began thinking about what he should tell them and still accept a ride.

An hour later, and a few miles further down the road, he heard a wagon and voices approaching from behind. It was Clarence Walker and his son James again, and two other people riding with them. When they got close, James called out.

"Hey Nayhoom, we thought we'd make a trip to Gamble's store and take you with us. Ridin's better'n walkin' any ol' day ain't it. This here's my sister Meg, and that there's our neighbor Justin Wade. He came along to help me ride shotgun, only we both got deer rifles."

"I really appreciate it. Ten miles is a long walk. Hello Meg, Justin, nice to meet y'all. Thanks Clarence, What is your horse's name?"

"Wilbur."

"Thanks Wilbur."

"Climb up there with'em Nayhoom. We gotta try an' get there an' back afore dark," Clarence said.

Megan was seventeen years old and had huge,

sumptuous breast. She was wearing a shirt with two top buttons missing. Her breast bulged like they might break another button and spill on out. She sat on a pile of sacks on the wagon bed floor. She also wore a red dress that was obviously too short. Justin, fourteen years of age, had positioned himself where his view was perfect for looking at whatever she might reveal up her dress. Nayhoom took a seat on the wagon bed where he could see over James' shoulder to the rear and the road behind. Up in the driver's seat alone, Clarence clucked to Wilbur and the rubber tires of the wagon began to hiss on the asphalt road.

"What kind'a work you do?" Justin asked Nayhoom.

"My wife and I worked on a vegetable farm over in Hillbrook."

"You come from all the way over there?"

"Yeah, through the mountains looking for Naomi my wife."

"Hooligans took'er, right?"

"They kidnapped her."

"Meg here needs a husband. You might be innerested. I'd go fer'er but I reckon I'm too young," Justin said.

Megan cast a demure glance toward Nayhoom. He smiled at her. "She'll make someone a good wife I'm sure, but I love Naomi and I have to try and get her back.

"I toad's'ye cornbread," James said, "he ain't innerested cos he's innerested in findin'is wife."

Justin threw a straw that landed on one of Megan's bare knees. She brushed it off and frowned at him. "You are so childish," she said.

Clarence was a good wagon driver. Wilbur never felt

the push of the wagon when they traveled downhill because Clarence had cleverly rigged the disk brakes so that he could apply them with a foot pedal. They made pretty good time all the way to Gamble's store. Nayhoom found a reason, early during their journey, to climb up and sit with Clarence. Bickering had continued between James, Justin and Megan and he tired of it quickly.

"How much further it is Clarence?" he asked.

"Just over the next hill, we bout there."

"I can't express how grateful I am for this ride. Maybe I can come back later and do something for you."

"Don't you worry about that. Just find yer wife and get'er away safe. We'll be thankin' bout'ya."

Nayhoom asked inside the store if anyone had seen two people on a four-wheeler. The young lady cashier and a young male helper had seen them. "He was a hooligan I thank cos she was handcuffed to'im until he came in to pay fer the gas they got. He cuffed her to the big motor-sickle then. He was a big'n, mean lookin' too," the boy said.

"Which way did they go?"

"They went south," the boy said. "I heard him tell her that Dahlonega wasn't too far away. I reckon that is where they headed. It costs twenty dollars a gallon but he bought an extra five gallon can of gas."

"What time was that?"

"Way before lunch sometime, it ain't but about sixty miles. They're there by now."

He went to the wagon and told Clarence and the others thanks and goodbye, and that he hoped to see them again soon. He then walked out to the highway for the long trip to Dahlonega. He thought he might catch a ride, but it seemed unlikely. Very few cars traveled the highway, and he was aware that he looked like a hooligan.

At two PM, and two miles down the highway, a car pulled in behind him and the driver tooted the horn. Nayhoom walked back to it and spoke to the driver, a woman about forty years old. "Hello mam. What can I do for you?"

"Probably nothing. But I can give you a ride. They told me back at Gamble's that your name is Nayhoom and you are looking for your wife. Is that right?"

"Yes, Clarence must have told them that, because I didn't."

"Who is Clarence?"

"The guy I rode to the store with."

"You want a ride? I'm going through Dahlonega."

"I sure do. Thank you very much," he said and got in the car with her. She pulled her quiet running, electric car out onto the highway and they were underway.

"My name is Celia Miller. I've never picked up a hitchhiker before, but the story they told me about you broke my heart, hooligans kidnapping your wife."

"Yes they did, a man named Ramar took her after that, and he has gone to Dahlonega with her."

"What can you do if you catch up with them?"

"I don't know. I'm just trusting that something will occur to me."

"You are hoping that God will show you a way."

"I guess so. I don't think about it like that exactly, but still, that is probably true."

"How do you think about it?" she asked, her bright blue eyes locked ahead onto the band of highway passing beneath them.

He looked at her, and she glanced over at him. "Do you pray?" she asked.

"I might and not think about it like that, think that I am praying. But I probably do. I'm not religious."

"I don't understand," she said.

"I just think that anything a person thinks about God can only be imagined. But that does not mean to me that what they imagine is not true for them, or for me. I think it very well could be. But even with that I think I can only imagine. But imagining, I think, is OK too."

"You lost me.

Two minutes in a car with a stranger and he was talking about God. He was a little amazed. "We, any of us, are just people, and small particles of a whole that is eternal. But our egos at times seem to be gargantuan, at least as big as to assume that we know something when really we are simply speculating, putting forth our best, and often educated guesses."

"Where did you read that?"

"I think I never have actually."

"You made it up?"

"Guilty," he said. "I mean I think it. Made it up, think it, what is the difference?"

"I don't know. I just believe what the bible tells me."

"Who wrote the bible?"

"Men of God."

"My suspicions about the bible start there."

"What do you mean?"

"Two thousand years ago, men were not a lot different from men now. Society has changed, but men still hold the big guns, the big sticks, and they are now, as much as they ever were, controllers and liars to others and mainly to themselves. I don't trust anything men have put their hands to. I'm not cynical, I believe, just cautious about the power of man, and where he is supposedly in charge."

"Man is a creation of God."

"And man created these horrible weather conditions. Do you want to say that God is ultimately responsible?"

"How should I know?" she said almost hatefully. "If I can't trust in God, who can I trust in?"

"Why should you quit trusting in God? The image of God, the one you carry with you, may need a bit of adjusting. But there are no good reasons that offer adequate grounds for thinking that there is no God. Some people attempt to dispel any idea that God exists. But their assumptions are just that, their assumptions. The same with people who profess to know that God does exist."

"What is God to you?"

"Anything and everything, existence both material and ethereal, all of existence."

"How do you know that?"

"I don't think I know anything. But I imagine that, and I think imagining is often a higher form of thought. Being right or wrong means nothing to me, unless I'm giving physical directions. I don't want to be wrong then. It might cause someone to walk off a cliff."

"My husband ran off with another woman. What do

you think about that?"

"It sounds like your relationship was not very good."

"Oh but I thought it was, until I caught them together."

"Do y'all have kids?"

"A boy, but he is grown and overseas."

"I'm sorry Celia. Do you know where your husband and she went?"

"No, and I don't care."

"It is hard for me to believe there are actually accidents in life, or spontaneous, even impulsive, acts of any kind. All things that happen are within the boundaries of a larger order."

"What are you saying?"

"We do what we do within an order that is beyond simple human understanding. I think our actions belong to a deeper order than any human contrivances could ever surmount. That does not mean that we are not responsible for our actions, I think we are, but the core of our actions runs deeper than can be easily comprehended."

"That makes no sense to me."

"I think we are more than the sum of observable parts. I think our simplest actions are aligned with more significant cosmic actions."

"Cosmic, what are you saying?"

"I'm not trying to be difficult. I'm trying to be simple. I think everything, every thought, every deed, action in the physical, material world, and the ethereal world, is of one grand order. And I think of that one grand order as God, not a he, she, or it, but all."

"Are you alright?"

"I'm fine."

Nayhoom's thoughts were clear to him, and had come together with a sudden rupture of insight. He felt a compassion for Celia that he did not realize he was capable of feeling for anyone. "I'm just saying be positive and compassionate with your thinking about everything, and everyone, including your husband and the women he ran away with. There is also much confusion in their lives too."

"How can that be?" she said. "They are off having the time of it."

"Everyone alive suffers with life. Life in this world is never easy, at least for very long. And I believe they are we. But in a rather convoluted way."

"Convoluted?"

"I'm not making any sense to you am I?"

"You are talking above my raisin'. I don't even understand some of the words you use."

"I'm sorry. Most of what I'm thinking about this is just now occurring to me. I'm just blurting it out. Do you still love your husband?"

"No! Yes, I guess I do. But he is gone from me, and maybe that is for the best. I'm getting over him. And so what is your wife's name, and how did she get kidnapped?"

He told her his and Naomi's story, from when he first met her until he last saw her riding behind Ramar on his four-wheeler near Green's Grocery. And he told her that a young guy at Gambles grocery told him they were going to Dahlonega.

"That would test my faith." she said.

"If I operated, functioned or got along by faith alone I think it would mine too."

"And so how do you operate? Do you believe in heaven and look forward to a happy afterlife with God?" she asked.

"A happy afterlife, hmmmm. I've never thought about a happy afterlife, and to me heaven is a man imagined thing. I imagine sometimes that life continues beyond death for any person, any living creature actually. That is my imagining. I know nothing certain about an afterlife, as I believe any person knows nothing. What can be known about something you can't know about? But I believe life can be lived to the fullest without knowing anything certain about an afterlife. It is the function of the imagination to provide ample inspiration in the place of such desired certainty. I think religion tends to diminish that innate function of the imagination. That is a paralyzing truth about religion. If religion were more agnostically oriented, things in general might improve for humankind.

"You have lost me again. But what if people imagine the wrong thing?"

"Wrong for who? What a person from China might imagine will most likely be different from the imaginings of a person from Tennessee. But I can't specifically know if the differences are wrong or right. I think how I operate is more akin to understanding than faith."

"Understanding what?"

"For example: nothing is nonexistent, only something exist, and the all which exists is referred to as existence. I understand that. And that something, any something that exists, is a part of all existence, eternally as one. I understand that all to be the totality of existence, the totality of being. And if it was OK to be born and struggle in this material world then it follows that it must also be OK to die and then."

"And then what?"

"For that we imagine. If we knew, we might not care so much about living."

"We might care more," she said.

"Yes, like I said: Imagine!"

"I disagree with your philosophy, but I sure do hope you find your wife."

"Me too. What is this town we are coming to?"

"Blairsville, Dahlonega is a bit further on. I live just beyond it about four miles."

"I don't have a clue where I should look first."

"Eat supper with me and then I'll take you to town, or near town, where you can go to a tavern that I heard hooligans hang out sometimes, and see if you can get some ideas. I'll drive around for awhile and then come back to get you, and you can come back and sleep on the couch, get an early start tomorrow."

"Thank you Celia. I'll do that."

Celia's husband was employed by a natural gas company. He was in charge of distribution and traveled frequently. Over the last ten years he had acquired a small fortune, and though he had left Georgia with a young woman half his age, he had left Celia with divorce papers to sign, the house, car, and a sizable accruement of cash in their home safety deposit box, inside their safe. Banks were, and had been for five years, basically out of business with the general public. It would seem that she would want for nothing. But she was unhappy, lonely and above all bored with her wealth. But she had no intentions of ever giving any of it up.

Nayhoom presented adventure and philosophical ideas very new to her, and yet he was also quickly becoming to her like a project, a kind of sociological project. But beneath that she really wanted to be helpful. She liked him and wistfully thought of him as a younger, second son.

*\*\**

The hooligans were growing in number all across the United States, and the name hooligan was catching on nationwide. Even the hooligans in the south called themselves hooligans. Their social philosophy, if it could be called that, was simple. They considered themselves to be champions for the have-nots of America, and their plight a war between them and the haves. That was their common decry. They took from the haves and gave to themselves, the have-nots. If you were the owner of things valuable, you had to be ready to protect them, or possibly lose them to hooligans. And you could lose your life. There was no real law enforcement in America anymore, accept for local police officers, and the efforts of the Minute Men and other locally organized militia groups.

Celia could afford to employ three young men to protect her and her things. They guarded her, when she was there, and her house, closely at all times, and each of the men carried automatic weapons and a cell phone, and was in frequent communication with the local Minute Men who were always armed and ready to do battle with the opposing hooligan gangs. She felt safe.

Violent skirmishes between the have-nots and the Minute Men had become more frequent. Firearms were easily obtained by way of the internet and the young, risk taking, Parcel Delivery truck drivers, who never traveled alone and carried automatic weapons. Fire arms commonly sought included automatic assault rifles, automatic pistols, and even rocket launchers. Other more powerful weapons were also readily available daily to anyone, including the hooligans, or the Minute Men, with, as it was often referred to, cold, hard, cash to pay with. And the hooligans were accumulating more and more cash constantly. As the membership numbers of both organizations increased, some people were beginning to call the situation another civil war.

If it came to civil war there seemed no question as to who would win. That would be the haves. But with the mounting number of hooligans, due to the ever increasing numbers of have-nots, and the enlarging of their cash supply from theft, and the constant improvement in the building of their hierarchy via the enhancement of their communication abilities, there were many who thought the haves should not be so presumptuous. A real divide was taking place all across America.

Blairsville seemed deserted, and Dahlonega was worse. The downtown area of Dahlonega was small, and all the stores were empty and locked up, though many had been broken into and much of the stored merchandise stolen.

Only a few brave, possibly foolish, men were out and about.

"I hate driving through this town," Celia said. "A woman is totally defenseless and a common target for creeps."

A few miles further they pulled into her long driveway. At the top, a hired man guarding her house came forward carrying an automatic assault rifle.

"That is Cletus. He is one of the men I pay to protect me. They do a good job." Cletus waved and she drove into the opening door of her garage.

"You don't smell very good Nayhoom. Would you like to get a bath?"

"I've thought about that. But if I'm to mix and mingle with hooligans, trying to gather information about Naomi, I'd better smell, as well as look the part of one of them. I need a bath, but for now I'm going to forgo taking one. Can you stand it?"

"I'll try. There is a tavern near town where rough types hang out. I can take you there."

"Can we go now?"

"Don't you want to go inside, rest and ready yourself first?"

"I'm ready now, if you will take me."

"I have to go to the bathroom. I'll be right back. I'll take you, but you have to return with me later. Will you do that?"

"I'll certainly try."

She drove him to a well known, road tavern on the outskirts of Dahlonega. "I'll come back by in one hour. Will you be out here on the road?"

"I'll try, but how can I know what might happen in there? If I am not, try again thirty minutes later. If I'm not out here after a third drive by, thirty minutes after the second one, I'll just have to get back to your place any way I can. Tell your guards that I may come walking in there tonight sometime. But I'll try very hard to be out here somewhere on the road in an hour. I may be further on down a bit, so look for me down there. OK?"

"OK."

"Thank you Celia."

At four PM the tavern had not yet attracted the bulk of its evening customers, but many had arrived to partake in the moonshine and/or stout made by locals, and others. A live band would usually show up at 6PM to play on into the late hours. Quite a few customers were sitting in booths sipping on homebrew while a lone girl, obviously drunk, was on the stage alone. She wore revealing clothing and sang loudly out of tune, and acapella, to a gathering of men, also drunk: *Want you look at my butt? Please look at my butt. It loves you sooo much.*" Nayhoom sat on a stool at the bar and told the bartender he was just resting and couldn't afford a drink anyway. The bartender smiled and poured him a small glass of homebrew.

"On the house buddy, sip it while you rest."

"Thanks," Nayhoom said, and took a sip.

When the bartender came back by he motioned for him to come closer.

"What is it buddy."

"I was wonderin' if you could tell me where I might join up with the hooligan bunch in this area."

The bartender looked at him hard before answering.

"What's you wanna join up with them fellers for?"

"They stand for getting back what I lost," Nayhoom told him.

"They don't none of'em hang out here much. They do over near Niles Acres. They's a big bar like iss'n over that'a way called Poker Hole. That's the name of it. But hit's a rough house. You better know ye shit before walkin' in'ta that place."

"Where is Niles Acres?"

"About ten mile on out the highway there. Anybody over that way knows about Poker Hole. They play a lot of poker ovar," he said and laughed.

Nayhoom sipped his drink and thanked the man and left the tavern. He was certain he would find Ramar at Poker Hole, and from that, hopefully, Naomi.

He walked out the highway, away from the tavern, and sat on a bank that rose to a parking lot. To his amazement Celia came along only fifteen minutes later.

"I just drove around. I've been by here three times already. I hoped you would be out here sooner than an hour."

"That is not a place he is likely to be. But the bartender told me where I probably can find him, and then maybe Naomi."

"Where?"

"A tavern called Poker Hole. Ever heard of it?"

"I've heard of it. You can't go out there. They'll kill you!"

"I don't have a choice. He has Naomi and I must get

160

her back."

✳✳✳

The two very large men guarding her house waved, and by a remote on her dash she opened the garage door. After parking they got out of the car and went inside. Celia's house contained many conveniences, many appliances for making life, her life now alone, easier. An array of solar panels in a fenced area adjacent to the house in the back yard provided electric energy for charging a grand assembly of batteries connected to DC to AC inverters. The door to the inside of her house from the garage opened with a remote produced from her pocketbook. Her house was air conditioned, and a rush of cool air enveloped them as they went inside.

In the kitchen where they entered, she clapped her hands and the lights in the room came on. She clapped twice and soft music began playing through hidden speakers. She went straight to a cabinet and took out a bottle of Gin. "Would you like a drink Nayhoom?"

"No thank you. But a glass of water would be good."

"The glasses are up there," she said pointing, "and the water is there. I'm going to have a gin and tonic."

They sat in her spacious living room to talk and sip on their drinks. "Have you lived here long Celia?"

"Five years. Is that long?"

"I guess it is. Time is what you make it I think."

"That is probably right. When I was a child I thought

it would take forever to become as old as I am now."

"How old are you?"

"Why should I tell?"

"I don't know. Maybe I shouldn't have asked."

"I'm forty-one. What can it matter?"

"Isn't it better to be forty-one than to not have lived quite that long, say to thirty-nine?"

"Hmmm, thirty-nine, let me think, the last three years have been shit, so maybe not. But I'll take what I have."

"Me too. Dying will come soon enough even if it comes several hundred years from now. It will be now then too."

"It will won't it. You think deeply to be so young. Why is that?"

"Why not? The ocean is deep, but if you like to swim, it doesn't matter how deep the water is."

"Good answer. What is Hillbrook like? I've heard of it."

"It is a small town, but the people there take care of one another. We live on a vegetable farm on the outskirts of it. I really can't tell you much about the downtown area. It is small, only a few stores and many of them are closed down now."

"You and Naomi could move to a larger town, where more people and things are."

"I guess we could, but we like it on Fred Hilliard's vegetable farm. We work there, and we like that also."

"Doing what?"

"Growing vegetables for ourselves and the people of

Hillbrook."

"What kind of future is there in that?"

"Future? We are both satisfied with one moment at a time, because we both believe there is really nothing else. Anything else is basically imagined. The past is but memories and the future is just a concept of an imagined, though believed, reality. Only this very moment actually exists, and I suppose you could make the argument that this very moment is also just a concept, a least a concept believed."

"I'm tired Nayhoom. I need to go to bed. You can sleep on the couch in the living room. It sleeps great."

"Will you take me out to Poker Hole in the morning?"

"Yes, right after breakfast. If you are hungry tonight, just look in the refrigerator in there. I'm sure you can find something. Wake me up early. Just knock on the door at the end of the hallway. Goodnight."

"OK, Goodnight. How do you turn the music and these lights off?"

"The switches are on the wall over there, or you can just clap your hands once for the lights to turn off, twice for the music. That is how you can turn them back on too. Goodnight?"

"Goodnight."

He slept very little that night. His mind was busy dealing with what might happen at the ill named tavern, if he would find Ramar and Naomi, and if there would be a struggle of any kind. He was aware that he and Naomi could both be killed. He tried to think of other possible ways to approach the dilemma. Nothing availed itself and he was left with but one alternative, and that would be to go and deal with the situation there, however it, or what, might occur.

When morning finally arrived he searched the kitchen cabinets and found a jar of instant coffee. He had not had coffee in months. He micro waved a cup of water and stirred in a spoonful of freeze dried coffee granules. But after two sips he poured the coffee out. That Naomi was probably locked away somewhere and unable to have the luxury of a good cup of coffee, made him sick at heart. He was also very hungry. But for that he would wait until Celia was awake and with him.

When he could wait no longer he went down the hallway and tapped on her door and called out her name.

"OK," she said. "I'll be out soon."

***

Poker hole was a log structured tavern, one half mile from the main highway. At the turn-off to it from the highway he saw a large sign with a crudely painted hand below the lettering, pointing the way east down a long, asphalt driveway. After putting the cell phone Celia gave him in his backpack, he got out of her car at the sign.

"In forty-eight hours this is where we'll be, I hope, unless I call you sooner. Thank you for everything Celia. I hope to introduce you to Naomi soon. I've memorized your number, I'll call."

"Be very careful Nayhoom."

"I will."

After returning home Celia made a stiff drink and called a friend of hers who was a major player in the local Minute Men organization. His name was Tom Dewey. She told him about Nayhoom, and about Naomi's abduction by a man named Ramar, and that Nayhoom was going to the highway tavern called Poker Hole. And if he found them he would attempt some sort of rescue, and she was afraid he would be killed. She asked Tom for his advice. He told her he would think about it and call her back soon.

What Celia did not know was that Tom was friends with Boris Storm. Bore had just returned to the farm and had communicated by phone with Tom twice already the previous night. Tom knew about the raid on the hooligan mountain camp, and that a woman Bore thought a lot of had been abducted by a cage fighter named Ramar. He called Bore immediately and told him what he had just learned.

"Poker Hole is a shit hole," Bore said. "I can be there in four hours with fifty men and plenty of fire-power. If you can round up a few, and I know you can, we can wipe that place off the map. But I don't want Naomi to get hurt, so we have to gather some information first."

"I'll find out what I can now and get back with you real soon," Tom said.

An hour later Bore's phone rang again. It was Tom. "He's out there, an showin' his big ass. Everbody's talkin'bout him. He likes to draw a crowd, likes to sing karaoke. They say he is horrible. He's been stayin' out there in a room with some woman, and he's got that pretty women, your woman, with'im. He keeps'er handcuffed. Come on down. Me and a few men will meet you at eight

PM at Deer Park and get organized there. What about that guy, what's his name?"

"Nayhoom?"

"That's it."

"I'll be watching out for him."

Tom called Celia. "We are going out there tonight with some men and see if we can get them. You sit tight and I'll call you back afterward."

Celia sat tight and sipped on gin tonics until six o'clock, and then she got in her car and drove back to the tavern, passing up the driveway to it, and driving on for another mile. She put her cell phone in her lap, turned her car around, and went back to find a place close to the sign and park.

\*\*\*

As soon as the tavern came into sight Nayhoom saw the back-end of Ramar's four-wheeler in a small wood framed shed attached to the rear of the log building. He crouched in the underbrush fifty yards away, the pistol bulging in his front pants pocket. He had walked through the woods instead of down the road, and was not seen by anyone arriving, and there were starting to be many arrivals. It was a weekday but the tavern was a gathering place, and drew large crowds even during the daytime, and all through the week as weekend days were now considered by most to be just other days.

Only a few cars were in the lot, but there were many horses and a few mules, even donkeys. There were pedal

166

powered bicycles, battery powered bicycles, and other battery powered, homemade vehicles parked near the tavern. And many more people would come, and go, throughout the day and approaching night.

The tavern was large to be just a tavern. It was a log structure built in 2010 by the family who would manage it to the present day, and it was situated on five acres of cleared land, most of which was a gravel parking lot that was choked in places with patches of weeds substantiated, fertilized, by numerous horse and mule droppings. The owners sickled the weeds from time to time, but weeds had still managed to maintain a strong hold.

Many solar panels were on the roof, providing a power source for the only available electricity. But in the evenings, after dark, candles and oil lamps were lit at each table, to provide ambient lighting, the beloved atmosphere for drinking moonshine and homebrew, and talking. It was one of the few businesses in Dahlonega that actually turned a profit in cash money. It was well known that many family dollars in Dahlonega went to Poker Hole.

Nayhoom watched and waited for night when he could sneak closer. In the late afternoon he saw a large shirtless man come out a door near the rear of the tavern and go to the four-wheeler. It was Ramar. He straddled the machine, cranked it, backed out, and left quickly. As he sped out the road to the highway he passed within only a few feet of Nayhoom.

Without hesitation Nayhoom went through the woods to the rear of the tavern, where he stayed hidden among pine trees. He saw a row of windows along the backside of the building. He took out the rifle scope and sighted each window. It was dark inside each and he could see nothing, though one window was raised. But the screen wire was dark and obscuring, and he could not see inside. He heard women's voices and thought one of them could have been Naomi's.

During a moment of emotional excitation, he bolted forth to the building and crouched beside the screened window. If anyone should walk behind the tavern he would easily be seen. But he had made the move and now, anxiously, he would listen for the voices. And then he heard from inside the room, through the window above his head, Naomi's voice: "Where could I go if I went out the window?"

He heard a door slam inside the room, and then silence. He peeked in and saw Naomi lying on a bed, her hands handcuffed to the metal frame of the bed. No one else was in the room. He whispered her name. She looked toward him and saw his face looking in through the screen.

"It's me. I'm going to get you out of here."

"Oh Nayhoom they will kill you," she whispered.

"There are no other choices. I have to try. Ramar is gone."

"But he only went a couple of miles away. He'll be back any minute."

"I'll wait in the woods back there for a better time. Do you know if he will stay here very long?"

"He said we are going up in the mountains tomorrow." She saw his gun. "Don't kill anyone Nayhoom. It's never worth it."

"But I might have to. I have a pistol."

"I think killing might be partly why we are still here. It stops now for me. I want nothing to do with killing from now on."

"I don't understand," he whispered.

"What do you actually trust about life, about living?"

"Trust?"

"When you were a child, who did you trust?"

"My parents."

"And now?"

"Well my parents are dead."

"What of their parents?"

"Dead too."

"So only the parents you had before they died?"

"I think I am a trusting person."

"But who?"

"You."

"Besides me?"

"Maybe there is no one. Why for God's sake?"

"There is everyone."

"I don't trust everyone."

"I know you trust very few, and maybe only me. But I mean everyone, everyone alive now and who has ever lived and will ever live, including everything that ever was or ever will be."

He thought for a moment. "I think I know what you mean."

There was a noise at the door to the room and he ducked out of sight. A girl entered and he dashed down along the building and got down behind a burn-barrel. He could see someone trying to look toward him through the screen. And then he heard the four-wheeler returning with Ramar. The person left the window and Nayhoom ran, unseen, back into the woods.

He lay on the pine needles among the pine trees behind the tavern, and looked up through the dark limbs to a blue sky and thought about trust, about trusting. To Nayhoom and Naomi God was not a He, She, or an It, but was everything in the material and ethereal world, including all in the cosmos, the sentient sensuousness of total being. All the people alive, and who had ever lived, life itself, and who or what would ever live, reflected in a metaphorical way his and her connection to, and belief in, God. That was their connection with the whole of humanity. In other words both he and she thought: they are we. By using the word they, Nayhoom and Naomi meant every living creature and thing.

That realization was at the core of his thinking throughout the remainder of the day. The four-wheeler was not cranked again and occasionally he heard the voices of Naomi and the girl. At Dusk it became obvious that the time for action would come soon, and he knew he would know what to do. He took the pistol out of his pocket, removed the clip and emptied it of bullets. He replaced the clip, and put the gun and bullets down inside his backpack. It stops now for me too, he thought. I don't need having killed someone on my resume.

\*\*\*

At eight that evening Ramar went into the tavern and prepared to sing the first of two songs he would sing that evening. It was a song he had written for Naomi and had practiced twice with the live band that often played at Poker Hole.

A girl named Lillian, who was Ramar's regular squeeze when he visited the tavern, lived in a back room and was a relative of the owners. She was charged with watching the girl, and a message was sent to her with instructions to take Naomi into the tavern to listen to Ramar sing a song he had written about and for her. Naomi had no choice of course, and after being led to the bar area she sat handcuffed to her chair at a table close to the stage.

Momentarily the band started playing the simple riffs Ramar had composed on a guitar, and he came from behind a curtain. He wore tight fitting, faded blue jeans, and no shirt, but had donned a brown leather vest and a black glove on his left hand. An automatic pistol was holstered at his side. The vest hung loose and open revealing his shaved chest and a gold chain connected to a shiny gold medallion inscribed with the words Born To Win. On his head he wore a large, brown, wide brimmed, Spanish style, leather hat. He had put dark eyelash liner on, and wore a pair of ornate, leather, cowboy boots. The crowd clapped and cheered as he strutted across the stage.

With the country sounding music playing softly, and a melodramatic look on his face, he held the microphone close to his lips. While holding the black gloved hand toward her, fingers spread, he looked endearingly at Naomi and sang:

*You, you, you,...you make me feel*
*Feel, feel, feel,*

She scowled at him, but he acted unfazed and continued:

*Like no other woman can*
*In this God'amighty world*
*Can make me feel*

The girl named Lillian was sitting with Naomi and looked at her, and then she shook her head. "What is wrong with you?" she said to Naomi. "Don't you know which side your bread is buttered on?" Naomi looked away, and then down at the floor.

*Has the truth of how I feel*
*Not always been in my eyes*
*You are the one*
*I have looked for all my life*
*There you are*
*Here I am*
*Here me*
*Feel me*

His song continued with other such unoriginal, maudlin expressions and Naomi would not look at him. When he finally finished he looked disgustedly at Lillian, and motioned with a thumb over his shoulder for her to take Naomi back.

She took her back, and then attached the handcuffs again to the steel bed frame and went back to listen to

Ramar's next song. He would begin it soon.

With his scope Nayhoom had been watching from the pine thicket, looking into the window at the dimly lit room. He saw when Lillian had taken her and had brought her back, and then cuffed her again to the bed frame. As Lillian was leaving the room and closing the door, he heard the crowd cheer loudly and the band began playing an old rock and roll tune. Though it was familiar, he could not think of what the name of the song was.

He dashed forth to the window and whispered to Naomi. "I'm coming in. Be ready to move."

Her cut the screen wire away and crawled through the window. Using the cutting blades of the pliers Doyle had given him, he cut the chain of the handcuffs. She followed him to the open window, and after he was out and on the ground he helped her crawl out and lifted her down gently. And then he patted her stomach softly. "Can you run?" he said.

"You lead the way, but don't let me run over you," she said.

He smiled and took her hand and they ran to the dark woods and then carefully, through the trees back toward the highway.

He was about to call Celia when they stepped into the road. Celia was close enough to see them and started her car. She approached quickly, but Nayhoom could tell by the way she drove that something was wrong. She was drunk. She hit the brakes too soon and stopped too quickly. Her head tilted forward like it was on a hinge. She looked at them staring back at her and grinned.

Nayhoom helped Naomi get in the back seat, and then went to Celia's open window. "Are you OK?"

"I'm drunk," she said.

"Slide over then. I'll drive. Just mash on the pedal?"

"At's right," she slurred. "An'n the brakes is righ'tair," she said pointing. She looked back at Naomi. "I'm Celia. Nayhoom has told me a lot about you. He sure does love you."

"I know, and I am very glad."

***

Ramar sang: *I can't get no, no satisfacto*
*I can't get no, no satisfacto*
...And then he began singing loudly, with great gusto and feigned emotion, some of words of the song:
*When I'm riding on my ride*
*and a man comes on my radio*
*he's tellin' me more an' more*
*about some useless information*
*supposed to fire up my imagination*
*I can't get no, oh no no no*
*hey, hey, at's what I say*
*I can't get no, no satisfacto...*

The front door of the tavern burst open suddenly and in came Bore, followed by several armed men. Ramar stopped singing and stared at the intruders with guns. He drew his gun and fired in their direction before running off stage. Gun fire erupted throughout the tavern, but Bore and his men were all bearing automatic weapons and within minutes they had the upper hand, with many of the Poker Hole customers lying dead or bleeding on the sawdust covered floor.

Ramar cranked his ride amid on-coming hot bullets from automatic rifles wielded by the Minute Men, and rode, now hatless, through the pine trees and momentarily emerged on the highway and headed toward the mountain hideaway of some of his hooligan friends. He had eluded the Minute Men and death once again, and he smiled to himself as he motored down the highway. He had lost the prettiest woman he had ever seen but only moments before had judged her completely useless to him. "I got all the pussy I need anyway. After all, I am the whore whisperer," he screamed as he rode fast down the highway to a road that would take him far into the mountains.

High in the ruby permeated, mountain hills above Dahlonega Georgia, on a curvy, winding road that he was certain he remembered well, he rode swiftly behind the two extended shafts of light streaming out from the headlights of his vehicle. All was well until he took a wrong fork on the black, asphalted, mountain highway. The wrong way took him to the edge of an overlook. There were no guardrails. Before he had time to think about his blunder, he was sailing out into the wild black yonder. His cry of astonishment and fear was lost in the great expanse of mountain air around him. The lights of his vehicle shot haphazardly and pointlessly across the starless firmament like wayward circus sky lights, down and then back around toward the dark clouds and then no lights at all.

\*\*\*

When Nayhoom, Naomi, and Celia arrived in her neighborhood it was obvious that something was wrong. They were met with a throng of people walking at the beginning of her street. An expression of shock was in each face they could see.

"Something has happened," Celia said drunkenly. "I see fire ahead."

Fire was ahead, and it was what was left standing of her house. Other houses in the area were burning also. Many of her neighbors had left weeks before because vandals came often to the neighborhood, breaking in homes stealing items before trashing anything they could.

Cletus, one of her guards, who had not been working that night, met them at her driveway entrance. Nayhoom stopped and the man approached the car. He looked frightened. "Don't go up there Celia. Bob and Jim are both shot dead. They called me when they were attacked and I came as quick as I could, but it was too late. They broke in the house before they set it on fire and took stuff. Your wall safe is out there where the garage was. They opened it with a blow-torch I reckon and took all your money and jewelry. There ain't nothin' up there worth goin' after."

Celia was absolutely speechless. "Thanks," Nayhoom said, and quickly drove away. They passed two other houses burning and saw several women and children in the yards and heard their wails and cries.

"That was all I had," she finally said. "What will I do?"

"You can't do anything tonight. You can go to Hillbrook with Naomi and me and think about what you can do tomorrow."

# CHAPTER FIVE

## RETURN

Celia passed out and slept all the way to Hillbrook. Nayhoom awakened her and walked with her staggering, almost falling twice, from the car into the house. There was a surprise awaiting them. The house had been made clean in anticipation of their return.

"It's clean!" exclaimed Naomi.

"Yes and someone cleaned the home sweet home sign and hung it back on the wall. Somebody cares and has been thinking about us," Nayhoom said. But he thought then that he would make a new sign, and bury the one hanging on the wall.

Celia was put to lie on the couch and Naomi covered her with mosquito netting. "I thought I might never see this home again," she said.

Nayhoom hugged her and kissed her. "We didn't have to die, and you are going to have our baby."

"Thank you for loving me."

"Thank you for loving me," he said.

They didn't sleep any that night. They sat together on the front porch on an old couch Steve and Patty had given them for that front porch. The excitement of the day, and the last few days, and then suddenly being free of fear and away from harm, had them both emotionally and physically charged. Nayhoom told Naomi about his experiences and she told him about hers. He told her about meeting Celia and all that transpired up until she picked them up near the tavern.

"She has nothing now," Naomi said. "What will she do?"

"She can't go to her son. He lives somewhere across the ocean. If she has no place to go we can check with Fred and see if she can live here on the farm. I know he won't ask her to leave. What do you think about her staying here with us until she can get settled somewhere else?"

"I was hoping you wouldn't mind," Naomi said. "But if she is an alcoholic she won't find anything to drink around here."

"Such is life," Nayhoom said. "It may be the best opportunity to get away from alcohol she has ever had."

"But it will not be an easy thing to do. She may think she doesn't need to be away from it. I've had experiences with alcoholics before. She may be in for a rough ride."

"Fred gets up early. I think I'll go up there at before dawn and tell him we are back, and that we have a house guest. He'll fill me in on all that has happened around here. I'll find some food for us while I'm up there too."

"I am very hungry," Naomi said.

"Me too."

He saw a light on inside Fred's home when he knocked on the door.

179

"Nayhoom! We have been so worried about you. Where is Naomi?"

"She is down at the house. We are both fine."

While sitting on the front porch, it took over an hour to tell Fred an abbreviated version of what had transpired since Naomi's abduction. And then he told about Celia. "She has absolutely nothing now. We would like for her to stay here on the farm with us until she can do better. Do you object to that?"

"Of course not," Fred said. "Do you think she would work? I can find something for her to do."

"She may have no choice. But it may be awhile before she is ready to work. Celia has always been able to somewhat pamper herself, and now she is not able to do that, and Naomi and I think she is an alcoholic. So, as you probably know, that puts a twist on how she will take to her sudden change of positions in life."

"I see. Well, things may also go easier than we both can imagine. We'll just have to wait and see how it all plays out. I know there is nothing in that house to eat. Let me box up some food for y'all."

"OK. I was going to ask because we are both very hungry. Celia might be hungry too after she wakes up."

"She is asleep?"

"Passed out on gin."

"Oh. Will she be alright?"

"I think so. It is probably not her first time."

"I want you and Naomi to know that we all welcome you two back with open arms. Take a few days to get settled. I'll tell Patty you will be back to normal soon.

And tell Celia I asked for her to come and visit with me."

"I will," Nayhoom said.

\*\*\*

Celia woke with a bad headache. She drank her Gin and tonics every evening but during the last evening she had completely overdone it, drinking almost a fifth of gin.

At first she was confused about where she was. She was absolutely aware that she was hung over, and then memories of the previous evening came to her, along with memories of seeing her burned and destroyed house, and that two of the men who had worked for her were dead. She remembered vaguely that she left Dahlonega with Nayhoom and Naomi, and she realized she must be at their house now. She called loudly for Nayhoom.

"You are awake finally," he said when he came into the bedroom.

"My house burned and Bob and Jim are dead."

"Yes. We brought you here to our house. You can stay for as long as you need to."

"I have nothing now, just that car."

"You have us. We will not forsake you."

"Thank you. What am I to do?"

"One thing at a time. That is all anyone can do."

"I don't know what that one thing is," she said, and started to cry. Naomi came into the room and sat beside her on the bed.

"You don't have to decide right now. You can stay here with us for now. It will come to you what you must do,

181

and we will help. Won't we Nayhoom?"

"Certainly we will. I'll see if we have some coffee."

\*\*\*

When Betty, Shirley and Harriet heard from Fred that Nayhoom and Naomi had returned they went in the afternoon to their house to visit and see for themselves.

"We thought y'all might be dead," Shirley said.

"We thought we might be too," Naomi said. "Was it you three who kept our house clean?"

"Yes. Did we do a good job?" Betty asked.

"Of course you did. It was such a great surprise when we first got home. Thank y'all very much."

"You are very welcome," Harriet said. "We were thrilled to hear Fred say y'all had returned unharmed."

"Is Bore at the dorm? Nayhoom asked.

"Bore doesn't work here anymore. He is now a Minute Man, and he lives somewhere else," Harriet said.

They visited for about an hour, and then the three girls left.

Bore was living with a man named Leroy Collins who was also a very active Minute Man in and around the town of Hillbrook. Nayhoom and Naomi had been away for only a little more than two weeks but already the Minute Man organization in the area had nearly doubled in size, and Bore had become a major player. His computer skills were his most effective contribution, but his large size and youthful daring was also much revered by other members. He felt as though he had acquired his life's calling and exerted great passion in his appointed duties, though often they were self appointed. But no one was paying any attention to that.

Bore contacted Fred Hilliard and learned that Nayhoom and Naomi had returned. He came to visit with them three days later.

"It was me and other Minute Men who attacked that tavern full of trash," he told Nayhoom.

"We didn't know it had been attacked. But we knew bad things were going down in a lot of places," Nayhoom said.

"How did you get away with Naomi?"

Naomi was sitting close by Nayhoom as he told Bore most of the story of their escape together, and about Celia picking them up. He told him about Celia's house and the death of the men who had worked for her. "Things are getting bad aren't they?"

"Yes, really bad. It is becoming like war, but a war that has to be fought. We can't let thieves and cut-throats take over the land, and they will if they are not stopped. It is as simple as that."

"I understand the logic," Nayhoom said. "I'm not certain how I fit in. But I am committed to Naomi and our unborn baby. I feel it is my place to protect them."

"So do I," Bore said, and looked rather questioningly at Naomi, who didn't know what the look was for.

"I'm very glad you have both returned safely," he said. "I need to go but I'm in contact regularly with Jason and Carl so I'll be hearing about y'all. I'll come back to visit sometime."

"OK," Nayhoom said.

"Thank you Bore," Naomi said. He shrugged a little and smiled at her. "I'm glad you are safe Naomi."

***

Two days later Celia was feeling a little better. She wanted to return to Dahlonega to somehow become more in touch with the reality of what had happened, but Nayhoom and Naomi talked her out of it, which was not hard to do. "You'll need that bit of money you have with you now, and the trip over there might be costly, and for what? You know where you stand as it is. There is nothing you can do except begin a new life, and right here is where you can do that."

"I am not a bad person," she said. "Why has God allowed this to happen to me?"

Naomi looked at Nayhoom and sighed. "There is no reason to think God is responsible for what happened," she said. "And besides, this may be an opportunity for you to find real happiness, somehow."

Celia started to cry. "Happiness is never going to happen to me. God is punishing me," she said.

There was a knock on the door and Nayhoom went to see who it was. He came back with Fred Hilliard. "Fred, this is Celia, Celia, Fred. She is a bit distraught at the moment. We've been talking about what she has lost and that there is still much in life to gain."

"There certainly is," he said. "Hello Celia, it is nice meeting you. Will you sit with me on the front porch for a little while? It is a little warm outside, but the air is fresh and it might do you some good. Nayhoom, Naomi, y'all don't mind do you?"

"Of course not," Naomi said. "I'll bring out two glasses of water."

Fred led Celia out to the front porch where he sat with her on the vinyl couch there. "I understand that you have lost much," he said.

"I've lost everything."

"Do you have faith in God?"

"Yes."

"Is that faith still intact?"

"I think so," she said, and looked at him with eyes flooded with tears.

"The will of God will never take you where the grace of God will not protect you," he said, and took her hand in his.

She wiped her eyes and looked at him. "I do believe that," she said. "Thank you so much. Those were words I needed to hear."

They talked on the porch for half an hour, and then they went back inside. "Thanks for the water," he said to Naomi as he handed her the glasses. Celia has agreed to have lunch with me at my place, and go there now with me. Do either of you have any objections to that."

"No we don't," Nayhoom said. "She will like your lunch far more than ours I'm sure."

"Would y'all like to come for lunch too?"

"No, we have much to do here, we should stay and get to it, but thank you," Nayhoom said. "Y'all have a great time."

After Fred and Celia were gone, Naomi caught Nayhoom's attention. "He saved the day," she said.

"Did you notice how happy Celia looked all of a sudden?"

"I noticed."

Celia stayed with Fred through lunch and then dinner. At dark she came back with him, and he said to Nayhoom and Naomi that because he had more room, an extra room actually, he and Celia had discussed the idea that she could stay with him. In exchange she would clean his house. She seemed very happy with the idea. She seemed happy period. Fred, it would appear, had worked wonders.

"Do y'all object to that arrangement?" Fred asked.

"No," they said together.

"It sounds like the perfect setup to me," Nayhoom offered.

"It's not that I don't appreciate what you two have done for me, I do very much. But this way I can earn my way," Celia said.

"We understand," Naomi said. "I think it is a wonderful idea."

"Naomi and I would like to get back to work Fred. Could I continue installing the cooling systems?"

"Certainly, David Porter, a new guy, has been working alone at it. He'll be glad to have help. Naomi, you're pregnant. You shouldn't be back out in the heat."

"I can't sit on my duff either. I need to work or I'll get lazy. I'll take it easy. When I get further along I'll have to stop until after the baby is born."

"I trust that you know best," Fred said.

"I can help with that baby," Celia said.

"I'm sure I'll need some."

When 3:45 in the AM came, Nayhoom and Naomi took a candle lamp, and walked to the gathering tree, and met with the others. David Porter introduced himself, and then Nayhoom and David went off toward the equipment shed together.

"I'm really glad to be getting your help. The installations are not hard work, but some of the holes I've dug were in hard dirt, rocks and roots and stuff. And it is so God-awful hot. I think it is hotter now than back in the summer. It's Thanksgiving time for God's sake. It's supposed to be getting cooler, but I think it is actually getting hotter. It is hotter this year at this time than it was last year."

"Yeah, and the ground is harder I think," David said.

They traveled in Fred's mule drawn wagon to a house three miles away. "These peoples' name is Simpson," David said. "And the dirt around their house is terrible. Right where we have to bury the barrel it is rocky as can be. You'll see. Get ready to sweat."

"There's no other place we can put the barrel?"

"No, just that one spot, you'll see."

David had been right. There was only one logical place for the barrel and the soil there was hard and rocky. "We'll do well to get this hole dug by tomorrow," Nayhoom said.

"Yeah, or maybe the next day. You had a bunch of hooligan trouble didn't you?" David asked while pecking at the hard chert infused soil with a pick.

"Yeah, they kidnapped my wife Naomi, but we were fortunate and didn't get hurt. A lot of people did though."

"It's just gonna get worse," David said.

"I agree. It all seems to be going in one direction."

"Yeah, straight down. I heard the hooligans had more than tripled in number this last year. They outnumber the Minute Men two to one now, and they say that might double again this year. It's liable to get to be each man for hisself. I've been thinking about heading out west, if I can get there."

"We've thought about leaving, but it is bad everywhere."

"Yeah, but out west there is more space to get lost in."

"Yeah, but for how long?"

"Who knows," David said. But it can't be long around here and it will be too dangerous to hangout. And your wife is pregnant, isn't she?"

"Yeah she is. I wish we could relax a little about that. But I reckon we can't."

Fowler Simpson, the man of the house, came out to check on the progress. "That dirt's a bitch, ain't it boys?" he said.

"Maybe worse," Nayhoom said. "You take that canoe out much over there?" A sixteen feet long, aluminum canoe was chained to the tree it leaned against.

"We ain't been paddlin' in two years. You wanna buy it?"

"How much?" Nayhoom said.

"How much you give?"

"I don't have any money."

"What's'chee got to trade."

Nayhoom thought of the pistol Doyle had loaned him, but he doubted that he would ever be able to get it back to him. "Maybe a .45 caliber, semi automatic pistol."

"I'll trade you even," Fowler said.

"Let me think about it. We'll be back tomorrow I'm sure. I'll bring the gun maybe, and show it to you."

He had almost decided he should try to return the pistol to Doyle when Jason came to their house that evening for a visit, and while there told him Hooligans had been seen encamped about ten miles away.

He did not sleep well that night. Dreams about hooligans attacking the farm, and his pregnant wife being taken again kept him mostly awake. He got up for a final time at two AM and sat out on the porch and decided her safety, their safety, was what he should consider, and the canoe could be very useful in that way.

He took the pistol with him that morning. Fowler liked it and the deal was made. The hole was finally dug by quitting time and he and David decided to wait until the following morning to put everything together. They loaded the canoe onto the wagon, and after he was home he put it under the house. While under there he found an old rusty machete blade. The handle had rotted away. Fred told him later that is was a corn knife his father had once used.

The back of the house sat higher on its foundation. A foundation door there, on the east side of the house, opened to the space beneath the kitchen. He shut the foundation door, folded the hasp back over the keeper, and dropped a bent nail into it. And then, after putting the long machete blade up in the front porch rafters, he went inside and told Naomi about the canoe and what he had been thinking.

Fred and Celia celebrated Thanksgiving with a big meal, and invited everyone working at the farm to join them. Many went, but Nayhoom and Naomi stayed at home. They had foul dispositions about Thanksgiving and Christmas. They thought of the celebration of either as being no more than an exemplification of human folly, folly in this country known by the phrase The American Dream, the same dream responsible for the incredible and exorbitant contribution of American carbon dioxide and carbon monoxide released into the earth's atmosphere.

Instead they stayed at home and talked about what their futures might be.

"It is war, no matter how you look at it," Nayhoom said. "It has already touched us here on the farm, but I believe it will return soon. I hope I'm wrong of course, but the numbers of destitute, starving, and sick people in this country is growing daily. And those people see the hooligan way of attack and seize as their only option of survival. I think it is only a matter of a short time and we will be forced to run."

"So do I." Naomi said. "What are you thinking?"

"As you know, that is why I got the canoe. And I want to collect things we might need to take with us, should we have to leave in a hurry. But we cannot take more than we can pack into the canoe and then pull to the creek. Fred said I could have that twenty pound bag of soybean seed left over from last season, and the ten pounds of mung beans. He wanted to know what I would do with them, and I said I wanted to keep them for hard times, and I do."

"What do we do after we paddle to the dam?"

"We get out, unpack, and then carry the canoe down to the river, and then all our stuff, and repack it. It is the only way I can think of to get away."

"I guess I knew that. We'll be seen on the river."

"We go down the river only at night."

"There really is nothing else we can do, is there?"

"If you think of something, tell me," Nayhoom said, "and we will do that instead."

After taking stock of the items he had in his backpack: matches, a hatchet and hunting knife, the wrist rocket, and split shot, pliers, rifle scope and canteen, they listed the items they would need and then scratched out the impractical ones. Nayhoom had spent a lot of time thinking and looking at an old tool catalogue for the tools that would be the most beneficial. He saw two things that he knew they must have. One was called a rebar, twist-tie tool. The other he saw in a camping equipment catalogue. It was called a fire starter, and was a small magnesium bar and a small, metal striking tool with a serrated edge attached. He didn't know if Brian could locate these things but he was going to ask him to try. And he wanted a roll of tie wire.

He explained to Naomi that tie wire and the twist-tie tool would make it possible to quickly put together a stable shelter. If he could get a roll of black plastic, the problem of making a shelter water proof could then easily be solved. He made sketches so she could better understand.

They made two lists, one of things they thought they had or could find on the farm, and the other list was of things they wanted Brian to look for. They called it the have not list. Nayhoom looked in his backpack and pulled out the wrist rocket and lead split-shot, the hunting knife, rifle scope, pliers, hatchet and canteen. These things he listed on their have list. He and Naomi further noted on the have list: two heavy blankets, large and small cooking pots with heavy lids, and their ten quart pressure cooker, which they kept in the kitchen to use until they might leave, kitchen cutlery, a coffee pot, cups, an assortment of vegetable seeds, matches, four different sized Tupperware containers with lids, two washrags, two towels, bath soap, raincoats, goulashes, extra clothes, blankets, two sheets, a thesaurus and dictionary, his 2030, fold-out map of the Southeast, the rusty machete blade with no handle, and a new roll of duct tape. There were many more things they wanted to add, but already it appeared that the canoe would be hard to drag and they had not yet acquired the things on the have not list.

These were: a baby book, a wild foods cook book, a roll of 6oz, ten by twenty' black plastic, or larger, A bow saw, two pounds of sixteen penny nails, a pair of heavy duty wire cutters and a pair of needle-nosed pliers, a small camp shovel, three plastic, five gallon, sheetrock compound buckets, two bastard files, and a roll of 300# test nylon cordage. Together they had taken much time discussing what they might need, and what they could do without. During the following day they would think of a few more items to add.

Two evenings later he went to the dorm to visit Steve and Jason, and his work partner David Porter. They talked awhile and then he got on the computer and e-mailed Brian about Naomi's and his adventures, and told him they were now safe and back to work. And then he typed the list of things he wanted Brian to locate for him.

A week later Brian e-mailed back that he had located all the items and wanted to discuss the details about obtaining them. Two hundred dollars would buy them, or, he wrote: *If you will install Fred Air in my widowed aunt's house I'll procure them for you. She has a well and plenty of pipe. I'll get the pump and fan and other things if you will just put it all together for her.*

It was a deal Nayhoom was glad to accept. He wrote back: *Sounds great to me. I'll get started as soon as you have the supplies and e-mail back.*

He dug the hole by himself the following weekend and installed the system Monday afternoon. Though it was December, Clara, Brian's aunt, sighed with obvious relief when the cool air began to fill her house.

The weather was a few degrees cooler than it had been during the summer, but cold, icy weather seemed to be gone from the environment for good. Fred was afraid to start a new planting until at least January, not for fear of frost or freezing weather, but he was afraid the seed might rot in the ground before it would germinate and sprout. But the greenhouses were active and the plants there thrived, and there was plenty of work for everyone on the farm.

The girls, Betty Shirley and Harriett, took care of

watering while the guys pulled weeds and kept the soil loose around the plants. The broccoli, bell pepper, squash and cantaloupe plants were growing great in the greenhouses while other plants were thriving and producing, but not quite as well.

Nayhoom and David thought they might never catch up with all the slated Fred Air installations. The makeshift devices worked well, especially considering the outlay of installation and then the cost of operating one. The people of Hillbrook without Fred Air considered themselves fortunate to be on a list for eventually getting it. And Nayhoom and David were glad their efforts were appreciated. It was very gratifying for them to do something so worthwhile and useful.

***

It was December the fifteenth when Fred and Celia invited Nayhoom and Naomi to dinner. They accepted and would come the following Tuesday afternoon. It was a sudden invitation and both Nayhoom and Naomi wondered about that. "I've never been invited to Fred's for dinner," she said.

"Neither have I. But we are now a married couple, so I suppose they just want Christmas company. And, I've wondered if this is going to be Fred's way of letting everyone know that he and Celia are hitting it off in a big way. They are you know."

"I know. I mean it was obvious to me they were right

after she moved in up there. And I am glad about it and glad for them."

"Me too. Should we take anything?"

"Celia said to bring nothing except each other."

Tuesday at one PM Nayhoom and Naomi knocked on Fred's front door and he answered it: "The Wadells! Good to see y'all, come in, come in. Celia, they're here!" he called out.

Celia came into the living room. She was wearing a new looking red dress, one that could easily be considered as sexy. It was tight fitting and cut low below the neck line. The cleavage of her breast was eye catching and Nayhoom almost blushed. "You look great Celia," he said.

"She does, doesn't she?" Fred said. "Y'all come on in and grab a chair. Celia, would you bring us some coffee? Y'all will have a cup want you?"

"Certainly," Naomi said. "We both like it black too."

"I've never seen the inside of your house Fred. It looks and feels great," Nayhoom said.

"Thanks, Celia has been keeping it clean for a change. I'm very proud of it."

Celia brought four cups of coffee and handed three out, and then she sat beside Fred on the couch, very closely, touching him even.

"I guess y'all have figured out that Celia and I are becoming very close. I'm very honored that she thinks highly of me."

"The same here," she said, and kissed him on the cheek.

"She has a good, big meal cooked. I hope y'all are

195

hungry."

"We are," Nayhoom said. "I had to scold Naomi for getting into the peanut butter just before we came. I have a lot more will power than she has."

"Phooey," Naomi said. "It is the other way around. But we are both big eaters, especially when someone besides us prepares a meal. I can smell what you have cooked, but I can't tell what it is."

"Spicy black beans, asparagus, sweet potatoes, coleslaw, whole wheat biscuits, white gravy, apple sauce, what else Fred?"

"I think you got it all."

"Oh, and coconut cake," she said.

"Good night in the morning," Nayhoom said. "That sounds wonderful.

"I'll be glad if y'all think it is just good," she said.

"I haven't had coconut since a year before I left the orphanage."

"It's been five years for me," Naomi said. "How did you make cake and the icing without eggs? I know Fred doesn't eat eggs."

"I experimented with mixing and cooking confectioner's sugar, tapioca, flour and coconut milk and ground coconut until I had the closest thing to icing I could come up with. The cake is made with self rising flour, coconut milk, brown sugar and vanilla flavoring, so it isn't white like it should be. But Fred said it was good. I made two cakes and he has about eaten the first one."

"It was good," he said. "You'll like it I'm sure."

"I'm sure I will," Nayhoom said.

When they sat down to eat Fred suggested they hold hands around the table, and that Celia say the blessing. They held hands and Celia began. Her prayer was not a short one. She took the opportunity to give thanks to the Lord for everyone there who had helped her through her recent ordeal, the loss of her home and possessions. And she prayed for the souls of the men who had worked for her and had died. And then she thanked the Lord for bringing Nayhoom and Naomi into her life, and for their introducing her to Fred. She was extremely thankful for her new home, and for the opportunity to get away from alcohol and the consuming of animal flesh. And then she said: "And thank you for the new love in my life." Nayhoom peeked at Fred and saw him smile, his eyes closed, his head bowed reverently.

Nayhoom and Naomi expressed great appreciation to Celia for her very fine meal. "This makes me want to be a better cook," Naomi said. "It is wonderful."

"I'm amazed," Nayhoom said. "These black beans are great, with just enough spice."

"I love it Celia," Fred said.

"Thank y'all very much. It makes me feel very special to have pleased everyone."

After eating they sat in the living room to talk. Celia brought coffee for all.

"The cooling devices are going well aren't they Nayhoom?" Fred asked.

"Yeah, they are now in high demand. We actually need help. There are too many to do for just David and me to keep up with."

"I'll see about bringing a couple of new folks into it," Fred said. "Naomi, would you like to work in the greenhouses for awhile with Patty? She is getting covered up and needs help. I can find someone to take your place in the fields. You're pregnancy will soon become a greater challenge than it is now, and you will need to start taking it a little easier."

"Sure I like Patty. We get along great. When can I start?"

"Tomorrow morning if you want to, I told her I was going to suggest it to you."

"OK, I'll get with her first thing."

"I want to tell y'all something. Celia and I are going to get married. We know it is sudden, but we have no doubts that we were brought together by God to be together. It is our belief that we should get married right away, and Nayhoom I'd like for you to be my best man."

"And I want Naomi to be my only bride's maid."

"Of course," Naomi said.

"It will be an honor," Nayhoom said. Fred laughed and shook Nayhoom's hand, and Celia got up and went to Naomi and hugged her. "Thank y'all so much."

"Can we make it a big Party?" Nayhoom said grinning.

"No, no," Fred said. "A friend of mine will conduct the ceremony, and we'll be married right here in this house with just you two and preacher Thad and his wife here with us."

"When?" Naomi asked.

"Christmas day, if that is OK with y'all," Fred said.

"It certainly is," Naomi said.

"We'll be here with bells on," Nayhoom said. Fred and Celia laughed.

After a half hour of small talk the conversation turned suddenly serious. They started by discussing the recent hooligan attacks in an area near Hillbrook Nayhoom had found out about through Carl, Jason and David who logged on to the internet each evening and watched live news feeds.

"It's getting bad all around," Nayhoom said. "Gunther is only a hundred miles from here. That is too close. And there are so many hooligans now. I wonder how Hillbrook could manage an all out attack."

"Yes, it all seems to be getting much worse, and so quickly," Fred said.

Suddenly Nayhoom related a torrent of thoughts that included information he had gathered talking with David, and Jason and listening to a world news cast on their computer: "Infrastructure is crumbling faster than it can be attended to. Roads, dams, bridges, electricity, clean water, city water is bad in many places and it is all getting worse everywhere. Polluted water is a major problem worldwide. Local springs are guarded by locals and sometimes deadly battles take place over the clean water there. Both poles are basically melted, and vast amounts of carbon monoxide is leaking from beneath the once frozen permafrost, and it is rising into the already exorbitantly, carbon infused atmosphere. The ocean levels worldwide have risen an average of over two feet. Many coastal towns and villages are now permanently flooded. New Orleans is basically a flooded ghost town. Malaria is quickly on the rise, especially in third world countries, but in places here in America also. Electric dams and coal-fired electric plants are sabotaged frequently, as are telephone land lines. Mobil technology is about the only telephone means of communication. Hospitals everywhere are attacked so often that doctors and nurses rarely go to work anymore. Fires, floods, wind, heat!! Cholera, malaria, tuberculosis, weird infections, pneumonia, and other diseases once controlled are beginning again to build and gather strength. Impossible to understand and control Flu strains are breaking out worldwide. Many, many, people are dying, especially the young and the old. I heard recently that people in Texas and Florida, what is left after the gulf has risen, are claiming that total anarchy is consuming their states. When will that be the case here?"

Fred had scooted to the edge of his seat. "I guess I didn't know it was that bad. If we ever needed prayer it is now," he said.

"We may have gone beyond what simple prayer can do. If you life is not a prayer, the way you live it, a ritualistic uttering of chosen words may be no more than a hollow and futile exercise."

"I agree," Fred said. "Prayer should be a constant link with God."

Celia moved uneasily in her chair. Fred looked at her.

"Maybe we should change the subject," she said.

"It certainly is not a pleasant subject, but it is happening," Fred said.

Celia stood up. "If y'all excuse me I think I will go clean the kitchen."

"Don't leave," he said. "We can talk about something else." Celia ignored him and went into the kitchen.

"I think I'll help her," Naomi said, and left the two men to talk alone.

"I didn't mean to upset her," Nayhoom said. "But I feel as though the world is sinking into oblivion. Well I don't mean oblivion. I'm just completely worried."

"Me too," Fred said. "But we have to trust in God."

"People all over the world are trusting in the God they are familiar with. Do you think that is good enough?"

"Matthew 12:30: you are either with me or against me, and he who does not gather with me scatters," Fred said. "That is all I know."

"So it is all or nothing, right?"

"It should be all, don't you think?"

"It may be too late," Nayhoom said. "The time for change has come and is about gone."

"Change?"

"A change in the way people think about life here in the material world. From the time you are old enough to remember you are told certain facts of life. Such as that you are born into an imperfect world where half of what you might encounter is good. But there is an evil side, an evil side to the world, and to people, because we are all sinners and have the evil potential in us, born that way. And it is up to each individual whether they let themselves be controlled by the evil side or the good side, with nothing being in between. And we all know what nothing is, nowheres'ville. You don't want to go there! As if we could, nothing does not exist, how could we go there? If it did exist, it would be something, but it is not something, it is nothing."

"Jesus saith unto him, I am the way, the truth, and the life, no man cometh unto the Father, but by me. John 14:6." Fred said.

"And Jesus came into the world to point the way, a way away from evil and toward the light of good. And Jesus believed that also it appears. I tend to think the rub with me starts with his supposedly saying I am the way and the truth and the life. No one comes to the Father except through me. Apparently he didn't say God, he said Father."

"Supposedly? He said it."

"How do you know? Nayhoom asked.

"It's in the bible written by men of God."

"Yes, and because I only have man's written word for his saying that, I am skeptical from the start. Who can trust men? Yes, yes, it is reiterated often that God would not allow such a flub-up. Men have been telling me that all my life. Where is your faith boy? God loves you and only wants you to obey him. It is a closed system, and men hold tightly to the draw strings, and the women and children of the world must obey. But who can actually know the intentions of God?"

"And so you are different?"

"It is not me so much that is different as it is different. Life is now different, made different by men. The same men who wrote 'I am the way, the truth, and the life. No man cometh unto the Father, but by me.'"

"But those are Jesus' words."

"So you've been told those were his exact words, and

you believe."

"He would never allow...." Fred caught what he was about to say and stopped.

"His actual words, long, long ago, may have offered complexities that men felt, thought, imagined, might be better expressed in a simpler fashion, one that the women and children could better understand."

"You don't know that."

"I don't not know it either. But knowing man, I highly expect something like that to have taken place many times, all those many years ago, and since. And the difference became the rigid backbone of the now Christian religion."

"The difference?"

"The manly augmentations."

"I'm not comfortable with this," Fred mumbled. He seemed very disturbed suddenly and couldn't speak distinctly.

"You see what you have done with your weird philosophy?" Celia said, entering the room suddenly. Naomi was just behind her.

"I guess maybe we should leave," Nayhoom said, noticing Celia's hateful expression.

"No, no, don't go," Fred said suddenly. "We have just begun to talk."

Celia left the room again and Naomi followed her.

"You are filled with criticism it appears. What is the answer to the problem as you see it?" Fred said.

"Man can't answer the problem. Man, it appears, is the problem. God can answer it though, and maybe that is what is taking place right now with the out of control weather."

"I'm glad to hear that you consider God to be a reality."

"Yes, but not the man upstairs bit. I think that perception is partially why we are dealing today with global warming, melting ice caps, acid oceans, impure water sources."

"Partially?"

"Selfishness is the rest of the equation, taking care first in a material way, of number one."

"I certainly agree with that. What is God to you Nayhoom?"

"To me, God is everything, all things material and all things ethereal, all places, allwhere, all of existence. Nothing doesn't exist, only existence exists, and there is an underlying order with everything. I think it can be thought of as Godly order. I think of it all as being God. And people are only part of the whole, a small part I think, but no less important than anything else, just as all things, all of life is important, and all parts of life are imperative.

"Men gave God legs and a manly head, so they could

more easily deal with the subject. And any thinking about a lowly beetle, or a dodo bird, being as important to the whole as man, has always been suppressed, snuffed out, before the idea could take root. But the root lives. It always will. The extinction of man may be but one more price paid that life might continue. Man is not the boss, man is the problem."

"So what do you think is the answer?"

"I don't know that there is an answer for the masses. Things already are what they are. But if there is an answer for the individual it will entail a major change in the here to fore hard held presumptions about what life is, about man being created in God's image, about the supposed idea that life is a struggle, almost a contest between man and nature, that only the strong survive. It has to stop being a man's world and start being life's world. Such long held Paradigms must be loosened and new thinking encouraged to transpire and develop. Either you do it or it does it to itself regardless."

"It?"

"Life, and life entire has more patience than any individual can ever imagine."

They heard Celia crying and Fred went to see what the problem was. Naomi came into the room and looked sort of frightened. "She is not doing well," she said.

Fred returned. "Celia is in a bad way. I suppose we had better call it an evening. We are very glad y'all came.

Let's get together soon and talk about Christmas Day, OK?"

"Sure," Nayhoom said, "anytime."

When they were walking home Naomi told Nayhoom: "We could hear y'all, and after Celia listened to most of your conversation she said that kind of talk just drove her crazy. And then she said that she needed a drink, and then she started to cry."

\*\*\*

Three days later after work, December the eighteenth, Fred came alone to see Nayhoom and Naomi. He wanted to talk about the wedding. They did, and afterward the three sat on the front porch and talked about other things.

"What do you think happens to people, their spirit after they die Nayhoom?" Fred asked.

"I certainly don't know, but I imagine the self we are all familiar with continues on in life, somehow, in some way."

"In life?"

"Yes. I know that death is generally considered by people, your everyday person, and especially people of the scientific community, as the end of life. But to me, to my way of thinking, Naomi's too, death is part of life and with life should together be thought of as the phenomenon called life."

"You got me there for sure. Can you explain that?"

"I can try. On this earth, the only place we can be certain that life exists, it requires the death of one thing to provide life for another. That is the known life process on this planet. To me that makes the two, life and death, as one thing, life.

"That simple?"

"That simple. And because an after death life of the spirit, or the self, cannot specifically be known about, only imaginatively theorized about, I think of imagining as actually being an elevated form of thought, though any substance of true thought there is most often cryptic or symbolic. And I am aware that imagining and thinking are not exactly synonymous. But much thinking, and mostly imagining, is always given forth by a person as to what might happen to them, their soul, after death. It is a common thing, and I think probably as natural as all of nature is natural. I imagine that whatever a person thinks and imagines about an after death life to be part and parcel to who and what they are, and an integral part of life itself. So, I see imagining as part of the life process, as well as being part of a person's belief system."

"Do you not fear Hell?"

"To me you are asking whether or not I fear some other people's beliefs, their belief that Hell exists. Hell may exist for some. There is obviously no way I can know for certain. But for me, and I'm sure Naomi thinks the same way, Hell isn't a reality, nor is Heaven."

"What then?"

"Life."

"But after life?"

"I don't think about before death and after life. I think about it but I don't contemplate it anymore. To me life is all that exists, which includes death. Just because I can't think about, and be certain of specifics about what awaits me, my self, after my physical death here in this physical existence, does not mean to me that my life, or my relationship with self, is over upon dying. Thus I imagine. To my way of seeing it, or imagining it, life has always been, and will never be over. I think of life as a continuum, which includes physical death."

Fred looked at Naomi and she smiled.

"I preach the word of God. I always have, I always will. "Y'all come up sometime soon so we can do a dry run of our wedding."

"OK, you pick the day," Nayhoom said.

\*\*\*

A few days before Christmas, at four PM, word came by way of an e-mail to Jason from a friend who lived near the downtown area of Hillbrook, that Bore had been killed in a violent shoot-out with hooligans at a roadhouse not far from town. Jason went to Fred's house and told him and was going to Nayhoom's house to tell them, but he stopped in the middle of the field when he heard gunfire close by. He ran back to the dorm, but heard no more after that one shot. "Someone hunting," Carl said.

"I guess so." Jason said skeptically.

Within the hour Fred and Celia arrived in her car and everyone living in the dormitories got in and Fred drove to a small church three miles away to attend the Wednesday evening prayer service. Patty and Steve Sorenson, and George and Beth Williamson, were already there. Only Nayhoom and Naomi stayed at home.

It was dark when Fred and friends left the church riding in Celia's car. A mile from the farm, they all noticed that the sky above the farm was glowing red, which could mean only one thing. Something was burning. Fred's house and barn were on fire, as were all the houses on the farm. They met Patty, Steve, and George and Beth, walking hurriedly on the road toward them.

"What is all that fire?" Fred asked them.

"Every building on the farm, our houses, your house, is burning. Hooligans!" Beth said.

A rifle shot rang out in the late evening air and the bullet could be heard as it buzzed very close over their heads.

"Get in the car," Fred said. "Just get in the best you

can, lay on their laps. We gotta get out of here!" After they were inside the car he backed up, turned around and fled.

*** 

They saw Fred's barn burning first, and then his house. That was enough. They ran out of their house carrying the pressure cooker. Nayhoom grabbed the old machete blade from the porch rafters, and ran with Naomi to the side of the house. He opened the door to the space beneath, and by the tie-up rope pulled the canoe out.

Naomi pushed it and Nayhoom pulled on the rope. The canoe slid through the dry leaves and woods pretty easily all the way to the Golly Gee. Naomi sat in the front while Nayhoom pushed the canoe out into the slow moving water. It was dark, but light enough that they could see the creek banks. They paddled quickly away from the farm.

When they reached the river and the dam, they got out to unload the canoe. The sky was bright orange directly over the spot they knew their house was. "They are burning it all," Nayhoom said.

"How will we ever know who is alright and who isn't?" Naomi said.

"We may never, because we will not come back."

# CHAPTER SIX

## RUN

For a little while, as fast as they could go, and with very little light to see by, Nayhoom and Naomi paddled the canoe down river. And then it became obvious that no one was coming after them, so they relaxed some and began to drift and talk.

"Where can we go?" Naomi asked.

"We go where we go," Nayhoom said. "We can't return."

"Do you think we will die?"

"Eventually of course, but I'm not worried. As you know we were born to live and to die, the two crucial elements of life. And in the larger scheme of things, what is time? I mean now is forever, or it may as well be. We live in the material world until we die of it. In the mean time we do the best we can to stay alive and healthy, but what is our ultimate goal?"

"We don't have one."

"That's right, just live," he said. "Living is the only goal."

"Just live," she said.

The sky to their left, toward Hillbrook was alight by the many fires burning in that direction. "I think it has finally come to all out war," Nayhoom said.

"Civil war," Naomi said. "The inevitable is happening. People in our part of the world have begun in earnest being at war with themselves. The haves against the have-nots."

They heard voices behind them. A man and his wife and child in a boat were gaining on them, and were very close. "Hello," the woman said from the dark. The man paddling was shining a flashlight on them. "Y'all seem to be in the same predicament we are in. Where are y'all going?" he said.

"We are just going," Nayhoom said, as the family of three pulled up beside them, and the man clicked off his light. "Where are y'all going?" Nayhoom asked.

"Chattanooga," the man said. They were both young, but older than the two Wadells. The man was very strong and the young woman very pretty, though his and her face was not visible. Their little daughter, five years old, was also very pretty like her mother, and she was acting shyly, hiding under her mother's arm.

"Why Chattanooga?" Nayhoom asked.

"I have a brother down there," the man said. "And he is our only kin. We have to believe he is still alive, but it is rumored that there is as much chaos in that area as everywhere else."

"Chaos? You mean war don't you?" Nayhoom said.

"We are trying to stay on the brighter side of things. Things are certainly chaotic, but I don't think it is war. War against who?"

"Man against man. Those who have, fighting those

who don't have. If you have something you protect it from anyone who tries to take it from you."

"We don't have anything," the man said. "We have our daughter, and that is all."

Nayhoom started to say that his little daughter was enough, and someone might try to take her, but he sensed that the child was frightened and thought it best to say nothing about it. "I like your boat, what I can see of it. Did you make it?"

"My brother made it. I have used it more than him. Maybe that will change soon. Are y'all eat'n these river fish?"

"Not yet," Nayhoom said.

"Well, good luck to y'all," the man said, and with deep, hard strokes started paddling away from them.

"Y'all take care," Nayhoom said to the dark shapes in the boat moving toward the middle of the river.

"I'm not going to eat any of these fish," Naomi said quietly.

"I'm telling myself I'm not either. But a man told me once that you would eat your own foot if you got hungry enough. We have beans for awhile, and I have the wild foods book. But we have to save some of the beans for seed. If we can make it until February we just might get some planted."

"Where?"

"Wherever. You rest Naomi, sleep if you can. I'll keep us going until morning, and then we'll hide and I'll sleep. We should travel in the canoe only at night under the cover of darkness."

"OK, but I don't think I can sleep."

"Try. Our baby needs for you to."

"OK."

Sitting in the very front of the canoe with their mound of valuables wrapped in black plastic behind her, she reclined against the bulk of it and looked up at the night sky. The moon was only half full, and appeared between the passing of high clouds, along with blinking stars. It has come to this, she thought. And we are going to have a child. And then she wondered if the person to be born was an old person or a young person. Either would have to be strong to survive in a world of irrational people. She wondered if the person to be born had a choice in the matter. From that thought her mind became involved with a myriad of details. The cooler night breeze on the river, and the gentle rocking of the canoe, soon lulled her to sleep.

Nayhoom could hear occasional popping sounds of gunfire somewhere in the distance on both sides of the river. With each pop he wondered if someone had been shot, and thought it very likely they had. The sky was bright with fire light in several places down river and behind. He also heard loud explosions and other sounds indicating additional kinds of turmoil. The chaos seemed to have aggrandized quickly. The tension had existed all along, and then had spread like wildfire. "Each man for hisself," David had said. Protect what you have or risk losing it. *People are acting like rats*, Nayhoom thought. He then remembered another verse from the Bible: *Be not deceived— God is not mocked— for whatsoever a man soweth, that shall he also reap.*

The wind from behind picked up and pushed them along without Nayhoom having to paddle much. He was quiet and cautious and kept his eyes alert for any movement on the river ahead and around him, and also along the banks of the shore fore and aft. His experiences with people during the past few months had taught him to beware of any and all human behavior. If there was to be any trouble it would be with people, with men in particular.

Twice he paddled to the right side of the river to be out of the way of gasoline powered boats going up river. If a light were to be shined on them they could easily be observed. But that did not happen. The idea that it might, forced him to stay close to the shore when it seemed safe to do so. He wondered what it could be like in the more populated areas along the river ahead, and considered that it may prove impossible to go very far downstream without being seen, even under the cover of darkness.

Before the attack on Fred's farm he had studied a map of the rivers and had been thinking that he and Naomi should go to the Tennessee River, and from there go down below Chattanooga, more than thirty miles further on. But that was a very long way and it was possible they would not make it before being discovered by hooligans.

*What is the point in distance anyway,* he wondered. *We can never go where the same problems with this life do not exist. One place is as good as the next.*

At three AM, after an uneventful time drifting, and slowly paddling down the Hiwassee, a Dark shape on the water loomed against the lighter shades of night directly ahead of him. And then they were suddenly there upon it. It was the capsized boat belonging to the people they had seen earlier and had spoken with. Nayhoom shined a small

215

flashlight on the man with a badly bleeding head, who was clinging to the hull.

"They took my wife and child," he said weakly. And then he let go of the boat and slipped below the surface of the water. Nayhoom could do nothing. He thought of going after him but he knew he would probably turn the canoe over with Naomi and their things in it. The man was gone, sinking fast to the bottom of the river. The woman and child were gone too.

Naomi did not wake up and he did not wake her. There was no point in doing that he thought. A hundred feet further downstream the river seemed to widen suddenly. But it was the mouth of a creek they had come to, a creek entering the river from the right. With no particular thought guiding him he turned in and began slowly paddling northward up the creek. After a few hundred yards he became aware that the creek could be taking them directly into the vicinity of danger, hooligans.

Nayhoom was not a person who purposely thought of faith as a guiding principle. He knew that faith was important and a part of everyday life. He believed that without faith in the sun rising, a person might always be afraid that one day it might not. And he considered it to be faith that allowed a person to eat the foods they trusted as safe to eat. Otherwise they might not eat. Faith was a function of life. Without a healthy measure of it a person could go mad.

The faith suggested by people he knew, faith he should have in a heavenly father watching over him and Naomi, did not figure into his attentiveness or imagination.

But, he never considered for a moment that his and her life was not as important as anything else within the totality of life. And that the same order which gave rise to stars, planets, flowers, animals, also gave rise to everyone including him and Naomi and all they had done and might do. If they were to suddenly de-exist in the material world, be killed, it would be a part of the same order, a living, functioning order. *Call it what you will*, he thought. He knew it was his imagination that informed him of such order, but he considered imagining to be a superior form of thinking, more superior than analytical and scientific thinking even, and the thoughts or imaginings of people about God and an afterlife to be a personal matter.

He abandoned his thinking about hooligans and paddled on. There was just enough moonlight to see by as the creek narrowed. There were no lights that could be seen anywhere along any horizon. They were away from city lights or lights of any kind. *This may be as good as it gets*, he thought. *We should stop somewhere near and tomorrow take stock of the local.* He dipped the paddle deep and pulled, and touching bottom with it he realized the creek was becoming shallow. Soon a mud-bar scraped along the bottom of the aluminum canoe. He paddled hard to his right until the front of it slid up on the muddy shore. Naomi did not wake up, and he sat still. After an hour and he had heard nothing, he sat down in the bottom of the canoe and leaned back against the seat.

He thought he could stay awake until daylight, but soon he was nodding off to sleep. He shook himself completely awake and stretched his arms and legs. Naomi woke up.

"Where are we?" she whispered.

"I paddled up a creek. We have to stop and stay somewhere. Populated areas are too risky. Maybe we should stay out here in the wilds with the critters and the bugs."

"I just now dreamed that we found a home."

"Maybe this is it," he said. "I'm falling asleep. Can you stay awake for awhile and let me nap?"

"Of course. I feel rested. I'll awaken you after awhile."

He went to sleep in less than a minute. He slept sitting on the floor of the canoe, leaning back against the aluminum seat. Naomi stayed where she had been while she was asleep, leaning back against their valuables wrapped in black plastic.

She wanted something to drink, but the drinking water was packed away. She thought coffee would be nice, but that was totally undoable. She could hear Nayhoom snoring softly. A meteor fell slanting across the sky. For a moment she felt comforted. But then she heard an explosion far in the distance and was reminded of the cold realities of human desperation.

Their baby was growing inside her. Her stomach was protruding a little now like she had known it would. She had seen the difference in her appearance immediately, but chose to not think about it just yet and wait until it was more obvious that her body was changing, and changing its look. That was happening and she now definitely felt and looked pregnant. She had several times been nauseated in the early morning hours and had thrown up. She thought at those times of herself as a baby factory. It seemed so true. But now she was out of contact with doctors, and he and she would have to deal with the uncertainties of pregnancy and childbirth without professional advice. It occurred to her that most of the people who had ever been born were born into this world without the aid of a professional doctor. But that was not a comforting thought. They did have the baby book which contained a lot of information about pregnancy and home deliveries. She intended to locate it among their things and start reading it again soon.

The night sounds were unusually quiet. A few animals were about but they were aware of the intruders and chose to stay hidden. It was warm, almost hot, but a breeze blew from the north and felt good on her skin. Nayhoom snored louder now and she listened, wondering if he was dreaming or not.

With her mind busy contemplating future possibilities, she sat peacefully through the rest of the early morning. And then it occurred to her that Christmas was only a few days away, but she was not certain how many. And she thought it did not matter if she knew exactly how many. Christmas had been exciting when she was a child, but for the past few years it had meant almost nothing except that it was an American Dream holiday that almost everyone she knew looked forward to. The idea that it was supposed to represent the birth of Christ and be a religious holiday had become laughable to her. She felt that Christ would be ashamed of the way people had placed him on a pedestal to stand for all they didn't have to deal with anymore because of his sacrifice. A sham, she thought. *People have turned his life into a sham.* And now the American Dream had become The American Nightmare. It fact the whole world, much of it trying to follow the American footprint, was having a nightmare with the realities of global warming. And there could be no taking them back. In time, a lot of time, nature could possibly return itself back, or forward, to a state unaffected by the handy work of man. But that could be thousands, even millions of years away, maybe never. Meanwhile struggle of an unusual kind ensues.

Words of a Christmas song came to her: *The weather outside is frightful, but the fire is so delightful.* She wasn't certain of exactly what irony was but she thought the concept of irony was probably exemplified by those words.

With first light Nayhoom awoke. He had slid further down along the bottom of the canoe, but there was no water there so his pants were dry, though he was a little cramped. He got back up on the seat and saw Naomi's back. She was looking straight ahead and did not move.

"Naomi, are you awake?"

She wasn't sure what she was. She thought she had stayed awake, but with his voice came the possibility that she had fallen asleep with her eyes open while sitting upright. She turned and looked at him.

"I think I'm awake now, but maybe I had fallen to sleep. It was very strange. I thought I was awake, but maybe I wasn't."

"We should pull the canoe up in the tall grass there and make something to eat," he said.

After they had dragged the canoe up and out of sight in the grass he decided to have a look around.

"Make a very small fire to cook the beans and I'll climb that tree and see what I can see."

"Don't go out of site," she said.

"I won't, I'm just going over to that tall beech there. You can watch me."

The beech tree had two trunks. One was dead, but the other was not, and it was that half that had the highest limbs. Climbing trees seemed to come naturally to him even though he had not been a tree climber as a child. He shimmed part way up the tree until he reached limbs that would support him. From there he went as high as he could, where he had an excellent view of the countryside in all directions. He waved to Naomi and she waved back.

The river was not far away and he could see where it veered left and disappeared in a westerly direction. To the north and back toward the east there were no houses or buildings of any kind, only mud flats and random pools and streams of water, backwater from the river and the creek. And the main creek meandered back northward through the mud flats toward what looked from his place in the tree to be at least two islands. Water seemed to be on all sides of the bigger island. He wasn't certain it was an island, but it appeared to be a lone wooded hill in the middle of a vast stretch of muddy waste land. *I should have seen this on the map when I looked at it, but I didn't.* And then he remembered that his map was not a new one. If they were to hide, this could be the best place they would find, even though other people may find it and want to hide here also. *One bridge at a time*, he thought. He looked around and memorized what he saw. *We might be here for awhile.*

It took the beans in the pressure cooker only an hour and a half to cook. Nayhoom was impressed with Naomi's immediate ability to maintain a small fire that kept them at a low boil. They ate and then repacked their things into the canoe.

"We should try and find out if those were islands I saw. If they were it could be the best place for us to rest and prepare ourselves for what to do next," he said.

"OK."

He paddled the canoe slowly up the creek. It took them about twenty minutes to reach what he had seen, but if the largest body of land was an island they could not tell by simply being there. It was large and would have to be walked in all directions to determine the borders. They hid the canoe and set out walking the shore line to find out.

The creek split around it, and there at the south end, among dead cattail stalks, is where they concealed the canoe. They thought the shallow section of creek that forked to the left of the wooded area might dwindle into the mud flats and be completely separated from the main stream. Only a walk along the shallow fork would show them.

The first thing Nayhoom noticed after hiding the canoe was one deer track along the shore of the main stream. "It looks like there might be deer around. I see raccoon tracks also. We'll have to keep our stuff hidden well from raccoons. Look that is polk salet. I've eaten some of that before. Maybe it is not as good as spinach, but it is good and I'll bet you will like it. There are no greens there now, but look at all those dead stalks. You've never eaten any have you?"

"No," she said.

"And look at that tree. I think that is an apple tree," he said. The leaves had all dropped, but many shriveled apples were still clinging to branches.

"It is, by jingos," he said, and pulled down a limb with several old, and leathery looking apples still attached. "Smell this one. I think it is still eatable. It isn't rotten, only dried out. This is amazing! We can eat these!"

# CHAPTER SEVEN

## AVALON

The larger body of land was an island, and most of it was a wooded ridge. At the base it was thick with vegetation and surrounded by the creek which split to course at different depths on each side. On the shallow side, the western side, the mud flats were more prominent and widespread than pools of water. During heavy rainfall the mud plane became inundated and looked convincingly from a distance like a large lake, or a large body of deep water. And there seemed to have been much rain lately in the area. The water was receding but it had not done so completely, so water pooled over the plane in many places, and at present water completely surrounded the island. After walking a short way Nayhoom suggested that they go through the woods, and up the ridge to the other side and see what was there.

While crossing the patch of woods to the other side, he saw muscadine vines. "Look Naomi, I think these are muscadine vines. They are all over the place. And up high there are muscadines still clinging to the vine. I'll bet they have dried out like the apples. We should try and get them."

"Let's do it later. I want to see the other side."

The island was only a hundred yards wide but it was

long, though they could not see yet how long. The muddy waste land in all directions looked vast. "This area must have been pasture land at one time. And then TVA flooded it. Why was it not on the map I looked at? The map was not that old. I'll show it to you."

And then they saw another apple tree, and then another. Both were at the edge of the woods. The limbs of the trees drooped low toward the water. Dried, shriveled apples were still on their branches. One was reachable and he picked it. "It is like the others, dried but not rotten. This is amazing. Birds have not pecked it either."

In all they would discover ten apple trees on the big island, which was about three hundred yards long and shaped like a banana, curving to the west. All the apple trees grew at the edge of the creek that split around the island and most of these trees were on the western side, along the inner curve.

Near the north end of it, they could see on another smaller island hill across the creek on the eastern side, several large cedar trees standing near the top with kudzu vines covering them almost completely. "You ever eat kudzu?" he asked.

"No I haven't."

"I have. I told you about it. Remember? It is good."

"I remember."

At the end of the main island they found a small pine thicket, only two hundred feet across, covering a hillock. The pine thicket was simply that, thick, very thick, with yellow pine trees of varying ages, heights and sizes. While standing in the center of it they could see down low, below the lowest branches, only small patches of the surrounding water and muddy country side, and the base of the hill to the east. They would soon discover that it was topped with several nut trees, a bit higher up the island hill than the cedars choked with kudzu vines. Sedge grass grew on its slopes. And a deep pool of water was at the northern tip-end of the island they were exploring, where the creek merged again with itself before trailing off and becoming smaller further to the north.

Across the pool in a north-westerly direction, there was another very small island, only a little more than hundred feet across. Growing in the center of it were several large hickory nut trees. Old and dead sycamores protruded from among limestone boulders at the shore. The outsized, limestone rocks jutted from the base of the steep shore line. They looked as though they had been placed there. The bare limbs of the sycamores reached like aged human arms to the sky.

"This is it," Nayhoom said. "Why don't we stay here for awhile and see what happens. We can camp here in the pine thicket and if anyone approaches they can easily be seen. Who would come here anyway?"

"We have," she said.

"True, but maybe no one else will. And if they do and are peaceful, we will probably get along."

\*\*\*

The creek would become too shallow for the canoe in the coming days, but at the time is was deep enough they could paddle all the way to the deep pool and pine thicket at the end of the island. They got out of the canoe, unloaded most of it, and pulled it with the remaining contents, up into the thicket, and then carried the things they had unloaded up among the sweet smelling conifers.

"It smells like Christmas here," Naomi said.

"Is tomorrow Christmas Day?" he asked.

"I'm not sure, but it is near."

"Merry Christmas," he said.

"Merry Christmas to you."

They didn't completely unpack their things right away, but kept out only what they needed then, a blanket to sit on, drinking water and the map he had mentioned, and put the other things back in the canoe with the rest. He used a dead pine branch to rake up a thick cushion of pine needles to spread the blanket over. They sat on the blanket and passed a bottle of drinking water back and forth while he unfolded the map and started looking at where they were.

"I can't believe this. The mud flats are right here," he said, pointing to a large section on the map. I would swear it wasn't here before. I've looked at this map fifty times and I never saw this vast stretch of mud flats. It is named Beakers Acers. I would have seen this I know.

"Well, there it is. I see it now," she said.

"I sure can't argue with that," he said. "But something is very strange about this. I've had this map for two months. I've looked up and down the river on it many times thinking about where we might go if we had to leave in a hurry. But here it is, and here we are! It is amazing to me!"

"Are you going to be alright?"

"I think we are safe here. How could that not feel alright?"

"I feel good if you do," she said.

"I do. I want to see your stomach, and feel where our baby is sleeping."

An hour later, with a steady breeze from the north blowing through the tree trunks and across them, and loudly through the boughs overhead, they shared a morning nap together.

After waking from the nap they walked around the area and discovered, less than a hundred yards back to the west, a cane break. Many long shoots of cane grew there and Nayhoom showed excited. I can build us a really nice place to stay with this cane. I have the twist-tie tool and a big roll of tie wire. Remember me telling you about how it works?"

"I remember. I will help."

"It'll be fun. I think we should build it back there in the pine thicket. We are basically out of sight there and shaded from the hot sun. What do you think?"

"It seems the obvious place. There is no manual we can go by, so we just have to do the best we can."

"I think we are doing that. Don't you?"

"Yes. How are you going to cut these?"

"I have that old rusty machete, or corn knife as Fred called it, that I found under the house. And I have a new file. I'll sharpen it up and start gathering cane tomorrow."

"What happened to Fred and all our friends Nayhoom?"

"I guess we can't know that, at least for now."

After returning to their blanket in the pines, Nayhoom got the machete and some tools out from where they were packed. "I'm going to sharpen this thing and start cutting cane today."

"OK. And I'll get our lunch started. We have food for now Nayhoom, but what about later?"

"It will be one thing at a time. I feel good about it. We'll manage."

"OK. I feel good too."

It took longer to sharpen the machete than he thought it would. It was very rusty, and he had to first remove the rust. He used the sandy creek mud's abrasive properties like a polishing compound, rubbing and scrubbing it over the metal with a chunk of moss, again and again. He was able to remove most of the loose rust that way. The machete was very dull and needed a lot of attention with the file. And it was hard to hold while he pushed the file against the blade. He was constantly adjusting the position of his foot holding the blade steady on a large rock. After an hour he was still at it, sweating and mumbling to himself. It was something he had never done before and he was very awkward with his attempt.

It was an hour after they had eaten lunch that he finally decided the corn knife was sharp enough to cut cane. He left Naomi in the pines and set out for the cane thicket. After a few whacks he realized that he would have to be patient and sharpen the machete better and put some kind of handle on it. The cane was tough and not easy to cut, and the bare, rusty metal hurt his hand. He thought he might wrap it with tie-wire and then wrap that with duct tape. He went back to the pine thicket, sat on the blanket and thought about what he needed to do. Naomi handed him a cup of water.

"What will we do for water?" she said.

"I guess we'll boil what's out there and take our chances."

And that is what they would have done. But the following day, while Nayhoom was cutting cane, Naomi explored the wooded hillside above the cane break and made a startling discovery. She hollered for Nayhoom who came quickly.

"What is it?"

"Look there. Is that what it looks like?"

"Unbelievable," he said, getting on his knees to inspect it more closely. A stream of clear water issued from the ground between two automobile sized rocks. It trickled down the wooded slope to the creek in the trough it had made down to the red clay, having obviously been trickling that way there for many years.

"It smells great. I think I'll try some."

"Why not? If you get sick, I won't drink any."

"Good thinking," he said, and scooped a handful up to his mouth. "It tastes great. If I don't die we'll know it is good to drink."

"My hero!"

He did not die. He sipped the water every day for three days, until their bottled water ran out, and then they both drank the water they had unbelievably found.

The next amazing thing they found, finding it together, was an old, nutting stone along the creek bank. There was no mistaking what it was. Nayhoom had seen one in an archeological magazine a few years before. "Indians made this. It is for cracking nuts on. You put the nut in one of these little pockets and crack it with another rock. They made these pockets with cane drills. You hollow out a length of cane, fill it with sand, and then, with a small bow, you spin it into the sandstone like you do a stick on a piece of wood when you're starting a fire. Now we need to gather some nuts. I think those trees over on that little island are hickory nut trees. We should paddle over there soon and find out."

The following day he suggested again that they go to the little island and investigate the trees there. They did and he had been right about them being hickory nut trees. He had seen their scaly bark from over by the pine thicket. "Nuts are everywhere," he said, "a great source of protein. With the soy and mung beans maybe you and our baby won't become anemic."

They gathered several pounds of nuts and put them in the canoe. "These won't last until next fall, but maybe we'll find other nut trees on the big island," Nayhoom said.

That evening they used the nutting stone, and using smaller stones like hammers cracked nuts until dark came. And then they put the nut meat in plastic bags and put the bags in one of their five gallon plastic buckets, and put the lid back on it. Then they bedded down under the pine boughs and listened to the warm breeze blowing through the branches overhead.

"I think we should wait a while before starting a fire after dark," he said. "I guess we will have to eventually, but for now, until we can feel more confident that we won't be seen, let's not light up the night with a fire."

"OK, she said. "How long will we stay here?"

"Long? Does it matter?"

"I guess that is the answer. What can it matter?"

"What matters is what happens now, don't you think?"

"Yes. But what is happening to us?"

"You mean other than having been thrown asunder by hooligans?"

"What exactly threw us asunder?" she asked. "I mean other than the hooligan attack."

"We are part of the reason I think, what we think and how we act. We, like everyone else, are never satisfied with life as it is. We have assumed it is our birthright, or something, to fiddle with the dials, as if life is some old radio that needs our fiddling. It doesn't, life itself has put up with the fiddling until now, until it has become over taxed with human meddling, the human experience, the American dream, which is basically the same the world over. And now that worldview can no longer be prevalent. There was a limit to the amount of carbon that could be dumped into the atmosphere, and a limit to economic growth, and limits to many other kinds of human expansion, but no one was paying close attention to limits. Everyone, including us, was too busy taking care of number one, and in a selfish, materialistic, way. Now the repercussions of that selfishness have become manifest, we have found the malleable, though finite limits of nature to be a wall too high for more human fiddling to surmount."

"We don't have much time, do we?"

"Time? I think time exists in human theory, human perceptions only. What was time before the first human? Eons, millions and billions of years have existed always. So what can this moment of life be other than a thought, a moment of human thought?"

"What happens to people when they die?"

"Of course I don't know that, and can't know. But I can imagine, and I do. But one's imagination about it is personal, I think, whether one thinks it is or not. But I certainly don't know that to be absolutely true, or an absolute fact of life. I think facts of life are relevant to the beholders. I suppose I also believe that if you think the world is flat, then for you it is. The scientist will argue that there are rigid rules of the road that must be heeded. But the scientific views held by scientists, and people in general, have found footing according to generalized world views held by people worldwide, largely imagined world views, that life is a struggle, man against nature. So science comes constantly to the rescue with answers and treatment. But I think the paradigm belief that man's life is a struggle with and against nature is, and has been misleading, and has led us to the destitute place we now find ourselves. Any life struggle exists within human perception only, and humans project that struggle, as they see it, onto all things and to everyone they encounter. The human view of reality attempts to reshape reality at large according to human will, and that attempted reshaping is, and has been, man's Achilles heel."

"I think that too," she said. "I am so sleepy."

Naomi dreamed that night, beginning immediately with fretful, snippet images of the day's activities, and then it quickly progressed into impressive encounters with dream characters she did not know.

The man's name was Jonas Ledford. He was a book salesman. He sold encyclopedias and dictionaries. *If you need an encyclopedia or a dictionary, I'm the man you should talk to,"* he told her.

*"Don't you know what is happening?"* Naomi said.

*"I know you are about the prettiest thing I have ever seen."*

*"Thing? I'm not a thing."*

*"A pretty thing,"* he said, as if saying that would make the necessary corrections.

*"You just don't get it do, you?"* she said.

*"Get what? I get how pretty you are, that's for sure."*

*"I don't need any books, encyclopedias or dictionaries. You can go and leave me in peace."*

*"You are in peace aren't you?"*

*"It is none of your business."*

*"Bitch!"*

She awoke for a moment and felt Nayhoom's hand touching hers. She took his hand and squeezed it. He squeezed back, and then she immediately fell asleep again.

\*\*\*

At different times, for two days, he cut cane and put

it in a pile, and then together they took it, an armload at a time, back to the pine thicket. There they stripped the cane of its branches and leaves, and then, while Naomi cooked soy beans in their pressure cooker, Nayhoom sat and made plans as to how their dwelling should take shape. After lunch he started cutting the cane into specific lengths, using one length of cut cane to measure the others with.

The biggest problem he incurred was how to secure the wickiup construction to the ground. He solved the problem by using a sharpened hardwood stake to first make a hole in the ground for each main upright piece. He used a large rock as a hammer to drive the hatchet sharpened stake into the ground. He then pulled it out and inserted an upright piece of cane. Each hole he made for the upright pieces was about a foot deep.

After the fifty, twelve feet long, upright pieces had been inserted, he had created a square around the spot their blanket had been spread in the center of the pine thicket. The square was about ten feet wide and ten feet long. It looked like a cage of some sort he was building.

"What are you making," she asked.

"A kind of wigwam, you'll see."

He sat on a blanket and with his wire cutters cut a hundred pieces of tie wire, each about ten inches long. And then with needle nosed pliers he put a loop at both ends of each piece. With these pieces, each looped at their ends, he would use the twist-tie tool to bind horizontal support canes to the upright ones, the ones pushed into holes in the ground.

The twist-tie tool was a simple handheld tool, a

wooden handle with a hole through it from end to end, through which had been inserted a metal rod— slightly smaller in circumference than the hole so it could spin inside it— bent at a forty-five degree angle where it came out of the handle. The rod, three inches longer than the wooden handle, had been heated, the very end drawn to a point and curved to make a small hook. The short pieces of tie-wire with loops at each end were each to be wrapped around two, or more, pieces of cane to be lashed together. The point of the twist-tie tool is then inserted in both loops, and with a stirring motion, the ends of the short piece of wire are twisted together until tight. If you twist too much, the wire breaks; stopping, after just the right amount of twisting, ties the cane together most efficiently.

Nayhoom was liberal with the wire ties, tying together almost any two, or more, pieces of cane that touched one another. This made the wickiup's frame-work very sturdy.

Naomi was soon helping. She cut short pieces of tie wire and with the needle-nosed pliers looped the ends before handing them to him. She also held pieces of cane in place while he secured them with the ties.

After bending the side, upright canes over to meet one another, and tying them together, the structure started taking on the look of a real wigwam. "Where did you learn to build a wigwam?" Naomi asked.

"I saw it in a book. I learned about the twist-tie tool from Fred. Is it great or what?"

"It is great!"

They tied supporting pieces of cane, like rafters,

along the length of the structure from the arched top down to the bottom, until it was sturdy and would shake only with force. "Now we'll cover it with black plastic, and then those cane branches," he said.

*\*\**

When the wickiup frame was finished, and covered with plastic, they sat on the ground a few feet away and scrutinized it admiringly. "Indians would like it I think," he said. "I am certain it is stronger than anything an Indian would have built, and probably more waterproof." Fred had told him that black plastic would last a long time. So he was confident it would be good to use.

And then, after wiring many foot long cane branches to hang perpendicularly  along each individual cane pole, they started at the bottom of the structure and hung each of these long, assembled pieces horizontally along the length of the wikiup, one a little higher that the preceding one, but overlapping it, up the side of the structure on both sides all the way to the top. Each assembly served as would a shingle, one overlapping the next. Nayhoom commented that the cane branch shingles would be useful in keeping the wickiup somewhat camouflaged and cool rather than dry. The plastic would shed any dew or rain. They cut windows in the lower half of each wall and hung black plastic curtains.

"If the mosquitoes discover us we're sunk," he said. "I wonder what Indians did about mosquitoes."

"I have dreams about Indians," Naomi said.

"So do I. What have you dreamed?"

"That we are Indians."

"Really? I have dreamed that too."

"And we lived here, on this island, only it wasn't an island, just a small hill next to the creek."

"I would never joke about this, but I have dreamed that too," he said. We had two children. And then the snow came, a blizzard. And then after that, after the snow melted, we left."

Naomi looked at him. "It was a long, long, time ago," she said.

He looked at her. "Yes, a very long time ago. I know it is only January, but I think we should plant some of our soy and mung beans very soon."

"OK, where?"

"Somewhere close to the creek so we won't have far to carry water."

"OK."

They moved most of their things into their shelter, leaving a few under the canoe nearby. Nayhoom raked up a big pile of pine needles and then took the needles inside and spread them evenly over the plastic covering the dirt floor. And then they made a bed on it with their sheets and blankets. "Home sweet home," he said.

"Yes, home sweet home," she said.

They heard a big clap of thunder. "It is going to rain," he said. They stepped out of the wickiup and went down to the creek. He pointed back to the south. "Look at that dark mass of clouds coming this way. We got the shelter built in the nick of time. It is going to pour rain."

A tremendous storm was approaching rapidly. It had not rained heavily in the area in several weeks, and this storm was massive in size. After the rain began it would not stop for three days. But it was an unusually warm winter. The temperature had not fallen below eighty degrees in twelve months. So staying warm was not an issue. And with the strong wickiup to house them, staying dry was now not an issue either.

During the second day, with the rain coming down in great waves, they stripped off their cloths and ventured into the downpour with washrags and a bar of soap. The thunder and lightning had subsided during the night so they felt safe about rinsing off in the deep pool. It was deep. Nayhoom blew air from his lungs and sunk to stand for a moment on the rocky bottom. "It must be about ten feet deep," he said after he came back up.

"I'll take your word for it. What was the bottom like?"

"Stony."

"Did you see any fish?"

"I didn't open my eyes. I couldn't have seen any anyway."

She laughed. The rain drops splashing into the water was loud.

With nothing much to do afterward, they stayed inside and kept dry, and read in their books, including the baby book. Naomi had been pregnant since the end of October and her thin body was beginning to show an ample rise in her stomach. "With no doctor we will be guessing what the baby will be, boy or girl," she said.

239

"It doesn't matter to me. No Klingons please. Ah heck, what can it matter? But I do hope it is human."

"With you being the father, who knows?"

He laughed. "I'll love it, him or her, whatever."

The rain poured for three days straight. The creek rose well into the pine thicket but didn't come too close to them and their new wickiup. "We'll have to wait until the water recedes to plant beans. I hope it is soon," he said.

"We have all those other seed too. Do you think we can keep it all watered?"

"We'll have to. What else could we eat?"

"Right. Maybe we can find some wild food," she said.

"I'm planning to. The book will tell us a lot. And I'm sure I saw Kudzu. We won't starve. But you need a lot of vitamins and minerals. We'll do our best."

"There is nothing else we can do," she said.

"Our worst."

"I hope we have already done that."

When the rain stopped the sun came out and shone brightly all around. It seemed as though water was everywhere, and except for the nearby islands, and the tree and ridge lines far in the distance, water was all they could see.

Nayhoom re-sharpened the machete, wrapped the handle with more tie-wire and duct tape, and cut more cane. He made shelves in the wikiup, all down the eastern wall. On these shelves they put all their useful items and cloths, which now included the ones they usually wore. It was Naomi's idea that wearing much clothing was now unnecessary. "Who will see us?" she said. "I'll wear my birthday suit, the one I was born wearing."

"OK, me too," he said. So most of the time from then on they were naked. Being naked seemed very natural and most convenient, and cooler. If they ventured very far from the wikiup they wore shoes and other clothes. But as the New Year rolled on they wore them less and less. Their feet became calloused and their shoes stayed on the shelf. A small loin cloth was all that seemed necessary to wear. And it was to discourage the few insects they encountered.

"I wonder why the mosquitoes are not so bad," he said. "I think I haven't been bitten even once."

"Neither have I. Maybe they have all died out."

"They are definitely somewhere other than around here."

After the flood water receded they started planting mung and soy beans along the creek. They figured it might rain again and the bean seed could be lost, but there was nothing to be done about that possibility, except plant a little higher up on the islands than they normally might. So that is what they did.

It was while digging in the loamy soil on the shore of the island hill to the east that he found a hoe made by Indians of long ago. It was fashioned from green limestone and still relatively sharp along its edge. "I saw one of these in an artifact book. All we need is a good handle for it and it will be usable as a hoe again. I can make a handle."

He found a small, six feet long, hickory limb with three forks at the end, which he pruned to the lengths he needed, and using the tie wire he fastened the greenstone hoe snugly in the three pronged crotch, and then pruned the hickory forks some more.

"Is there anything you can't do?" Naomi asked.

"Sing, I can't sing."

"I knew that," she said.

With the warm sunshine after the heavy rain, the ten apple trees, having gone dormant mostly from habit, began to bud and would soon bloom. The beans began to sprout as did the other vegetable seeds they had planted near the creek. The kudzu took on new life and many different kinds of wild greens began growing in the woods and near the creek shore. Poke sallet, narrow dock and chickweed grew abundantly. And they discovered several large stands of cattail not far from the wikiup. The wild foods book described the cattail plant as being eatable in many ways, the roots, shoots, seed pods, flowers and mature plants.

"If the beans do good we'll have plenty for food and seed," he said.

"Is there any reason why they won't do good?"

"We don't have fertilizer, and it will be hot. The weather is unpredictable, so who knows?"

"We have our own waste for fertilizer," she said. "Why not use it?"

"I don't know. People in far eastern countries have done that successfully for thousands of years. I suppose we could too. Does the idea not disgust you?"

"Not if it is just you and me," she said. "I can get used to that, I think."

"OK, let's give it a try. Why not? Waste not, want

not."

"You mean waste yes don't you?"

He sniggered. "Yes, waste yes, want not."

So they made a compost hole fifty yards from the wikiup. For awhile they both did their bodily eliminations in a bucket and carried it to the compost hole, which was two feet wide and dug down into the hard clay a foot below the top soil. They dumped it there along with vegetable scraps. But shortly thereafter he dug the hole deeper and built a cane outhouse over it. He dug a trench to the hole so they could approach it from outside the outhouse to collect the waste for putting it in the soil around the vegetable and bean plants. The plants reacted very favorably to the fertilizer.

At first they used every scrap piece of paper they had for toilet paper. And then that was gone and something else had to be found. Nayhoom began gathering fallen pine branches, the old ones without bark anymore, dry, gray, porous, and smooth. He cut individual pieces, sticks, with the bow saw, to ten inch lengths. He made a container with the popular bark of a downed tree and put the wipe-sticks in the container and hung the container on a wall of the outhouse.

This idea was all he could think of at the time. The smooth, gray, porous sticks, they would use like corncobs. He hoped he would eventually think of something better. But if the sticks worked well, there were plenty of them, and fresh ones fell from all kinds of trees frequently. After the bark weathered off of them they would be ready to gather, cut to length, and use.

"Those Oriental folks were smart about what they were doing," he said. "Our plants are growing great."

With March came the stifling heat. They were worried about all their plants when Nayhoom suggested that they cut more cane and build covers over them the way they had the bean plants on the farm. It would be a little difficult to do, but hard work would have to be their way of life if they were to survive.

In the evenings, until dark, they set in the wikiup and cut the cane to lengths. And then at first light they went to each plant and constructed over it a sun-shade. Four pieces of cane were plunged, or driven, into the ground around the plant, creating a square, and then short pieces were wired around that at the top. Leafy branches were laid across the frame and then wired securely to it to hold tightly against any wind that might blow. It was simple, and all the plants were shaded in three days time. It had worked at the farm and should work now, and it did. Only a few of the plants died, while regardless of the oppressive sun and heat the others thrived and produced.

By April Naomi was definitely looking pregnant. Her stomach protruded noticeably. Without a doctor to help her they compensated the best they knew how by reading constantly in the baby book until they each knew its contents by heart. "Think of all the people born since the first humans and there were no doctors available," Nayhoom said. "You and the baby are going to be fine. We are doing what we should do."

"We are doing all we can do," she said.

"What else is there?"

"That is all there is or has ever been for anyone," she said. "There are no exceptions. Life is difficult for everyone."

*\*\*

Using the wild foods book they started finding many more things on the islands to eat. Nayhoom insisted always that he first test eat anything they were unsure about, and she joked about it. "What could I do without you if you were poisoned and died?"

"Avoid eating whatever killed me."

"And I would then be OK?"

"I would think not," he said with a grin. "But it only seems right that I test them before you...and the baby."

As early summer developed, as it would in the strange, new, and hot environment, they searched all three islands looking for wild food. A tall pecan tree grew at the top of the island to the east, and another black walnut tree. No squirrels seemed to be on any of the islands, but some of the scattered pecan and walnuts had been broken and eaten at, by rats Nayhoom presumed. Another black walnut tree grew at the base of that same island on its far eastern shore. They found what the wild foods book termed May Pops, or Passion Fruit, growing in the weeds along the creek between the two larger islands. It would soon be a good source of vitamin C and other necessary vitamins. Blackberries and dew berries grew there also, and they grew on the sedge brush covered slope of the island to the east.

They found a persimmon tree, and elder berry

bushes at the tip end of the big island. "We'll have no wants for food," Nayhoom said. "These are magical islands."

"Did you ever read about King Author, Camelot and all that?"

"No, not really, he said. "I've heard some about that though."

"King Author went to an island called Avalon. It was a magical island. Apples grew there along with all manner of other vegetable foods. Author was taken there to recover from the wounds he suffered in the Battle of Camlann. Fruits and vegetables grew miraculously there. This place reminds me of Avalon.

# CHAPTER EIGHT
## LYONDELL CRAMMER AND
## RODNEY BOOTH

Lyondell Crammer and Rodney Booth were considered, even among many hooligans, to be the lowest of the low. Lyondell was a swindler, known to have swindled his widowed mother out of her only possessions, namely household goods and ceramic trinkets, and traded them for alcohol. She died soon thereafter from an unknown illness, but friends said it was of a broken heart, broken by Lyondell.

He was a petty swindler, a liar and a thief, and had murdered two younger men, at different times, for no other reason than being angry with them. He was crude of manner and at all times smelled badly because he seemed to never bathe. His face was always shiny with body oil and sweat. He was forty years old and going bald, but he had a large penis, which was his pride and joy, and what attracted Rodney Booth to him. Rodney was ten years younger than Lyondell, and he too was a nasty individual. He also had murdered people, several people, people who confronted him about his homosexual advancements toward either them or friends of theirs.

The two men met at a regular camp meeting of a Knoxville Hooligan band. They had both been drifting separately from one band to another, being essentially ostracized from each within days of joining because they were not loyal to anything, which was immediately obvious to those around them. Lyondell would invariably attempt pulling off some shenanigan deal with the wrong person. His dishonesty would be discovered and he would be labeled unworthy, and then expelled. Rodney's main problem was that he could never resist coming on to any and every man who smiled at him. He too was judged as a misfit and always chased away from hooligan organizations. They were not liked and they both knew it. They stood together at a bar, a ten foot two by twelve spanning that distance between two fifty-five gallon, metal drums. Their moonshine drinks were in aluminum soft drink cans.

Two burly men wielding drawn pistols, came up to them, grabbed the drinks from their hands and threw them on the ground, and pointed toward the guarded gate. "Don't'chuns never come back neither," one of the guards said as the two misfits were walking away from the compound.

Having been kicked out of The Bull Ross Number Fifteen at the same time, they found themselves walking south together down old highway eleven toward Chattanooga.

"Looks like we're in the same boat," Rodney said.

Lyondell, walking a few steps ahead, said nothing.

"We're together, we ought'a talk," Rodney said.

"I ain't got shit ta'say."

"Where you from?"

"Hicksville, where you from?"

"South Carolina. Where's Hicksville?"

"I made it up shit'fer'brains."

Near dark they stopped at a big highway sign close to the highway, but off it and up a small rise, and sat beneath it to rest and maybe stay the night.

"They said you had a big'n. Zat right?

"Big'n what?"

"Big dick. Zat right?"

"Hit ain't no damn redworm."

"Em'me see it."

Lyondell got it out. "Air it is I god. What's'ye thank."

"Damn nation! Ah'tair's sho'nuff a big'n."

"Hit's a real ass buster all right."

'You ever had it up somebody's ass?"

"Naw," he said lying. "You reckon hit'll go up yor ass?"

"Shoot yeah. I had'em bigger'n at'n up'air before."

"We'll less'see if she will."

"You got'ny thang to slick'er up with?

"Spit. At'll do'er want it?"

"Go slow till you get'er goin'."

"I know how ta'do'it I god."

"I thought you said you ain't never done it."

"I ain't," he said lying again, "but at don't mean I don't know how."

When morning came they went down to the mostly deserted  highway and started walking south.

"Chattnoogy's a fer piece from here. Hit's worth goin' to though," Rodney said.

"You suck my dick like you said you could, you can go wi'me."

"I thought I'z goin' anyways."

"I'm the boss ye see. What I say gets done. Zat settle hunkydoodle wi'ye?

"Emme see at dick again."

Lyondell unzipped his pants and pulled his penis out into the bright morning sun.

"You kinda fond'iss som'bitch ain't'chee?"

"Yeah, you the boss alright. I can take at dick an' ye orders too. How fer we goin' today?"

"We need food. I say we take some from whoever."

"At works fer me," Rodney said.

***

Just after dark, after walking all day down the mostly deserted highway, they saw a light on in a house two hundred yards off the road.

"A's food in at house," Lyondell said. "We need to check'er out."

"Fine by me," Rodney said. "I could eat the ring out of a cat's ass."

They walked up into the yard around the house and stood behind a tree and tried to see in the lit window. But they were still too far away. "We gotta get closer'n iss if we're gonna see in," Lyondell said.

"You creep up'air'n'look, an'I'll stay here," Rodney

suggested.

Lyondell look at him in the waning light of near dark. "Good plan shit'fer brains," he said, and pulled a small, .22 caliber pistol out of his front pocket and flashed it before Rodney's eyes.

"Damn, you got a pistol" Rodney said.

"You damn right I do. At big ol' weed whacker hangin' on ye side won't do ye no good at a distance."

"Guns are hard to come by or I'd have me one."

"You watch ol' Lyondell work. I'll be back directly." He crept from tree to bush until he was standing alongside the lit window. Rodney watched patiently. Lyondell peeped in the window and saw an old man walking around in the room looking for something. He watched for five minutes while the man searched under magazines, behind books, and in drawers. He wouldn't have turned a light on, but he had lost his house keys and was looking for them. He walked close to the window and looked out into the darkness of the front yard area. Lyondell ducked back out of sight. When the old man turned to go away from the window Lyondell looked in, took aim with the pistol and pulled the trigger, shooting through the window glass, hitting the man in the back. He fell dead. The bullet had entered his heart. Lyondell watched, ready to run away if someone else entered the room. He thought no one was going to, but just as he was standing up a little ten year old girl opened a door and came in. She went to the old man and saw blood on his back and then she ran back to where she came from.

He waited a full five minutes more without hearing

another sound or seeing anything or anyone through the window, and then he trotted back to where Rodney was.

"Let's go in," he said. Rodney nodded.

The front and back doors were locked, but the window with the bullet hole was easy to remove broken glass from and open. They crawled in.

He had told Rodney about the little girl and said they had to find her, and then search the rest of the house for other people before getting into the kitchen and the pantry. They went from room to room in the old five room house. In the last one, a bedroom, they found the little girl with her twelve year old sister hiding under the bed.

They had been left by their parents with the mother's father while her husband took her to a midwife's house to deliver their third child. Leaving the girls alone with her old man was not what she and her husband wanted to do, but it was an emergency and they weren't supposed to be gone for very long.

"Come on out little girls," Lyondell said disdainfully, in a phony, patronizing, child-like voice. The girls started crying and Rodney got on his knees and grabbed an ankle of each and roughly pulled them out from under the bed. They were screaming.

What Lyondell did to the two little girls before shooting them in the head was completely perverted and utterly senseless. Rodney watched the gross forays with morbid curiosity.

"They both'er in permanent lala land now," Lyondell said, and put his pistol back in his pocket. "Now less get us som'm ta eat."

After raiding the pantry where they found canned goods, dried beans, and a full unopened fifth of scotch, they also found, in the old man's bedroom, a semi-automatic .22 caliber rifle and a big box of long rifle, hollow-point, shells for it. "I'll take iss gun I God," Lyondell said, and put the shells in the pillow case with what they had taken from the pantry, and tucked the rifle under his arm. "Let's get some gone," he said.

They were only about a mile away from the house when Rodney suggested that they drink the liquor. "Let's drank at whiskey," he said.

"It ain't whiskey goddammit, it's scotch."

"Same thang."

"It ain'ta same thang shit fer brains. It's scotch, a big difference. And air probably ain't enough for boff'us ta get drunk on."

"It don't take much fer me. I get drunk quick," Rodney said.

"Not me. I could drank iss whole bottle an'n some."

"Really?"

"Yeah really."

"I like to fuck when I get drunk," Rodney said.

"You like ta fuck anyways dont'chee?"

"At's a fact. When we gonna drank it?"

"I'll say when goddammit. But not now. We gotta get far from at house. A's other folks lives air an'a coming back soon. A'll put somebody on us fer sure."

# CHAPTER NINE

## AVALON

In the early morning, just after daylight, Naomi bathed naked in the shallows of the creek while Nayhoom watched. "Cleopatra had nothing on you." he said.

"I hope not. She was kinda ugly."

"You mean she didn't look like that old actress?"

"Elizibeth Taylor?"

"I guess. A pretty woman."

"No, she was homely looking they say. But she had power."

"You have power."

"Are you flirting with me."

"You bet'cha. Is it working?"

"You bet'cha," she said. "Why don't you get in here with me?"

"Will do," he said, and took the loincloth off, and waded out into the water with her. He took the bar of soap from her hand and started soaping her back.

"That is the last of our soap. How will we wash when it is gone?" she said.

"I saw several yucca plants on that island over there. Indians made soap with it somehow. I'll look in the book and see if there is anything about it in there."

"This place is absolutely miraculous. So far everything we need has been right here. Does that seem strange to you?"

"Miraculous is a better word than strange. The map made a believer out of me. I don't want to fight with it."

"Neither do I. I love you Nayhoom."

"And I love you."

She was bathing as early as she was because it was cooler then than at any other time of the day, and still it was hot, and very humid. They would both rinse sweat off twice more before bedtime at dusk. They went to bed early, but not always straight to sleep. Lying on their pallet they often talked until much later, but almost always were awake and up drinking tea before first light.

They drank tea made beforehand by soaking roots, and/or dried plants, in a Tupperware container of water set out in the sun. A fire was rarely needed anymore, and if one was required it was made during the daytime, and made usually to cook beans in the pressure cooker. And a small cooking fire had to burn only a little more than an hour. But lately they had started soaking the beans in water and sprouting them in another, large, Tupperware container.

"Bean sprouts are better for us than cooked beans, don't you think?"

"Yes," Naomi said. "And we can learn to like them just as much."

The seeds they had planted along the creek had germinated and the bean and vegetable plants were thriving. They planted near the creek so they would not have far to carry water, and in the extremely hot weather the plants

255

required a lot of water. The composted fertilizer was working better than they thought it would, and the following year it should work even better because it would have had more time to compost.

The apple trees, all ten of them on the big island, were putting on small green apples abundantly. The muscadine vines were also growing fast and muscadines formed copiously along each one. They had already picked a few, and a few small, green apples, to add to the daily tea mix brewing in the sun, to give it a sour and yet somewhat sweet taste.

Naomi put her loin cloth back on. Her stomach protruded a little out over the top of it, and Nayhoom patted it. "We can't know if it is a girl or a boy until it is born in August or September."

"I have an old calendar I've been marking. It is not current, but that doesn't matter. When it is the exact time for being born, we will know," she said.

"I'm sure you will," he said.

"You will too because I'll tell you."

"I never get tired of reading the same things about child birth over and over."

"Neither do I," she said. "We'll be prepared."

\*\*\*

As darkness descended and they lay quietly in the wikiup, they heard again, far in the distance, the sounds of explosions and gunfire. "Will it ever end? I guess I know the answer but you can lie to me," she said.

"It will end alright. But everything else might end with it."

"That is not a lie. Why can't people just stop and look at the situation with honest eyes?"

"Honest eyes?"

"Do you know what I mean?"

"Yes. Society has a forward momentum unto itself and people in general believe there is nothing else but that forward march of society. Time and death and battling with nature are most important to the average person. The average person is the poster child responsible for perpetuating that social illusion. Dick follows Harry following Tom following Mary and Jane following Dick."

"Circles?"

"Sure. You have to be somewhat nonsocial to actually get somewhere, but the trip can be quite lonely, so few go. Many set out, but few continue. Hence there is social gridlock, a human log jam that stays stagnantly in place. But no one pays any attention to that. Ever forward and upward, more economic growth, more and more, bigger and better, more expensive, more carbon dumped into the atmosphere! The illusion continues. And then the end comes and everyone is amazed. People, in general, are like misbehaving children without parents. But try and tell the average person that. Of course expressing that is not a problem unless you intend to stand in the way of progress. You can be killed for less. Now there is just chaos, desperate people against people trying to maintain some semblance of the status quo, all amid the atmospheric catastrophe caused by belief in the presumption that getting ahead is equal to winning out over nature. And people like to speak sagely about Mother Nature, like they know something about a her, an earthly mother. That is all just more male propaganda believed and cherished I think."

"I'm glad we are here," she said.

"Me too."

\*\*\*

In the coming hot days of summer Naomi would become more aware of her pregnancy, and so would Nayhoom. And they had been increasingly concerned with what the purpose for their lives might be, now that it seemed that people everywhere were falling prey to one kind of anarchy or another. But of course they could not actually know what was taking place in other parts of the world, or other parts of their county even. But they could hear sporadic gunfire, especially at night, and occasionally they heard very loud explosions.

"Our purpose is now our child which is coming into this world very soon," Naomi said.

"That is the only good reason to hang tough," he said.

"I agree. We have to be strong for the baby, the new person to be."

"We are safe now, and there is no reason to assume that will ever change. But of course it might," he said. "All we can do is live life one moment at a time. That is our existence. When change occurs, it just does. Change is to be expected, at some point down the road. Hopefully change will be favorable."

"Do you ever pray?"

"I guess I do," he said, "but not specific prayers. I don't ask for anything. I don't pray expectant prayers, just prayers of acknowledgment."

"Acknowledgment?"

"I think of all things, anything, as being a part of God, and I do not think of God as being an entity unto a Godly self, in any sort of way, or being different from the lowest form of life. Nor do I think of God as a supreme being you can put an order in to and expect something in return. And actually I think of anything, even the non living things, rocks, clouds, rain, soil, wood, as being as much a part of God as a person, or animal or tree is. All is God, and God is all."

"I think that too."

"I know. And that you do has much to do with why I love you so much. I am selfish about loving you I know. But I have no choice. I love you greatly and it is done, a fact of my life. I think I might be totally lost without you. I never want to find out for sure."

"I love you that way to Nayhoom. We came together because we have always been doing that, coming together. Coming together is who we are. And I believe that we will be coming together eternally."

"So do I, and death is not any sort of measuring rod."

"So if I die giving birth to this child, you will go on?"

"Yes, especially if the child lives. But you are not

going to die giving birth."

"You know that?"

"It won't happen."

"I don't believe it will either. It is good to know that you don't believe it."

"I most certainly do not. Our lives are all that is."

"There can't be anything without you and me."

"And nothing is nothing, nonexistent. Only existence exists, which means only God exists."

"Beautiful," she said. "People depend so much on there being an afterlife, life is life, before birth and after death. This life we live is an afterlife. Birth may be an after death experience."

"Of course it could be. I have wondered about that. But I know answers about it are not to be had, only imagined. Why would an afterlife be so important if there is no before and after? And my imagination tells me that before and after applies only to people alive in the material world. Like time, it only exists for one who perceives time. There is no reason to think time is a cosmic constant or that the concepts of before and after are paramount realities, or that the laws of math exist without the perceptions of them. The concept of time occurs to people, people who are especially concerned with time. Before and after: one person's ceiling is another person's floor.

"Life can be lived to the fullest without knowing anything certain about an afterlife. It is the function of the imagination to provide adequate stimulus in the place of certainty. Religion tends to diminish that function of the imagination. That is a crippling truth about religion. If religion were more agnostically oriented, things in general might improve for humankind."

Naomi sat up straight on their bed. "That life and death are together life is never considered," she said. "Neither is the idea that eating animals is the same as eating yourself, or that the world is you and the responsibility of intelligence is yours, it is all you."

"I think that," he said.

"Is it just us that think that way? Could we be completely out of bounds?"

"How can we know?" he said."

"We can't. We can only imagine, or take man's word as truth. And man is currently suffering anarchy. How true has man's take on life been?"

# CHAPTER TEN

## LYONDELL AND

## RODNEY

Lyondell was tired from walking but he didn't want to admit it. "We probably ought'a rest. You probably bout had it aint'chee?

"Naw, I'm good for awhile," Rodney said.

"Well less stop fer awhile. I don't want'ye to go sissy on me."

"Shor, where ye wanna stop?"

"Under this tree comin' up'll be fine I think."

They had just crossed the bridge over The Little Tennessee River in Loudon. The town was deserted, a few lost looking and destitute type people lumbered along the empty streets. Lyondell and Rodney were sweaty and filthy, and their clothes were ragged, and they stank badly, so the few people they met while walking, men mostly, turned their noses away and tried to ignore them. Near the outer edge of the old business district they sat under a large tree with bare limbs hanging out over old highway eleven, and rested. Lyondell breathed heavily.

"We need some thangs," he said.

"I'd like a big long ceegar," Rodney said.

"You dumbass. We're about starved and you're thankin' bout smoking."

"I ain't had no smokes in two days. I need some."

"You need a total overhaul is what you need. I'm talkin' bout food goddammit."

"We'll have'ta steal it."

"I know we'll have'ta steal it goddammit. I'm thankin'. We need to hit another house, as soon as we see one that looks like there won't be no trouble. We bout got shot last night cos we got careless, you got careless. You talked to that goddamn dog and he got to barkin' when you left'im. Don't fuck with pets, OK?"

"OK. He just looked so sweet and lonely."

"You're just like some goddamn girl. We gotta thank about stayin' alive goddammit. Do you unnerstan at?"

"Yes."

"OK then, leave the fuckin' pets alone, OK?"

"OK. You want'chee dick sucked?"

"No I don't want my goddamn dick sucked. I want a goddamn bologny sammich, with lots a mayo squirtin' out all around. And some beans cooked with fat meat, an' a big ol', tall glass of cold sweet milk. Ah shit, I gotta quit thankin' bout food. They ain't none, an' they won't be none till we find some."

"You bout ready to go?"

"Hell no! I ain't bout ready to go! I'll tell'ye when I'm ready!"

"Ok."

Thirty minutes later Lyondell announced boisterously that he was ready to walk on. Rodney was laying in a grassy place close by sleeping.

"Hey you, homo erectus, you ret to go?"

He raised his head. "Sure Lyondell, I'm ready."

"Well lets get."

They trudged on down the highway until it started getting dark. Neither had eaten in over twenty four hours and Lyondell was feeling weak and faint. He had to stop again. He was ten years older than Rodney, but he still would rather maintain a false position of superior strength and endurance.

"You're lookin' a bit peeked Rodney. I say we stop fer a while more."

"I'm OK Lyondell. I can go fer awhile longer."

"I say we stop fer awhile. They ain't no damn hurry. We need to thank about findin' a place to stay the night anyway."

"OK. Them people's leavin' at house up yonder.

Reckon a's anything air fer us?" Rodney said.

Lyondell saw the two men walking down the sidewalk away from the house toward the highway. One carried a flashlight and the bright beam swayed in time with the man's walking. They turned and started walking south down the highway away from Lyondell and Rodney.

"We'll go see I God," Lyondell said.

Except for a light in the living room the house was dark. Lyondell peered in the window and saw a pretty woman sitting on a couch reading a magazine. "I'm gonna get me some'at damn pussy," he told Rodney quietly. "Less just knock on the damn door an' see if she answers."

"OK."

They knocked and the woman came straight to the door and opened it.

"Good evening mam, may we come in?" Lyondell said.

"No, of course not. Who are you and what do you want?"

Lyondell pointed the rifle at her, and the two men pushed their way into the house past her. Inside Lyondell shut the door and turned to her. "I want me som'at damn pussy I God. An' you gonna give it to me. Grab'er Rodney."

"Rodney grabbed her arms and held them tightly behind her back."

"Brang'er back in this bedroom," Lyondell said pointing with the rifle to an open doorway and a bed just beyond. Rodney shoved the woman toward it while still holding her arms behind her, and she screamed. Lyondell came back to them quickly and slapped her hard across her face.

"You yell again and I'm gonna choke the shit out'a'ya," he said. She struggled against Rodney's grasp, but she did not scream again, right then.

"Sit on the bed there with'er Rodney an' keep holdin'er."

Rodney did as he was told to do, grinning while he did it. He sat on the side of the bed with the woman in his lap, her dress hiked up high on her thighs, while Lyondell stood before them and unzipped his pants. "Come on out little python," he said, as he pulled his penis out into view. That is when the woman screamed again. She was thirty-five, and very pretty, and very frightened. Lyondell slapped her hard again. If you don't wanna die keep at dick sucker shut. I won't tell'ye again. Nex time I'm just gonna break yor goddamn neck. Ge'tem panties off'er Rodney, I'm gonna pour the root to'er.

A light flashed on the wall behind Lyondell and Rodney saw it. He let the woman go and jumped up from the bed and ran to a window opposite the one in which shone the light. "Them men are back Lyondell, we gotta get ou'tis winder," he said. Lyondell had not yet figured out what the problem was. And then he heard the men enter the house and speak to the hysterical woman who had run back into the living room.

"Less go now," Rodney said, and Lyondell hustled toward him and they got out just as one of the men entered the room. The man went to the open window, but Rodney and Lyondell had run into the shadows out of sight.

In his haste to screw the woman Lyondell, and also Rodney, had failed to notice a small staircase in the kitchen that lead to an attic room where a fourteen year old boy was staying. He heard his sister scream and using his cell phone he called his brother-in-law who was one of the men who had just left.

"Goddamn that was close," Lyondell said after they were far enough away and knew they hadn't been followed. "Goddamn I'z want'n'ta fuck at bitch."

"You was wadden ye?"

"Goddamn I'm hungry. We gotta find som'm quick 'fore I starve. I should'a shot the whole fuckin' bunch of'em. But you got me in a goddamn rush. I'll take at dick suckin' now."

# CHAPTER ELEVEN

## AVALON

They walked daily, together, over the islands until they knew almost every square inch of each. The walks were originally intended to be searches for food, but food was now not a problem to find. So often they strolled along the beaches and through the woods, just enjoying the serenity and peacefulness somewhere in the backwater mud flats of the Hiwassee River. They enjoyed a menagerie of birds and other small wildlife present on the islands, but larger animals, deer, coyotes, even dogs, were never seen, though they had seen a few deer tracks.

There were many trees that Nayhoom regularly climbed to look all around for possible signs of approaching intruders. He had not seen even a hint of that. But he often saw on the far horizons, many plumes of dark smoke rising into the sky, and he could hear gunfire and explosions. Signs of war and violence, he thought, anarchy. He considered his number one priority to be keeping Naomi and their unborn child safe.

At the first of her pregnancy Naomi was amazed at

being pregnant. She talked to Nayhoom about it being a mystery and about the wonder of it, as if something magical was taking place within her body. And she worried a little about the possibility of miscarriage. But now, far into her second trimester, she concentrated on being positive about her body and the future birth of the child. She was often very pensive, even withdrawn, thinking about the awesome things to come, birthing a baby and raising a child there in the wilds. And when the baby moved inside her Nayhoom always wanted to be there and put his hand on her distending stomach and feel it.

She was now less active and Nayhoom had to be more active, but he did not mind that. In fact he often insisted on doing the chores she was usually responsible for doing, and she would accuse him of babying her. But they did not argue about it, or about anything. She knew she was now more vulnerable, and fortunate that he was willing to be helpful beyond what was normal. In fact she felt more worried about him, and what he might be experiencing with her pregnancy, than she would otherwise be.

But he was doing well, and was busy almost all the time, gathering food, watering the bean plants and other vegetable plants, and making things for Naomi and the baby to come. He made a bassinet with cane and tie-wire, and made a crude rocking chair that was sturdy but unattractive compared to the ones they had seen. He had cut small but strong hickory limbs, and whittled the ends to fit holes he had bored in the frame work with his bow-drill, a damaged flint arrowhead for a bit. He had recently found the broken point along the creek bank. And then for extra strength he secured the joints of the rocking chair with tie wire and draped a blanket over it. "It works," Naomi said. "I'll rock the baby with it and that will be wonderful." He was satisfied and proud.

Naomi was having many strange dreams. They were often bizarre and frightening. She dreamed several times about the birth of the baby, and twice she dreamed that it was born dead. And she once dreamed that instead of a person, the baby born was a little puppy like the one she had when she was a child. She told Nayhoom that she was becoming afraid to go to sleep, afraid that she would have another frightening dream. He held her for awhile as she lay on their bed every night. He held her there each night until after a week she felt a bad dream was less likely to happen. But holding Naomi was no problem for him. He loved her and enjoyed the closeness.

They read "Your Baby Book" together, trying to determine what vitamins she needed, and that they could obtain from their garden vegetables and the wild plants they might find on the islands. It was obvious that some things she needed were unavailable, but her attitude was that their true needs, including those of the baby to come, would be provided somehow by the Great Spirit. "We were shown this place of refuge, we will be shown all else. I'm not worried about vitamins," she said.

"Then neither am I," he said.

"If I was seeing a doctor regularly he would try to make me eat meat and cheese, and drink milk, and take all manner of medicines. And I wouldn't and there would be conflict."

"Doctors are like everyone else, they are under the illusion that life is a struggle between man and nature," Nayhoom said.

"Yes they are. It may not be obvious to some, but to me it is obvious that how you obtain your food is also what you are eating when you eat. If you shoot a pig and eat it, you are also eating the act, the shooting. The shooting of the pig is also part of your diet. If you allow someone else to do the shooting for you, that is part. You are what you eat. Every life form is that. Something happened sometime early on in the evolution of humans, I think it may have been empathy, when some of the animals began to consider what others might be feeling and experiencing. They then quickly became human. But with time slowly, the empathy got sidetracked in favor of a more animalistic progress, up, up, and away! It has since been a manly progress, as early to late man considers himself to be cast in God's image."

"I understand that," Nayhoom said. "That is my

understanding of the journey of man as well. And it seems obvious that all people take the concept of time very seriously."

"Before people there was no concept of time," she said.

"That's right," he said. "And now the clock and the watch are like small idols. Time is of paramount concern, especially where one's life is concerned. Many people consider this their one life to be all there is so it must be lived to the fullest, whatever that means. It means get it now because the opportunity to get it will soon be over. Even though it can be argued convincingly that an absolute ending of one's life cannot be an absolute proven fact, other than the obvious physical death. The average person finds comfort imagining an afterlife of the self as existing in some far off place for dead souls. And that imagined place is always imagined to be a marvelous place. With the Christian religion it is heaven and has streets of gold. Man's idea of a final resting place. What does anyone really know about final?

"Forever is movable, it moves. If there is no actual past, except in memory, and no future, except an imagined one, that leaves now as being the only time that really ever is, or was, which means to me that now is forever at any moment, past, present or future. It moves like a living being, so forever lives. It is the Great Self!"

"And so you think time and the Great Spirit are one?"

"I think now and the Great Spirit are one."

"Now, yes," she said. "To see God all one must do is see now. And that seeing can always be improved. And The Great Spirit wishes to be acknowledged, or acknowledge itself, with more and more clarity. But there is so much strife and confusion. People are locked into their habits, their notions, it appears."

"Their imaginations are locked, and society is responsible for that," he said. "Society rules the day, and the person, and that is a shame. Each individual has within their means the ability to be beyond the clutches of society. If you have imagination you are free to use it, use it in thinking about life, about God, about a continuation of self. It is the influences of society that tells a person they must think of God the way they are suppose to, the way they were told to think about God. But living in this material world cannot be about knowing explicitly what you are supposed to do. However, a free imagination will lead a person in a direction that is specific and meaningful for them, but few use their imaginations for that. The cowboy way, or the equivalent, rules, all over the world, and most people follow."

"You talk about a universe per person, an eternity of universes. What do you mean by that?" she asked.

273

"An eternity of universal concepts, one per person, a cosmic shuffling of identities among life forms, from experiencing one individual's universal concept to another's, add infinitum, residing for a time in one, and then in another until cosmic intention is appeased."

"Do you mean an actual, physical, universe?"

"Of course," he said. "Physicality is just energy formed solidly. The cosmos is eternal, which means to me there is room for every person's actual universe that is now, or ever was, or will ever be. Knowing where exactly each is at any moment is not the point, and not something that one mere life form can know specifics about anyway."

"What would you say to the people of the world if you could be heard?"

"Why, with the concepts of eternity and an endless cosmos so magnanimously in your face would a person, or a people, put all their faith, their belief, in the concepts and hypotheses of a humanly conceived science. Is it just because they can't imagine beyond those concepts? That might be the answer to the question: they can't, or won't imagine beyond. Man must feel in control. That is the cowboy way. To imagine is not control. When you round up the doggies and put'em in the corral, that is control. Imagining is for sissies. Men do not imagine. Man is a doer, man acts, whatever that means. Well, to me it is now obvious what it means. Well what the hell are you saying, someone might ask. I'll try to be there when the lights of life throughout the world go out entirely. It will be easier to answer that question of yours then. But you could answer it for yourself right now.

"I imagine that all current life forms, after dying, spill back over to an ethereal existence, and from there is born back into a material existence. Whether that is an instantaneous thing or a much longer process, on this earth or another, I will not venture a guess. Time or place is not important. But each or any identity might interchange, or exchange, with another, who could know? How an identity changes at death cannot be known to one living in the material world. Where were you before you were born? Where and when other than The Great Here and Now?

"But life to my imagination is an oscillating process of life to death, to life, from the material to the ethereal and back again, on and on. The oscillating from living to dying constitutes the life processes of the Great Self. Death seems presently meaningful and dire to a single living being, but not to life itself, the Great Self. The death of an individual is only a small, even infinitesimal, but integral part of life's processes, the living processes of the Great Self."

"How do you know this?" she asked.

"I don't. I imagine it. What can ever be known to be absolute fact?"

"I understand what you say, and lean decidedly in

those directions also. I believe we have finally come to share the same universe, two people among the multitudes. But are we the only ones who do?"

"We can't know the answer to that question," he said. "How can that be known? And what does it matter?

"Respect of a new paradigm reality is the only hope for the ultimate survival of people. And that is not indicative of just this one life. Life is continuous. Death is merely change, a change which may alter the main trajectory through the transitions of living, which includes death. People in general think of life as something that is happening to them. As I see it people are happening to life. Living in the material world charges each individual with responsibility. They are ultimately responsible for how they perceive life, and for continuing or discontinuing paradigm opinions. Without action taken to change the current paradigm assumptions, total extinction of humankind from this earth may be in the near offing. The action required is that people, a person, change their paradigm philosophy of existence, the general assumption that humankind is, in a divine way, special. For Christians an individual can either establish themselves for heaven or for hell, and are originally created by a God in His image. People the world over, in general, believe that people are divinely special when, as per the new paradigm reality needed, they are but one aspect of the natural, physical

276

world, no more essential that a dodo bird."

# CHAPTER TWELVE

## LYONDELL AND

## RODNEY

"Your eyes look like two blubbers in a piss pot," Lyondell told Rodney when Rodney awoke that morning after their night of drinking half a gallon of expensive rum. Lyondell drank most of it, which was after Rodney had passed out.

"My head is so fucked up," he said.

"Yeah, well that ain't the rum I god. That is just you," Lyondell said.

"Did you fuck me in the ass last night."

"Is a anybody else around?"

"I thought so. I remember at."

"Well glory be, and I declare! You don't say? Ain't at som'm?"

"My head hurts."

"Cut the mother fucker off. At'll stop it."

"Who'd suck at dick'en?"

"Oh I'd find another dick sucker. The world's full

of dick suckers."

Rodney looked defeated. "Is they anything ta'eat in'air?"

"They might be. Why don't you go look. An' brang me som'm."

"What?"

"I don't know goddammit. Som'm good. See if a's any cake?"

"Cake?"

"No Goddammit I said a rake. Yes goddammit cake. I could use some."

"I could use it to stuff in that shit mouth a'yorn," Rodney muttered as he was walking toward the kitchen.

"What, what was that?"

"I'z talkin to myself," Rodney said.

"By got you better not'a been talkin' ta'me, goddammit," he said. Rodney shrugged and went on.

They had broken into an upper middle class house belonging to a man named Ralph Spencer and his wife Len. They were away in another state. Lyondell figured the house had not been lived in for awhile. The furniture had all been covered with sheets. The refrigerator was basically empty, and very little food was in the pantry. But there were canned foods, and he and Rodney had wasted no time opening cans and eating the contents with spoons. And then they found the rum.

They could have bathed while they were there, but neither one did. They were used to their filthy smells and like bad little boys they both hated to take baths.

For no other reason than wanting to, Lyondell built a fire on the kitchen floor just as they were leaving. A hundred yards from the house they looked back, and watched the flames burst through the kitchen window. And then the whole house went up in flames. Lyondell laughed, and then Rodney laughed.

It was near dark and they were just beyond the town called Sweetwater. The interstate highway had been blocked for over two months with wrecked cars that had not been hauled away. There was little traffic on the interstate anyway, and what traffic passing through slowed at the wreckage and crossed the medium to the opposite lane until the hazardous wreckage was behind. Lyondell and Rodney avoided the interstate and walked mostly along the highway, old highway eleven.

A short distance further south down the highway a man called to them from a barn near it. "Yo, you'ns got time to help a feller out?" he called out.

"Reckon he's got'ny thang we want?" Lyondell said.

"E might," Rodney replied.

They went up to where the man was, to see what he wanted and to see if he had something they wanted. He was younger than he had sounded and Lyondell immediately became defensive. "We ain't got much time. What is it?" he said.

The man suspiciously eyed the .22 caliber rifle that Lyondell carried. "My old cow is giving birth in there, but she can't get the calf out. I'm pretty sure the cafe's dead, hit ain't movin' a'tall. But it is just stuck half in and half out. I'z want'n y'all to help me pull it on out. Will yuns?"

Rodney was ready to help, but Lyondell stopped him from saying he would. "What's in it fer us?" Lyondell said.

"I got a twenty dollar bill you'ns can have," the man said desperately."

"Well why didn't ye say so," Lyondell said. "Less pull'er out."

When the dead calf was laying on the manure and mud packed floor of the barn stall the man pulled his wallet out and took from it a twenty dollar bill and gave it to Lyondell who gawked in the dim light at the man's billfold and the other denominations he could barely see in it.

"If we hadn't come along that cow might'a died too," he said.

"I expect that's right," the man said.

"So it ought'a be worth more'n twenty dollars to'ya."

"What?" the man said, putting his wallet back in his

back pocket. "I ain't made'a money."

"Less take another look ah'tat wallet an' see."

The man backed away and Lyondell raised the barrel of the rifle to be pointing at his face. "Get it back out goddammit."

A voice was heard near the barn entrance. Someone was coming into the barn. "Dad, you in here," the voice said.

When Lyondell looked out the stall door toward the sound of the voice, the man bolted out behind him and into another stall. "He's got a rifle Jimmy, get out," he said.

Lyondell and Rodney ran out that end of the barn. Just then a shot rang out and a bullet passed very close to Lyondell's head. He ran as fast as he could, back toward the highway, with Rodney passing him.

They ran down the highway in the near dark until Lyondell thought he could run no more. When they stopped running and were resting, another shot rang out and Rodney took a bullet in his left upper arm, which had stopped the bullet from entering his chest. They ran off the highway into a field and continued trotting across it. Rodney was holding his arm and cursing, and slowing down, while Lyondell, breathing heavily and running awkwardly, drew further and further away from him.

Two more shots were heard and the bullets whizzed over their heads. The moon had come up in the east and was shedding light on them as they hurried across the very large pasture. "We gotta get to them trees," Rodney called out to Lyondell running several hundred feet in front of him. But Lyondell didn't stop running until he was safely among them. From there he watched Rodney come staggering up beside him.

"We made it I god," Lyondell said breathlessly.

"You did, but I got shot."

"It's just a flesh wound."

"Yeah, my flesh."

"Well don't be belly achin' about it. Hit'll be alright."

Other shots were fired at them and the bullets passed through the branches above their heads. "We gotta get again," Lyondell said, and took out running through the woods away from the approaching pursuers. Rodney followed.

They were essentially running blind through the small forest and had no idea where they were going. They ran until Rodney was only barely trotting while holding his arm, and he was now ahead of Lyondell who was blowing hard and trying to keep up. When they had to stop they listened for sounds of the ones chasing them, but heard nothing coming through the woods.

"I gotta rest," Lyondell said. "If I don't I'm gonna die. I don't hear nothin', do you?"

"I hear my heart beat'n's all. But we oughta walk on anyways."

"I can't, not for a minute anyways."

They rested for two minutes and Rodney said he had to get help or he was going to bleed to death. "I'm goin' on, I got to," he said.

Lyondell still couldn't talk loud so he just kept his disagreeable words to himself and followed Rodney at a somewhat fast walk. The woods were dark and they had to be careful about running into trees, which both did several times. Soon they came to an open field and crossed a barbed wire fence into pasture. A dim light shown several hundred yards away and Rodney headed toward it. Lyondell followed, breathing hard and wheezing every step of the way to the house from which shone the light from one of its windows.

"A's somebody in'air. I seen'em," Lyondell said when they got there. "Hit's an old woman, I see'er."

The seventy-five year old woman was by herself. She lived alone in the house her deceased husband had built for her thirty years before.

You make noise here outside the winder an' I'll go around to yon winder and break it. When she comes to see what's what, you break iss'n an'n one of us can get in," Lyondell said.

"Don't you hurt'er," Rodney said. "I need'er ta help

me. She looks like my ma goddammit."

"I won't. She can help us both."

Lyondell broke the window and the woman grabbed a shotgun and went toward it. And then Rodney broke the one he was looking in and the woman turned toward him and aimed the shot gun."

"Drop that gun old woman or I'll shoot'ya," Lyondell said from the window behind her, his rifle trained on her back."

She aimed the shotgun at him. "You do and I'll scatter you out inta the yard."

"Ma!" Rodney called from his window. She turned and looked at him. "I ain't yor maw shitass. I'll shoot you too."

"I been hurt an' I need yer help's all we want. Let us come in. I'm bout to bleed to death. Lyondell there won't hurt'ya."

She looked at Rodney. The light in the room cast enough light on him and his arm that she could see the blood. She turned toward Lyondell. He pulled his rifle back through the window and gave her an exaggerated look of innocence. She looked again at Rodney, at his face, and saw that he was indeed in pain. She leaned the shotgun against a kitchen counter.

"Y'all come in'a front door. Yuns gonna have ta fix eez winders."

They entered her house. Rodney was feeling faint. She pulled his shirt sleeve up and looked at the wound. "Who shot you?" she said.

"I don't know who it was," Rodney replied.

"What the hell was y'all'a doin'?" she asked.

"We weren't doin' nothin'," Lyondell said. "That bullet just came out of nowheres, a stray."

"You're lyin' dickhead. Yaws doin' som'm you ought'n have an' somebody shot'im. I know shit when I see it."

Rodney's legs buckled and he grabbed her arm to keep from falling. She held him up. "I'll have to dig at bullet out. Can you take it?"

"I got no choice," Rodney said feebly.

There was a knock at her door. "Yuns get in the bedroom there. I'll see who it is," she said. They went into the bedroom and closed the door and she went to the front door. Lyondell put his ear to the closed door and listened. He held his rifle ready.

She opened the door and there stood the farmer's son and a friend of his. "Hiddy miss Decker. You had any trouble round here?"

"What kine'a trouble?"

"We're lookin' fer two men at tried to cheat my Dad. They ran iss way."

"I ain't seen shit... Is that it?"

"I reckon," the boy said, and back down the two steps. "We might check on'ye later."

"Suit yerself," she said, and closed the door."

When Lyondell and Rodney came back into the kitchen, the old woman named Annette, spoke to them. "It was that Ralphs boy at shot'ye wasn't it. At's a .22 wound an' he totes a .22.

"We never tried cheat'n nobody. They got the wrong idea," Lyondell said.

"When I want yer opinion dickhead I'll ask ye fer it," she said. Take a seat air, what's ye name?"

"Rodney."

"Rodney, I gotta find my tweezers, ah'nin I be rat back."

"OK."

When she started probing in the wound Rodney passed out.

"You killed'im," Lyondell said.

"I never killed'im. He ain't dead. Go sit in the livin' room yonder till we're done."

"You hurt'im an' I'll hurt you old woman."

Annette put her tweezers down and stepped up close to Lyondell. "You might be one of the stupidest dickheads I ever seen. You harm one hair on my head an'em Ralphs'll tell my son bout'yins an' he'll hunt ye down an cut yer fuckin' heads off with that church key he wears fer'is neckless. He's Dead Head Fred Decker. I'm guessin' you've heard of'im. My son ain't no queer like you'ns. I know he's a queer," she said pointing at Rodney. An' you are just plain stupit, an'a queer too I betchee. Now go sit sommers else, out of my face."

Lyondell had heard of Dead Head Fred. He was one of the men responsible for kicking them out of The Bull Ross Number Fifteen hooligan camp. Dead head Fred was know by that name because he had all the old Grateful Dead albums and played the CDs over and over again. He was also known for removing his enemy's heads with a bottle/can opener he wore around his neck on a string. He was big, and hairy, and mean. Lyondell did not want him as an enemy.

With Rodney out cold and Lyondell sitting quietly in the living room, Annette was able to finally dig the small piece of lead from Rodney's bicep. When Rodney regained consciousness she made him drink from the jar of straight moonshine she had washed the wound with, until he again passed out on the couch in the living room, this time it would be until morning. Lyondell saw and smelled the liquor and ask her if he could have some.

"Hell no you fuckin' moron. I hated givin' him some, but he had to have it. You sleep on the floor there, an' tomorrow you're gonna fix my winders."

"The glass is broke," he said.

"I got winder glass in my shed. You wake me up tonight an' I'll shoot'ya. You gah'tat?"

"I got it."

\*\*\*

Annette was awake and up at four thirty. Both Lyondell and Rodney snored loudly while she made coffee and fried side meat. She scrambled eggs she had taken from her hens nest, and then woke them up. "Yuns eat, an'en fix my winders an'en get the hell on away from here. Coffee's made and breakfast is cooked. Get's'yin's asses up."

Rodney whined and tried to gain her sympathy that morning at the breakfast table. But Annette was not falling for it. "I probably shouldn't even have helped yuns. Your messed up arm is just tough shit. This ain't no hospital an' I ain't no damn doctor. Yuns fix my winders an'en I want yuns gone."

"What if I get sick?" Rodney said.

"I've done all I'm gonna do. After yuns eat and fix my winders I never wanna see yuns again. Is at clear?"

They both nodded and finished their breakfast. She brought the window glass in, and an old rusty can of window putty that her husband had bought three years before he died, three years back. The lid on the can was rusted, so when Lyondell finally got it off he discovered that the putty was drier than it should be, but still usable. He was hoping to find it had dried completely.

He tacked in the glass, and then chewing the skin on the inside of his mouth, Lyondell labored with a rusty putty knife, applying the old putty that was not very pliable. It was ten AM when he finally finished.

"That is the shittiest putty job I ever seen. But at least I got winders again. Now yun's get on away from here," she said, shooing them out of her house. "You'll be lucky I don't send Fred after yuns. Don't look back goddammit." Annette slammed the backdoor and they walked out of her yard and into the woods.

Rodney complained for awhile about his arm, but she had done a good job cleaning the wound with moonshine and binding it with pieces of clean, white, sheet cloth. And she had even given him a small bottle of moonshine to put on it later, warning him to not let "dickhead" steal it and drink it.

## CHAPTER THIRTEEN

## AVALON

"I dreamed that the time was long, long, ago and we were Indians, primitives, way before Tennessee was a state. Our people lived on these islands, and we were married. We were Yuchi, children of the sun." She was telling him this for a third time.

"Yes," he said. "And you died from typhoid fever. And I died first from a gunshot wound to my head."

"What are dreams?"

"Unsolvable mysteries. You may imagine what they might be and hit the nail right on the head, but I think that in this material world you can never know for sure. I say dream away and don't worry about them. Dreams are great."

She was well into her third trimester, and was as she said: "As big as a bear." Nayhoom told her again and again that she was beautiful, and he meant it. The total affair of pregnancy was beautiful to him. Beauty was all he could see. But she was very uncomfortable most of the time so he had to acknowledge that and be agreeable. He pampered her, bathed her, petted her, and repeated over and over again that she and the baby were going to be just fine.

They talked often about the name their child should have, and had settled on Nadine, if it was a girl, and Nathanael if a boy. It was no secret that she wanted it to be a girl, and Nayhoom wanted a boy. But both he and she were resigned to accept whichever it might be. "A person," Nayhoom said, "a person."

They were reading "Your Baby Book" more often now and reading it together. They shared a certain amount of confidence, but both knew the delivery might be extremely difficult to deal with. But negative thoughts about it were most often replaced with positive ones. "We are doing everything as well as we can. And that is all anyone ever does," Nayhoom said. "You and the baby will be just fine. I know it!"

The apples on the ten trees were getting larger and it would not be long before they would start turning red. Muscadines were heavy on all the vines they found and would soon be ripe enough to eat. Almost all the blackberries, dew berries, wild strawberries, and elderberries they had found were now gone, they having picked and eaten them. Many of the vegetable plants they had planted were still growing and producing: bell peppers, tomatoes, okra, broccoli, squash, cantaloupe, all their beans, including green beans, and onions. Nayhoom had tried to dry many vegetables, but the atmosphere was too humid for the drying to last very long. Mold grew on the sliced and dried vegetables after about ten days. But the soy and mung beans were drying out very well, they thought. And they hoped the apples and muscadines would dry in the trees and on the vines like the fall and winter before. It was uncanny, he thought, that they had, especially under such humid conditions, but he could only hope they would continue to do it.

Two weeks before she would deliver, Nayhoom had a dream like the one she had told him about. They were Yuchi Indians and lived on the islands they were now on, though many other members of their group lived around them. Naomi was sick with typhoid and he was with other Yuchi men guarding the village constructed behind a tall, log pole, palisade fence surrounding the island. He stood watch with his comrades in a log pole tower near the fence. They had been attacked twice by marauding Cherokees and their cohorts, white men from parts unknown.

He hadn't heard the shot firing the bullet that struck him in the head, but he could hear the three guns his people owned, firing loudly nearby. And then he was above the commotion, floating alone over their village. And then, suddenly, Naomi was there beside him and they went higher and higher until they could hear the gunfire no more, and then they went south together, high in the dark

night, in search of peace and serenity.
    He told her about the dream and she cried.

# CHAPTER FOURTEEN

## LYONDELL AND RODNEY

"Lou'azzy, you ain't got no clothes on. You get yo'self back in iss house an outta at tatah patch. Don't you know em'tatahs got eyes. An take iss dishrag an wipe yo'nose. If a's anything I despise it's nas'ness."

Rodney didn't completely understand what Lyondell was saying. It was supposed to be some sort of joke, but Rodney got caught up in the contorted way Lyondell looked when he told it. "I don't get it," he said.

"You wouldn't dumbass. It's a goddamn nigger joke. Shit!"

"Niggers are evil."

"Who ask ya?" Lyondell said. "Gim'me another slice at dog. Dog ain't sa'bad. Steak would be better, but kay sa'rah, sa'rah."

"Huh?"

"Fuck you Rodney. Gim'me some'at meat goddammit."

They thought they might starve until Lyondell shot a hound dog trotting through the woods. They skinned and gutted it and rammed a hickory pole up its rear end and placed it on rocks to hover over a fire and cook. Rodney was chosen to keep it turning while Lyondell slept.

"I ain't never eat no dog before."

"No shit," Lyondell said. "I figured you was raised on dog."

"Hamburgers mostly. Ma never cooked much. That ol' women we met looked a lot like my Ma."

"I should'a just put'er in permanent la'la land. There ain't no way Dead Head Fred could ever find us. If she was dead she couldn't tell nobody shit I god."

"I'm glad you never did though."

"You would be."

"She saved my life."

"Yor breakin' my fuckin' heart."

They slept away from the fire pit that night. The air was hot and humid and the hot coals made them sweat more. When morning came they found that some animal, or animals, had dragged the last of the cooked dog away. There was nothing to eat, so they trudged on through the forest until they came to a creek running south.

"I bet'chee at creek'll take us to the river. Hit can't be too far," Lyondell said.

"If you say so," Rodney said.

"I say so goddammit. Yon way," Lyondell said, pointing south down the creek.

It was hard for them to travel along the creek. Weeds and briars grew thickly beside it in places, and in other places the ground was muddy and wet. But it was true that the creek would eventually take them to the Hiwassee River, Lyondell had been correct about this. And following the creek kept them away from more populated areas where many hooligan types might give them a kind of grief they did not want.

"We get to Chatnoogy an' I got lots'a friens air," Rodney said.

"Dick suckers I expect. Right?"

"You'd like at wouldn't ya."

"We gotta get som'm ta eat. Do you hear music?"

"Yeah," Rodney said. "A's somebody up ahead."

As soundlessly as they could go that morning through the dry leaves and weeds along the creek, they crept closer to the music they heard. When it became evident the source of the music was only a few hundred feet further, they got down and crawled on the ground. And then they saw a trickle of smoke from a small campfire. It rose, curling into the branches of trees along the creek. They heard men talking and Lyondell pulled the safety back on his rifle.

One of the three men, three Black men, heard a crunch in the leaves to his left and looked directly at Lyondell, who knew he had been seen, so he rose with the gun pointing at two of the men sitting on the ground. The third was out of sight in the woods pissing. Neither Lyondell or Rodney saw the third man.

"Howdy," Lyondell said, and Rodney rose up beside him.

One man nodded. His name was Walter Wheeler. He was forty-five years old. His two companions were Jerome Ballinger, thirty-four, and Jerrod Lackey, age twenty-seven. It was Jerome who was a hundred feet away hiding now behind a tree and watching. The three men had been neighbors and were run out of the small town they lived in because they were Black. Many Black people had lately been killed just for being Black people. The three men had lost their wives and children to Hooligans, and were running now, trying to stay alive.

"We heard yer music and came to see what," Lyondell said, still pointing the rifle at them. Rodney looked terrified.

"Yun's got a radio, er som'm?" Lyondell asked.

Jerrod Lackey turned his small, battery powered recorder off. Neither of the two men spoke.

"Yun's got'ny thang'ta eat?" Lyondell asked.

"We ain't got nothin'," Walter said, and looked over at Jerrod who shook his head. "We just out her lookin' fer som'm ourselves. What's y'all doin?"

"We're lookin' fer som'm too. Any pussy about?"

Jerrod smiled. "We ain't got zilch, includin' pussy," he said.

"Well what's yuns been eaten?"

"Nuts mostly," Jerrod said.

"Ye hear at Rodney. They like nuts like you do. Rodney here's a nut man, well a nut boy. I ain't rat sure how manly e'is. Yun's got som'm more ta eat don't'chee?"

"Like he said," Walter said, "we ain't got zilch."

"Well then what good are'ye to me?" Lyondell said, and started pulling the trigger on the semi automatic .22 rifle, firing off several shots. Walter and Jerrod slumped over dead where they sat on the ground. Lyondell went to Walter to see what he might have in his pockets and Jerome came running out of the woods straight at him. Lyondell, having found two cigarette lighters in Walter's shirt pocket, heard Jerome running but did not see him coming from behind.

When Jerome, with his walking stick raised high in the air to strike Lyondell in the head, was only a few feet from him, Rodney jumped to his feet and ran at Jerome, his machete held high with his good right hand, and with the first slicing swing hit the stick. The second one cut across Jerome's face. He fell holding his face and Rodney wacked him several times in the neck and head. And then when he knew Jerome was done for, he continued whacking at his head, ten or more times. When he stopped he was out of breath, and Jerome was most definitely dead. Lyondell just looked bewilderedly at Rodney.

"Dammmm, you went ber'zerk didn't'ya."

"Niggers are evil," Rodney said.

\*\*\*

The batteries on the small recorder lasted only another hour, and then the recorder wouldn't work anymore. Rodney threw it down. "I never liked that music anyways," he said.

"Nigger music," Lyondell said.

Later in the day Lyondell shot a squirrel. Rodney skinned it and roasted it over a fire, and Lyondell ate most of it claiming that he owned the gun and was the chief provider of food, so he needed the food before Rodney did. Rodney took the lesser parts and did not complain. And then Lyondell shot another squirrel and Rodney cleaned and cooked it also. "I get most'a this'n," he said.

"You do? You suck my dick if I let you have most of it?"

"Shor," he said. "How far's the river?"

"Fifteen'er twenty mile I guess."

"We need a boat."

"Well steal one on the river sommers," Lyondell said.

"I like you altitude," Rodney said grinning.

Lyondell knew Rodney had made a kind of joke, but he wouldn't acknowledge it. "When I get rich I'm gonna have me a bar. Yes sir, it'll be licker up front and poker in the rear," he said.

Lyondell's attempt to be funny passed over Rodney's head without making the slightest impression. "Get drunk, an'nen go back an' lose yer money, right Lyondell?"

"Well fuck ol' fuzzy! You never even caught that a'tall, did'ya?"

"What?"

"You gonna eat'ny'at squirrel?"

With their hunger somewhat appeased, Lyondell sat on the ground and leaned back against a tree while Rodney serviced him sexually. And then they waded on through the mud, weeds and briers along the creek toward the Hiwassee River.

# CHAPTER FIFTEEN

## AVALON

Hard rain had poured down, and it would continue raining for several days. The standing water around the islands was two feet deep. It looked like a gigantic lake all around. And it was a time in which Nayhoom worried about people in boats coming to the island for whatever reason. What the reasons might be, he could only imagine. But he climbed his trees often, even in the pouring rain, to look in all directions for possible visitors. There were never any.

Naomi was very uncomfortable. Her stomach was distended almost grotesquely, and she had trouble even walking. She was constantly tired and haunted with mental visions of a disastrous delivery. She sat a lot in the rocking chair Nayhoom had made for her. He waited on her patiently, and listened to her complaints about discomfort. He was worried about her and fought back a constant urge to feel panic when he thought about the delivery to come. He was caring and thoughtful, and she realized this, and it gave her confidence. She was confident that he was capable of handling the magnificent event to come, and she now wanted it to come quickly and be over.

Contractions began early in the morning before daylight. He was not sleeping and neither had she been, and they could only hope the baby would wait until it would be light enough so they could see. A fire for light would not be bright enough and a fire would make it too hot in the wikiup if they built one in the never used, center fire pit. But they knew that it might be necessary in order to see.

But the baby did wait. After the sun had risen they went outside to a pallet he had laid out for her, a pallet of two blankets on a thick layer of pine needles. She sat naked on it and lay back, and then he put a folded blanket under her hips. The contractions were coming quickly now and they knew birth could happen any minute. He had warm water, nylon cord, and several clean rags ready.

With the sun rising barely over the top of the hill to the east, her baby's head emerged through her vagina from the birth canal. Nayhoom found its shoulder and help it through, and then quickly it squirted out, slipper and wet.

He tied the umbilical cord with the nylon cord, and then cut it. After wiping the baby girl with clean rags he laid her on Naomi's chest to hold. He looked for the afterbirth but instead of finding that he found a foot, and then another foot. She was delivering twins. He almost panicked, but now was not a time to do that, so he stayed with the emerging, second baby, a boy, until his head was free and he was fully born. All was well. Both babies cried the way they were supposed to. He had tied the umbilical cords successfully, caught the shared afterbirth, and helped to kept Naomi calm through it all. She lay on the pallet with both babies cradled in her arms and watched their sucking motions.

"They need to eat and I have no Milk."

"The book says you will make milk quickly now that they are born. They will be OK. Don't worry. They aren't the first babies to be born."

"But they are our first," she said.

"Well, that we know of, right?"

"Right."

***

For several days Nayhoom was very busy taking care of all the normal chores by himself. Naomi was busy with the two babies they named Nadine, born first, and Nathanael, born five minutes later. They both weighed exactly six pounds each. He had made a crude weighing device just for weighing the baby, now two babies. It was a simple balancing apparatus much like scales. He had the baby book that he knew weighed exactly one pound, and ten rocks that one at a time balanced with it to weigh one pound each. The babies each balanced the crude scales at six pounds.

She made milk quickly after their births, just as they had read. Her breast became large and very hard. The twins suckled veraciously. He spent as much time as possible just watching them suck. "Accept for their births, that is the most amazing thing I think I have ever seen," he said. "It is spellbinding."

Nayhoom and Naomi were proud, happy and enthusiastic about the future life of their children, including their own future lives, living primitively on an island, three islands actually, in the backwater mud flats of the Hiwassee River

# CHAPTER SIXTEEN
## LYONDELL AND RODNEY

The high water had receded. Lyondell and Rodney came through the woods beside the creek and stopped when they saw the great expanse of mud stretched out before them.

"Where the hell is this?" Rodney said.

"The river is just beyond that mu'dair. I used to play around here when I was a little kid. We might find us a boat somers along the river thar. You ain't scared of a little mud are'ye?

"Lead on Daniel Boone," Rodney said.

It was more than a little mud. There were times when they both got stuck up to their knees, and as it turned out it was easier walking in the creek than across the mud plane. The creek was not very deep and the bottom was stable. They discovered this when they stood in it to wash away their muddy feet and legs.

"Hell, let's just walk in the creek I god," Lyondell said. "Fuck a bunch'a mud!"

"I'll fuck some," Rodney said.

"You probably would."

It took about an hour for them to come close to the islands. The creek was still shallow where they were. They were a hundred yards from the main island when Rodney pointed to the southern sky. "Looky yonder ah'tat big ol' cloud yonder. At's a rain cloud."

"Well, shit fer brains, you figgered at out all by yor self. Goddammit now go on."

"Hit's'a coming iss way fast too."

"A little rain won't hurt us, do us good."

All the sky was blue, except for the fast approaching dark cloud. Dark gray folds of clouds rolled over one another other like lava flowing from a volcano. "That looks bad to me," Rodney said.

"I don't hear no thunder. We'll be fine. Move on."

But Rodney didn't move on, and Lyondell didn't try and force him to because he too became transfixed watching the approaching, dark clouds. They were coming exceptionally fast, unnaturally fast, and he and Rodney were becoming a little frightened. There were no loud booms of thunder, no strikes of lightning, just the oncoming, churning, mass of dark clouds very high up in the sky.

"That don't even look like rain clouds," Lyondell said.

They stood still in the creek as the cloud mass came nearer until it was directly over the big island, though very high in the sky. It blocked out the noonday sun. And then it stopped moving and remained, roiling and churning over the island. Rodney and Lyondell looked at one another in amazement.

Nayhoom was sitting in the wikiup on the floor mat they had made together with kudzu vines, watching Naomi and their babies in the rocking chair he had made for her. She was breastfeeding Nadine and Nathaniel. It had suddenly become much darker outside and darker in the wikiup. Nayhoom was watching intently. The matching sucking sounds were quite loud. "That is how, in one way or another, it has been for all life," he said. She smiled at Nayhoom and he smiled back with great pride.

A long, dark, violently twisting cord of wind came down out of the cloud like a thick length of hemp rope, lower and lower, directly over the pine thicket.

"That looks like a damned water spout," Lyondell said.

"What's a water spout?"

"A tarnada over water."

It was long, coming from very high up in the viciously agitated mass of clouds above the island. It came down with a kind of corkscrew motion, spinning incredibly fast, and bore directly into the pine thicket. An extremely loud noise erupted when the twisting wind encountered the trees. Pine needles, debris and other things rose violently up into the vortex, creating a very ominous sound. Rodney put his hand on Lyondell's shoulder, and Lyondell did not move.

The twister was there only ten seconds, viciously twisting, and churning, and sucking. And then it receded slowly, back up into the dark mass of clouds above. Pine needles and river cane leaves rained back down all around for several minutes while Lyondell and Rodney watched. And then the dark mass of roiling clouds began moving again on to the north, and soon out of view beyond distant trees. The sun again shone brightly.

Lyondell shook Rodney's hand from his shoulder. "You wadden scared was'ye?" he said.

"That was awesome. I ain't never seen nothin' like at a'fore."

"You ain't, well where you been? A fluke'a'nature's all at was."

"A what?"

"A fluke goddammit. Yor useless as tits on a bore hog. Don't you know nothin'? Ess go ov'air and get outta'iss goddamn creek ."

Where the deep pool began they had to get out of the creek and onto the bank of the island to the east, and walk along that shoreline. They came to a place across from the pine thicket where it appeared obvious the creek was shallow enough they could cross over.

"I see a canoe ov'ar," Lyondell said. He hefted the rifle down from his shoulder and readied it for any trouble they might incur. "You go'head," he said. "I'll stay here where I can watch with iss rifle."

"Ain'choo goin over too?"

"I'm goin, but there might be somebody there an I can see'em better right here. Go'head, I'll be right behind ye."

Rodney knew Lyondell was scared, but he went anyway. "A ain't nobody ov'ar. A'd'a showed a'selves by now," he said as he crossed the shallow creek.

"This is a damn good canoe," he yelled back at Lyondell. He went up into the thicket and found only a bare spot on the ground where the wikiup had been. And then he followed a path away from it until he came to the outhouse. "They's a shithouse over here," he yelled back at Lyondell. "Come on over. I'm gonna take a shit."

He did, and when he was finished he stepped out and saw Lyondell walking up to him.

"Damn, a shit house," he said. "I need'ta take one to."

"I warmed the seat up far'ye," Rodney said.

"Shit'fer'brains, it's a hundred and twenty in the goddamn shade. I think the seat was already warmed up."

"I just wanted to do somethin' nice far'ye."

"If you want to do somethin' nice for me, go shoot yourself," he said.

"Who'd suck at dick'n?

"Oh I'd find somebody. There's plenty of dick suckers in the world."

Lyondell turned to go into the outhouse and Rodney pulled his machete, and with both hands, and all his might, he brought it from high over his head downward with a calculated swing, slicing it into the back of Lyondell's balding head. As Lyondell fell Rodney held tightly to the machete handle and the blade came loose from his skull. He wiped the blood on the machete blade onto Lyondell's clothes.

"You probably would ah'tat," he said, "cept now you're in permanent lala land. My brains at shit. But yours are gunna be soon enough."

He rifled through Lyondell's pockets, finding the twenty dollar bill and the pistol, the cigarette lighters, and a few shells. He took it all. And then, after also taking the automatic .22 rifle, and the box of shells he had been charged with carrying, and putting all the items in the canoe, he dragged it with its two paddles along the creek until he came to water that was deep enough he could launch and get in and paddle. He then paddled to the river and downriver toward Chattanooga.

## PARADIGM

Not long afterward, at sometime after mid-century, the planet would essentially shrug in many ways. It would then be prepared for life's new beginnings. Time would again not exist.